Bodie or Bust

Debbie Madison

Copyright © 2009 Debbie Madison

ISBN 978-1-60145-897-1

All rights reserved. No part of this publication may be reproduced, stored in a retrieval system, or transmitted in any form or by any means, electronic, mechanical, recording or otherwise, without the prior written permission of the author.

Printed in the United States of America.

The characters and events in this book are fictitious. Any similarity to real persons, living or dead, is coincidental and not intended by the author.

BookLocker.com, Inc.
2009

Chapter 1

"Are you or ain't you with me?" Candice whispered, tucking tight her masculine physique and wiping the pelting rain from her view.

Kitty hurried to the open saloon window. Numbing rain slapped her face as her young, deep-green darting eyes peered into the darkness. "Where are we going?" she yelled, tightening her hands over her head as frigid rain stole her warmth.

"I don't know!" Candice replied. "All I know is I hate this place. Let's get while we can!"

Kitty's thin frame disappeared from Candice's sight. All she could see now was the thick, splintery windowsill.

Kitty's pale arms strained to lift a heavy valise. Without hesitation she threw it out the open window, her eyes widening as she watched it fall.

"Hurry up... Jump!" Candice hollered in a panicky voice. "We've got to get." Heart pounding, she screamed, "Now!"

Kitty slowed then twisted toward familiar footsteps. A soft knock sounded on her door, then grew louder. "Open up, Kitty. Men are waiting. Open this door now!"

Heart racing, Kitty's wet body shook as roaring laughter and the pungent smells of male suitors tore through the saloon and her consciousness.

Hurrying, but studying the ground below her first-story window, with a full grin Kitty tucked, legs dangling, and jumped. Her body plummeted as splintery wood tore at her clothes and silk stockings.

"I will find you!" A strong voice shouted from above. "You can't get away from me... I own you!"

Both young women glanced upwards, then hollered in unison, "Get up!"

A team of horses bolted, sending their wooden buckboard jumping. Both women grabbed at the buckboard's wet, slippery seat.

"What the heck are we doing?" Kitty cried as she shared a fast glance--and then a giggle-- with Candice.

Kitty looked up and screamed, "So what do we do now?"

Candace's eyes fell, as she barked, "Wasn't this your idea?"

A deep scowl formed on Candice's tired face as her left hand kept grabbing underneath their swaying wooden seat. "I borrowed this from the livery," she yelled. "Here-- put it on." Her thick, masculine arms tossed a moth-ridden, heavy wool blanket at Kitty, while her deep blue eyes focused on their surroundings.

Straightening her aching back, Kitty's thoughts raced as nature teased, lifting and sailing her newfound warmth upwards.

"Why did you treat him like that?" Candice barked, catching Kitty's attention.

"Wouldn't you?" Kitty snapped, her voice quivering.

"Never!" Candice yelled, throwing Kitty an uppity look. "Especially as good as I saw him taking care of you."

Was I wrong?" Kitty's head fell forward. She sighed. "All I ever wanted was true love.

Thoughts growing, her young eyes tightened. She screamed, "I hate it out here! He was just a man." Nature toyed with her swaying body as she mumbled, "Men don't want wives. All they want is our flesh! I hate them all!"

Wind screamed, muffling the slap of the heavy, frigid rain that pulled at the women's comforts. Thunderbolts of light shot across the horizon, briefly exposing their darkened surroundings, ripping across the sky, exposing the muddy path and slowing their horses.

"Where are we going? I can't stand the cold! Let's go back!" Kitty screamed, her dainty head falling, her scantily dressed body shuddering.

Candice's thoughts were on Jack. She knew her husband wouldn't let her go. His comfortable smile and hard hand drove her onward. Head tipping, slowly falling on Kitty's shoulders, she softly yelled to the horses, "Get up!"

Mud flew, grabbing hard, slowing their buckboard. Leaning tight, teeth chattering, both women stilled as their buckboard carried them far away from familiar comforts.

"Is that a light?" Candice's cried. Hands shaking, she pulled back on the slippery leather reins.

Both women cautiously peered into the distance. When their horses caught a glimpse of the light, the buckboard jerked abruptly to the left. Heart leaping, Kitty's back straightened as her thick, stubby fingers grabbed at the jumping reins. Lowering her voice without a sign of panic, she calmly hollered, "WHOA!"

"Where the heck did you get these horses from?" Kitty barked, her fingernails digging deep into the soaked wooden seat.

"I borrowed them from the livery," Candice hollered back, tucking her body for warmth.

"We need to get farther away!" Kitty screamed, slapping wildly at Candice. "Turn them back…towards the road…now!"

The horses picked up speed. Their panicky, high-pitched voices screamed. Rocks flew. The wagon leaped

"I hate y--!" Kitty's words ended abruptly as mud pelted her fair, delicate skin. Raising an eyebrow, she cried, "This is all your fault!"

"My fault?" Candice shouted as her thick physique repeatedly jumped, slapping hard on the soaked wooden seat as they hurled over the rocky terrain. Voice rising, she screamed, "You think you can do better? Here." She threw the slippery reins at Kitty, her eyes following the snaking leather.

"I don't do horses!" Kitty snapped, slapping wildly at Candice. Ducking and leaning, Candice's growing laughter erupted, echoing off the narrowing canyon walls as Kitty's waving arms missed their mark. Lights of comfort grew in the distance.

Wood and screaming metal teased their buckboard. Their horses leaped, shooting both women upwards as their buckboard flew over a downed tree.

Kitty's thin frame twisted, flying up and backwards above her seat.

Candice's thick, heavy body fell, slamming, curling onto the buckboard's shaking floor. Head dangling dangerously close to their horses' thundering back legs, a musty odor gnawed at her senses. Heart racing, she wildly grabbed at the flying reins.

"Whoa!" a deep, heavy voice hollered, drawing both women's attention away from their racing hearts.

A man lifted his weathered face to numbing rain, a sizeable man who cautiously glanced up at his gloomy surroundings while scratching hard at his thinning, wiry beard. Hands shaking, he grabbed wildly at the slippery leather and hollered, "WHOA!" Peering deep into the slowing wagon, he demanded, "What the heck are you two doing out in this weather?"

Their soaked linens exposing their physical attributes, Kitty and Candice lifted their spinning heads as their frigid, shaking bodies inched upwards.

Eyes staring long at young flesh and then glancing guiltily about, the man Josh, quickly led their horses forward into his rickety, leaning barn. An unnatural wide grin filled his face, as did a twinkle in his eyes.

"Who are they?" a high-pitched feminine voice hollered over a fierce wind. Slowing her movements, swaying body tucking, she pushed forward, grabbing wildly at the shaking barn doors.

"I'll take care of the horses!" her husband shouted, his voice deepening. "Get back in the house!"

Kitty moaned, grabbing Josh's attention. Wind screamed, shaking and threatening his barn's very existence, seizing his thoughts.

His callused, weathered hands trembled as he touched the women's creamy flesh, in ungentlemanly ways. His focus didn't falter. Neither woman stirred. His heavy eyes widened as he lifted Kitty's skirt.

"Huh?" Kitty's mind stirred as she felt his weight pressing down. Her stomach turned as she caught a whiff of his rancid breath. Boots still on, Kitty screamed, "No!" In a blur, she wildly slapped at her surroundings. Josh's eyes fell as he pulled and pushed hard on her tiny frame.

"Is it family?" an excited voice hollered. Josh's wife challenged nature, hurrying back to the shaking barn doors.

Silence set his wife's mind racing. Fist rising, pounding on the shaking barn doors, she loudly yelled, "Josh, can you hear me?"

"Don't come in!" Josh hollered weakly, heart racing, catching his breath. Sweat pooling, dripping, his shaking hands grabbed, Kitty's thin linen skirt. Thoughts exploding, he hurried as he heard his wife's voice deepen. Lowering his head, he cautiously opened the heavy, trembling barn doors.

His wife's short, thick stature didn't slow her. Soaked, her eyes widened as she excitedly asked, "Is it your family or mine?"

Her husband's slow response and reddened face set her mind racing. She pushed him aside as she peered inside the buckboard. She calmly said, "It's not family. They need to get."

Josh's back straightened and his eyes widened. "No, no one can survive out there! They can stay until mornin'." His voice grew louder. "They can stay until this storm passes."

"No!" Head lowering submissively, his wife cried, "If it ain't family, they need to get!"

When Josh didn't respond, she screamed, "So what are you waiting for? Open those doors!"

When Josh hesitated his wife frowned. Calm and lightly in tone she said, "Josh, we have enough to care for. It's not our business."

Wind screamed, shaking their barn's very existence, grabbing their thoughts.

Breath slowing, shoulders dropping, Josh pulled hard at his shaking heavy barn doors. Numbing rain slapped his face. He hesitated. His wife leaned forward, focusing on the closeness of their house.

Kitty slowly rose, closing her spread legs. Tears pooled in her green eyes as she straightened her clothes. A scowl grew on her face. Head wobbling, her back tightened. She barked, "Where the heck am I?"

Josh turned, as did his wife, and with shame in his eyes he slowly replied, "Nevada."

"Stop...or I'll shoot." Gun cocked, Kitty's tiny hands shook, focusing on the man and woman. Eyes darting, she heard Candice moan. Thoughts growing, she screamed," Now you get, before I shoot you!"

Josh scratched his head, focusing on his wife's thick physique, immediately shielding her. He stared, his thoughts confused. Announcing its presence, the wind demanded attention, teasing, growing.... Tucking, he grabbed his wife's heavy waist, sheltering her, moving quickly.

Kitty's body teetered as her knees buckled, sending her downwards. Her hands kept fully extended, the gun still raised and aimed. Candice's head lifted, watching Kitty.

Eyes darting, Candice's stomach turned as she caught a glimpse of the rancher's head disappearing into the darkness. "Is that Jack?" she asked, her voice trembling.

Kitty lowered her quivering arms.

"Give me the gun!" Candice demanded, grabbing at Kitty's hands. "I'll kill him this time."

"Is he alone?" Candice asked. "How the heck did he find us?" Mind racing, adrenaline rushed, awakening every inch of her wet, shuddering, fatigued body.

Chapter 2

"Wake up!" Huddling, curled like kittens, Candice quietly whispered, "We need to get." Voice softening while stroking Kitty's thick blond curls, she said, "Kitty…Wake up…we need to ge--. Her words dropped as strong, angry voices sliced through the opening barn doors.

Heart jumping, Candice took in her surroundings.

"No, I'm not that kind of girl," Kitty softly replied.

"Huh?" Candice's eyes darted as she grabbed at shadows, feeling for the gun.

Their horses stirred.

"Wake up!" Candice cried. "Jack's back…and he brought friends."

"I might…" Kitty said giggling. "Where did you say that spread is?"

"Are you sick?" Candice snapped, rocking Kitty back and forth. "Can't you hear them? They're coming! Get up!"

Sunlight pierced the openings of the dilapidated barn. Candice welcomed its warmth.

Her red, untidy hair fell forward, blocking her view as her hands found the gun. Cocking it, she studied her surroundings. Kitty's slow movements grabbed hard at her thoughts.

"Don't shoot!" a strong, deep voice shouted. "We're comin' in."

"Kitty, get up!" Candice whispered, her voice deepening. "Jack's here!"

Kitty raised her arms and her fingers danced in the air. She mumbled, "Why, I declare. Is all that money yours?" Eyes still closed, a smile widened on her face.

"I hate you!" Candice snapped, slapping at Kitty while tossing her thick blonde locks backwards.

Barn doors slowly opened. Light engulfed the barn, grabbing at the women's shadowy surroundings.

Candice's eyes, caught in blinding light, saw glimpses of thick moving physiques.

Their horses' necks jumped, shaking the buckboard. Throwing Kitty a quick glance, Candice's voice deepened. She yelled, "Hang on!"

"Haah, Haah!" The team bolted, jerking the light buckboard as Candice kept slapping the reins. Her gun hand tightened on the shiny metal.

"Whoa! W-H-O-A!" deep strong voices hollered as masculine arms waved at the team.

"Get up!" Candice yelled as the team slowed. "I'll shoot!" she screamed, her voice cracking. "Get out of my way!"

"Grab 'em."

"No!" Candice aimed and squeezed the trigger. The explosion startled the horses.

Bodies flew, dashing for cover. Kitty raised her spinning head and yelled, "Why, thank you, gentlemen. We had a lovely time."

Men still sprawled in the dust were drawn in by Kitty's soft voice and the tease of her golden hair. Kitty threw them a kiss, waving goodbye.

Weaving and crawling into the buckboard's front seat, Kitty calmly said, "Candice, you really have to work on your short temper. Are you trying to get us killed?"

"My temper!" A scowl deepened between Candice's widening light blue eyes.

"That was Jack." Her loud, testy retort lingered.

"See, you're doing it again," Kitty calmly said, nonchalantly dusting off her weathered dress while fussing with her hair.

"I'm dumping you off at the next saloon!" Candice snapped as she urged the team faster.

"Smell that? I'm hungry. Let's go back," Kitty cried, grabbing at the snaking reins.

"Are you crazy?" Candice's head shook. She pulled her arms as far from Kitty's as the reins would let her.

"That wasn't Jack." Kitty raised an eyebrow. "That was the rancher and his cowhands."

"No it wasn't," Candice hastily replied. "It was Jack."

"No it wasn't. Why... I can smell that hog farmer from a mile away." She shook her head. "It wasn't him."

"You don't think I know what my husband looks like?" Candice's voice tightened.

"See, you're doing it again." Kitty threw Candice uppity looks, slowly saying, "Did you bring the champagne? My head hurts. I need a drink."

"That was Jack," Candice insisted angrily. "And what does a pig farmer smell like?" Expecting an argument, Candice glared at Kitty.

Kitty's eyes filled, as she softly replied, "Like pigs. That wasn't Jack."

"Yes it was."

"When's the last time you smelled a pig farmer?"

"When was the last time you saw a pig?"

Thundering hooves silenced their argument.

"Where the heck are we goin'?" Candice asked as her voice softened.

"I don't know," Kitty quickly replied, still gloating from her last remark.

"Then why the heck are we headed south?" Candice snapped.

Kitty studied her green surroundings and took in a deep breath, a twinkle growing in her eyes she said, "Matt said to head to California. He promised me, I'll be rich... overnight!"

"And you believed him?" Candice laughed, shaking her head in disagreement. "You should have married Smitty. He was an honest man."

"I'm not a farm girl," Kitty screamed. "I can read and write...he was...." Unable to find words, she settled the matter by saying, "I didn't love him."

"Love? What do you know about love?" Candace screamed angrily, noticing her friend's tears pooling, head falling.

Softening her voice, she gingerly asked, "So... what will make us rich in California?"

Kitty's head inched upwards as she wiped wildly at the tears pooling in her alluring deep green eyes. A glow and smile Candice had missed seeing on her friends face grew. "Everything!" Kitty screamed. "Gold, silver, saloons… and…the best champagne in the entire world… all the way from Paris."

Kitty's excitement lightened the pensive lines on Candice's sagging face. Her tiny voice strengthened. "He promised I wouldn't have to do any more men pleasuring. He…." Her voice calmed as a light in her eyes grew. "He said he would marry me."

"All right," Candice replied, still watching their back. "How far is it to California, then?"

"We have to head south …and then east…and…." Kitty's young eyes lifted, floating. "I'm not sure after that," she admitted. "But we'll get rich. Throw them reins at me," Kitty demanded…confusing Candice. "I reckon you're tired. You sleep…I'll head us good."

Candice nodded in agreement, dropped the reins, and Kitty took them. "Why is everything out here dusty?" she yelled. "Don't you know how bad dirt tastes?"

A bird appeared from nowhere, crossing her path. "Where are you going?" Kitty softly asked, eyes following it. Its wing caught the edge of their flying buckboard. The bird crashed and fell under her wooden seat.

"We need to get," she whispered, glancing down at the flailing baby bird. "Don't die. I'll take care of you," she promised.

Pockets of sunlight piercing through dense branches of mature pine trees danced across their shadowed path, offering a taste of warmth.

Kitty glanced at Candice.

"Where did you say…we're going?" Candice asked drowsily.

"I told you!" Kitty replied, rubbing her forehead. "California!"

"Is it far? "Candice asked, her heavy eyes drooping.

Kitty didn't answer.

Clouds lifted and sunshine teased… grabbing, drinking in moisture from everything it touched. Musty, lingering odors blanketed their drenched surroundings.

The passing storm had left its mark, uprooting, twisting, and spinning everything it had touched.

Slowing the team and glancing downwards, Kitty's left hand grabbed at the stilled, tiny bird. "I'll name you…I'll name you Lucky." Color slowly returned to her pale face. Nodding, she exclaimed, "Yes…Lucky. That's a good name."

"Oh!" Kitty's eyes jumped as the baby bird began to wobble. "Don't you fret. I'll take care of you."

Delicately scooping it up into her hands while spreading her pleated skirt, she laid the bird alongside of her left thigh, offering it warmth. The chick curled, pressing against Kitty's leg. Carefully folding a piece of her thin silk skirt upwards, blanketing the bird and leaving only its tiny head exposed, she excitedly shouted, "I've always wanted a bird. I love you, Lucky."

Loud explosions of rapid gunfire ripped across the landscape, spooking their team. Bolting, ears perking, blindly running, Kitty hollered, "Hold on Lucky," her hands grabbing at their jumping wagon.

"Candice, wake up!" Kitty screamed. The horses took off at a dead run. Pushing Candice's leaning body away, her small delicate fingers tightening on the reins, she shouted, "I don't do horses! Wake up!"

"Huh?" Candice's neck flew backwards, jolting her senses. "Why are you running the team this fast?" she muttered, her head bobbing. Yawning, wiping sleep from her hollow eyes, Candice shot a fast glance at Kitty. "What the heck are you doing?" Candice's heart jumped as her eyes focused on Kitty's leaning body that was sheltering the flopping baby bird.

Adrenaline flowing, Candice's hands shot at the flying reins. "Are you crazy?" she screamed. "Help me…grab the reins!"

Kitty's didn't budge or offer help. Her swaying body demanded her attention as she focused on the safety of the baby bird.

Gunfire erupted again, this time within throwing distance. Their horses' thick necks jumped, ears pricking, legs slowing.

"What the heck's wrong with you? I knew I oughtn't have brought you." Candice's eyes fell on a small log cabin in the distance.

Adrenaline flowing, her body leaning dangerously low, and her fingers grabbing in all directions, snapping at the slowing reins, she hollered, "Don't shoot! Your gunfire frightened our horses. Whoa," she shouted at the horses.

"Stay inside," a tall shadow of a man shouted, his shotgun aimed at the fast-approaching buckboard.

"I smell food. STOP!" Kitty popped up. "Give me those reins," she snapped, almost knocking Candice's round physique out of the slowing wagon.

"Don't shoot!" Candice screamed. "My friend is sick. Don't shoot."

"I'm not sick," Kitty shouted, pulling hard at the reins, using all the strength her petite frame could muster. "I'm hungry." In a screeching high voice she added, "S-T-O-P!" The horses' ears turned. Following the command, they stopped in their tracks, surprising and shooting both women forward.

"Hold on, Lucky!" Kitty cried.

"Huh?" Candice's foothold gave way and her arms flew over the front of the buckboard. She landed belly down on the back of the horse directly in front of her.

"What are you doing?" Kitty calmly asked, watching her friend fly forward. "Why…that's dangerous. That's not how to stop a horse."

"I'm going to kill yo--," Candice's words fell, her face dropping.

Casually tidying her golden locks, ignoring heavy footsteps and deep voices closing in, Kitty yawned, stretching her pale, thin arms. "Oh," she softly cried, "I almost forgot about you, Lucky. Are you dead?"

Footsteps rushed to Candice's sprawled body. "How do you know she's dead?" an immature male voice asked, poking Candace's dangling legs.

"How sick was she?" a deep voice asked, stepping closer. "She sure has red hair. I ain't ever seen a girl with red hair." Cautiously stretching his left hand out to touch it, his right hand fidgeted above his unbuckled gun.

"Did her sickness make her head red?" The young one asked, thinking out loud. Everyone within hearing distance slowed their pace, a few stepping backwards.

Kitty sighed, staring at her tiny bird's red breast. With a puzzled expression, she quietly replied, "Maybe."

Whispers flew. "Then you need to get on yer way." A double-barreled shotgun focused on them. Cocking the barrel, a short, limping old-timer rapidly approached.

Everyone within his gun's spraying distance scattered. "Them two are real handsome. I wonder where they're goin'. I wonder how much they charge?"

"Hey, Andy," a stout drink of water whispered. "Don't them horses look familiar?"

"Jake," Andy roared, "You ain't seen a woman in so long you called them horses, not whores."

"Huh?" Jake's ey brows lifted as he said, "If them are mares ..." he scratched his head, then his hairy neck, his eyes jumping, purposely working the men, "I'll take this one." He loudly chuckled. His laughter was contagious. The camp's men fell in line, following him, circling the buckboard, staring.

"We have our own problems," the old-timer shouted as a familiar yearning grew in the young men's eyes. Hands shaking, sweat pooled and slowly trickled, falling into deep folds of weathered skin. "These women are sick." Head spinning, his eyes followed the moving men his gun still focused on Kitty. "You heard her. You want to die, red?"

Candice moaned, surprising nervous gun hands.

"Look!" Kitty's back straightened as her cheeks reddened. "Lucky is alive. I didn't kill him."

"I hate you," Candice's yelled, shocking and confusing her captive audience as her spinning head rose.

"Ma'am, can I help you?" Dashing forward, a young gent with thick black hair pushed a few men aside, extending his bulky arms toward her.

"No, let me help. I'll make ya feel right t' home," another gent shouted, slapping clouds of dust off his faded, striped shirt.

"No! Pick me. I'm tellin' you, I'm older; I'm first." Arms rose, swinging wildly in all directions.

Taken aback, Kitty's lips tightened, watching all the men fussing over Candice.

Stretching while slowly standing and dusting off her skirt, sunlight pierced Kitty's layered clothing, exposing her feminine attributes. Heads turned abruptly as men lifted their hats, staring. Voices froze and eyes widened as the men gazed at Kitty's silken golden locks playfully catching the sunlight.

Mesmerized, the men's numbers grew. Using a well-rehearsed line, Kitty daintily said, "We haven't eaten for days. We don't mean to be a bother." Eyes closing, with a dramatic exit, Kitty faked a fall. Her body became limp. Men flew to her rescue, arms grabbing and pushing.

"What do we do?" most mumbled, entranced by Kitty's youthful beauty.

"Feed em'," a stout prospector shouted.

"What fer?" a gruff, raspy voice bellowed. "We need our food. Let's just have our way with 'em and then send 'em on their way."

Smiles appeared on the dingy bunch's faces, some chuckling and most nodding in agreement.

"I take this one." Big Jake's slow deep voice drew attention as he lifted Candice off of the back of the horse like she was a feather. Men's eyes followed, guns hesitant.

"That ain't no horse," Andy shouted, his eyes focusing on Candice."Put her down. It's a woman."

Big Jake's huge body slowed.

"Put her down!" Andy demanded again, his gun aimed. He was concentrating hard on not shooting the woman. Andy's gun fired, creasing Big Jake's bulging arm. Men leaped for safety.

"You ain't taking my friend," Kitty sprang up, hands pulling a loaded derringer out of a hidden pocket in her skirt. It exploded, adding to a growing ringing noise in her ears.

Blood darkened on Andy's face, his eyes stilling, falling.

"Get away!" Kitty yelled, eyes darting, the gun pointing wildly.

"She's mine!" Big Jake stepped forward. "You all get." The men stepped back, minds racing as a skeleton of a woman challenged them.

"That's my only friend!" Kitty cried, the gun falling from her shaking hands. "I'm not good at this... I'm just hungry. Oh why don't men want wives?" she screamed, stomping and losing her composure.

Big Jake's head turned. "I'll marry you," he said, still carrying Candice like a piece of meat over his back.

Jumping out of the wagon, her fancy shoes sticking, and lifting her skirt over the muddy ground, Kitty said, "Okay...but can I eat first?"

Abruptly turning, she ran back to the buckboard and grabbed her gun.

Men erupted in laugher watching Kitty's unfeminine steps as she chased after Big Jake.

"I bet she kills him," a shaky voice shouted.

"How much?" Voices exploded and gold dust flew while changing hands.

"What about Andy?" a strong, serious voice demanded. "Are we gonna let a girl get away with that?" Voices settled and the betting slowed as the men resumed scratching and pulling on overgrown facial hair.

"She's mighty handsome," an old-timer said. "I'd regret killing something that handsome."

"I ain't got money, but the last tomcat that tried to tame me... missed.

"Did you win that bet?" a loud voice asked, laughing quietly.

"What bet?" Amusement rippled through the men, as did the enticements of spring.

"What you got?" a keen-eyed younger miner loudly asked.

"Two mules...but I ain't bettin' them both. How do I get my money if I win?"

The men stirred, bets increasing.

"She's a girl," a loud voice chuckled.

"I'll bet ten to one!" Old-timers shared glances.

"What the heck are you bettin' on?"

Heads raised and eyes locked.

"We thought you were dead!" an unsure, voice replied.

"You were buried," another miner, added. "I saw it myself."

"What's all the ruckus about?" Men's eyes darted and heads turned.

"Big Jake's got a girl runnin' after him."

"No!" a deep voice shouted. "He's got *two* girls. One to marry and one to shoot."

"I change my bet!" an excided voice hollered. "I'm betting on Big Jake."

"What fer? She ain't big enough to kill him."

"But she's purty enough to." A man chuckled.

Betting resumed with fervor.

Hips dipping with each slow step, the man studied the crowd. "Where's my brother?"

Voices froze... eyes cautiously lifted.

Gun unbuckled, right hand twitching, he commanded, "Where's Andy?"

Men moved, blood flowing to their trigger hands. "We didn't kill him," an old-timer shouted. "The whore did."

"Where is she?" he demanded.

"She's with Big Jake."

Heads turned, pointing down the muddy path leading to Big Jake's fortress.

"Nobody gets away with killin' my brother." His face darkened with angry blood. He spat disgustedly into the street saying aloud, "I'll kill them both."

"Don't kill them both. They's purty whores. Leave us one."

"You're buttin' yer nose into his business," a crusty voice shouted.

Men around him nodded in agreement, lining both sides of a muddy path following Andy's brother.

"I saw you go into the tunnel," someone said. The miners collectively asked, "How did you get out?"

Staring long, trying to keep his thinking unclouded, he pressed forward in total silence. Big Jake was the kind of man you wanted on your side. He wasn't challenged much, but memories of his last tangle still lingered. The men resisted the warmth of Big Jake's log cabin, even in the freeze of winter. He was not the sort to be reckoned with.

Mud grabbed at his boots, adding to his limp. "How the heck did you let a whore kill you?" His rounded shoulders lifted, his rage returning. "Pa would be ashamed!"

Leaning wide, balancing his busted body with each step, he slowed. With fluid motions, his hands flashed to his holster.

Miners froze, their minds racing. Eyes dropped, hands fidgeting around their waistbands.

"You think he'll shoot us first?" they said.

"What fer?" the crusty old-timer barked. "He's gonna need the shots he's got left to kill Big Jake.

"Which whore you reckon he'll kill first?" a betting man asked.

"I hope it's the short one," one replied, eyes growing, scratching hard. "I'd give my last year's diggin's for that golden one. She's sure handsome. I ain't never touched gold hair."

A slow-speaking man supposed, "You reckon she's from around here?" Not used to companionship, he agreed with himself, saying, "I bet she came all the way from California."

"Ya reckon she'll marry Big Jake? I ain't ever been to a weddin'. I hear there's good vittles…and you don't need to pay in gold dust."

"I been to my sister's weddin'." Eyes slowing and fingers less jumpy, the miners grabbed at the thought.

"Is it true?" Men straightened their backs, ears yearning for more.

"Was she handsome?" Deep lines shot across foreheads, eyes narrowing, caught as they were in thinking.

The young one calmly replied, "Yep."

Thoughts drifting, the men's faces eased. Squinting, grabbing at comforting rays, smiles crept upwards as they looked forward to the fight.

Chapter 3

Heart jumping, Kitty screamed, "I'll shoot!" With her shoes sliding, sinking into the mud, her steps slowed. Ears still ringing and gasping for breath, she asked, "You said you would marry me. So where are you taking my friend Candice?"

Big Jake's powerful legs plowed a deep, wide path through the mud, his feet never slowing.

Stopping, breathless, face reddening, Kitty screamed, "Are ya or ain't ya gonna marry me?"

As Big Jake froze, his thick neck twisting, his eyes settling on Kitty's face, the miners' movements also slowed.

Kitty caught Big Jake's eyes. They were cold, granite hard. His massive features and emotionless gape set her mind racing. Years of whoring had taught her how to sum up a man with just a quick glance, but Big Jake's hooded, beady eyes were hard to call.

Stomping in place, flinging mud all the way up to her neck, she demanded, "Big Jake, you just let Candice go!"

In one fluid motion Big Jake heaved Candice off of his shoulder like a sack of potatoes. Her body slapped the hard, soggy ground, slowly sinking.

Laughter erupted as the miners cautiously approached.

"Are you the whore that killed my brother?" The miner's eyes darted, trigger fingers itchy.

"Huh?" Kitty slowed, her slender physique twisting. Her eyes widened as she gulped hard. Muscles tightening, she screamed, "I hate it here!" She hoped for a quick distraction. Grabbing for her hidden derringer, she lost her balance, her body flying backwards, splashing bottom first in the mud.

"I'm bettin' on Big Jake," a gruff voice hollered.

Bodie or Bust

"Give her a real gun. She ain't never gonna kill him with that pea shooter."

Quiet laughter grew to guffaws as the betting men's arms flew. Agreeing with quick handshakes, they listened nervously. Nodding, then disagreeing, they changed their bets.

"No girl can kill Big Jake." The clarity and certainty in the man's voice rang out, grabbing the other men's thoughts.

"Get up, whore!" Andy's brother Robert yelled while grabbing at Kitty's golden locks, paying no mind to Big Jake's close proximity.

Slapping wildly at Robert's hands, Kitty screamed, "I was just hungry! Let me go!"

Big Jake's thick shoulders straightened, catching the miner's attention. Betting slowed as voices stilled. He threw a hard look at Robert. "Let go o' my wife," he demanded, his voice hard as stones.

Old-timers stepped a few paces back. Younger men in ragged work clothes cautiously crept closer, hands poised next to their loaded gun belts.

Bad luck, which had set in for one of the younger betting fellows, offered a speck of change. "She's a feisty one," he shouted. "I'm still bettin' good about her killin' him first."

"No," an old-timer drawled, eyeing the situation. "I think she's gonna marry him."

"What fer?" Somebody yelled back.

"You asking me?" A smile crept onto his weathered face, "Cuz…she's a girl, o'course."

His quick response caused the men to scratch their heads, most nodding at the thought.

"You git!" Big Jake's slow, deep voice assaulted every ear within hearing distance. Eyes darted left, then right, jumping from Robert to Big Jake.

"Those ladies are mine. You git now!" he shouted.

Robert held his ground, his face darkening with rage. "She killed my kin! She can't git. I don't have a fight with you. You can have the other one, but this one's mine."

Miners scattered as they ducked for cover, their eyes widening, faces tightening.

Candice stirred, moaning. Kitty's eyes fell from the men's faces to Candice.

"I... don'..." words came slow, "like... guns." Big Jake's simple response instilled confidence in Robert. He drew, aiming dead center at Kitty. He figured he had a second or two before Big Jake could reach him, and he had plenty of bullets.

Big Jake sprang like a wildcat, flattening Robert, his gun drawn.

A gunshot exploded.

Big Jake's body rocked as Robert kicked, pushing Big Jake's enormous body away.

Men cautiously rose. "Is he dead?" a crusty old-timer asked.

"He can't be," another one insisted. "That's Big Jake. You could shoot him to ribbons and he'd just walk away."

Men drew closer, their minds awhirl.

Candice's eyes slowly opened. She surveyed her mud-laden clothes. Confused, she cringed at all the approaching lusting eyes. With her voice quivering she asked, "How far is California?"

Kitty heard her and giggled softly, her gun still raised.

Big Jake shook, frightening the women. Men stepped back.

Kitty cocked her gun, watching Robert drop to his right knee.

Robert aimed and shot, the bullet buzzing by Kitty's left shoulder. She fired, hitting him in the chest. He dropped to both knees and fell backwards, his eyes stilling.

Big Jake sat up, caked in layers of gray mud. Blood stained his red plaid shirt, trickling down his left arm.

"He didn't kill him," the betting man announced. "He's still alive!"

What about Andy's brother, Robert?" another old-timer asked, "Did he kill the girl first?"

"Is Andy's brother dead? Who killed who first?"

The miners congregated like bees to honey, swarming amongst themselves, all insisting they'd won their bets. They paid little mind to Big Jake, Kitty, or Candice who were still plopped a few feet apart, layered in mud.

Head spinning, Candice cried, "Who put me in the mud?" as she wiped the sludge off her blouse. Eyes tightening toward Kitty she screamed, "You did this on purpose...didn't you!"

Scooping a handful of wet mud, she threw it at Kitty. She missed, hurling the goo much farther than she had planned.

Both women watched in horror as the muddy wad landed directly on Big Jake's cheek.

"What the heck did you do that for?" Kitty hollered. "He just saved my life."

"Cuz you put me in the mud!" Candice barked. "It's not funny!"

"Funny?" Kitty laughed, hands scooping, taking aim. "I'll show you fun--" Before she could finish her words, wet mud slammed into the side of her head, knocking her forward.

"What the--?" She turned, facing Big Jake, and got a second bombardment, mud hitting her directly in the face.

Candice howled, grabbing the men's attention. Big Jake roared, shouting, "I like my wife."

"I still win that bet!" a man shouted. "He's gonna marry her just like I told ya."

"She ain't gonna marry him," another shouted.

"How come?" an old-timer asked, scratching his four-day-old beard.

"Cuz…" the miner hesitated, then shouted, "cuz she's too purty!"

Miners turned to size up Kitty's beauty. She looked like a mud-laden tree stump. They roared.

"Which one was the blonde one?" a curious voice asked.

"I know it's not that tall one!" someone shouted, chuckling as the men stared at the three live piles of moving wet mud.

"It's time to work," an anxious voice hollered. "Summer ain't gonna last forever."

With the fun over, the men nodded, heading off toward their claims.

"That's the most fun I had all year," a young, slim miner insisted as the men settled into their backbreaking routines.

"I told you women are trouble," another warned. "Did you forget about Andy and his brother?"

"It's them women's fault. When they show up, men die. We need to warn them away."

Talk slowed to mumbling as the men split off in different directions into the nearby hills.

A miner known for his streak of bad luck stayed, eying the situation. A grin crept across his greasy, heavy eyebrowed face as he thought about working women and gold, lots of gold. His back straightened.

"Ma'am, may I assist you?" He offered his arm and said, "My name is James."

Kitty glanced up at him curiously.

"You must be exhausted," he said. The sympathy in his words caught her attention.

"I am," she sobbed, looking him over and smiling a little.

"Ladies," he insisted, "I have a delightful tent, pitched by a spring, and the softest, cleanest bed in camp." His eyes narrowed. "I would offer you more if I had it."

Kitty eased her body from the mud. Stepping closer, the man offered his hand and then his handkerchief saying, "It's a pity you've had to be around these sorts. You deserve the finest of everything."

His words were music to Kitty's ears. Holding her head up high, she softly said, "It's refreshing to find a gentleman in these parts."

Candice's rounder figure slowed her escape from the wet muck. Breathless she turned to notice the blood on Big Jakes arm. "You're hurt." Determined, she attempted to stand up, her muscles tightening as her legs shook.

Big Jake, still wallowing, laughing, throwing mud, paid no mind to either woman.

"Where you going?" Candice yelled, watching Kitty's feminine retreat.

Head lifted, chin pointed, Kitty arrogantly called over her shoulder, "To a gentleman's tent."

Chapter 4

"He's a bad sort!" Candice yelled after Kitty and her, "gentleman."

Big Jake caught her words, eyes blinking, his manner changed. "Where you takin' my wife?" he growled.

Kitty's steps didn't slow.

"I hate you!" Candice screamed, her body floundering as she sank deeper into the muck with each attempt to stand.

"You're funny." Big Jake clapped.

"Are you stupid?" Candice angrily shouted at Big Jake.

Her words echoed off of the rocky, mountainous terrain, easing the miners' boredom. A few slowed, turning sharply. Others listened intently, quietly chuckling as the feminine voices teased them.

"I...Big...Jake...! Wife, come back!" In a swift movement Big Jake stood, his eyes wandering toward Candice.

"I ain't your wife!" Candice spat. "And she's my friend."

Big Jake's eyes locked onto Candice's face. Slowly he said, "I'm hungry."

"So am I," Candice admitted in a softer voice, her eyes watching the huge man.

Big Jake reached down with his bleeding arm and grabbed onto Candice's wallowing, thickly muddied body.

"You come, we eat," he said, throwing Candice onto his back like a slab of beef in one quick, effortless movement.

Her heavy build sent his knees shaking, slowing him down.

"Let me go!" Candice screamed, kicking and squirming. "Kitty's my friend. I need to go with her. Let me go now!"

Then, eyeing his bloody shoulder, her squirming slowed. "You're bleeding," she said, her voice softening. "You're hurt."

Kitty's constant chatter caught more than one miner's ear.

James purposely walked Kitty in circles, gold dust settling deep into his thoughts. He figured he's just found the mother lode.

"How far is your tent?" Kitty stopped, breathless. "These hills and that thick sun are tiring me."

In a sympathetic voice he replied, "If I had a stronger back, dear lady, I would carry you." Glancing about, he sensed the men's hunger, their eyes tracing her every movement. "It's not much farther. A cool bath and a comfortable bed will..." His carnal thoughts caught the best of him.

Kitty's blush was hidden under layers of mud. Teasingly, she said, "Well, I do declare, you haven't been around a lady in some time, now, have you?"

At a loss for words James cleared his throat. "That's my stake," he told her, pointing toward a tent in the distance.

Picking up his pace, Kitty's arm shook as her thin frame swayed while he pulled her along. Abruptly stopping, he announced, "Madam, welcome to my humble tent."

Winded, Kitty murmured, "Thank you." Her head fell, spinning. "I just need a minut..." she said, voice fading. The next moment found her in a dead faint.

"Don't die on me, whore!" James demanded, turning sharply.

Towering trees cast shade twenty or thirty feet across their path. In the thick of the shadows a tan, simple tarp stood out.

Face darkening, eyes hardening, he yanked, then pulled...and with no response, kicked at Kitty's thin physique.

Stepping back he hollered, "Get up, whore." But then his voice eased as he remembered the miners' close proximity. Kitty didn't move.

Knowing he could drag her a short distance, he wondered if she would wake up. Thinking about her screaming and hollering didn't bother him. He knew his laughter would calm the men's sympathetic thoughts and bring in gold...lots of gold.

Glancing down at Kitty, he slowly pulled out a chaw of tobacco. Darkened fingers slid it inside his right cheek. The comforts of shade and the familiar clench of his jaw occupied his thoughts.

"Where's the whores?" an angry voice, hollered, ricocheting off the steep canyon walls.

Minds stirring, the men's labors stopped. "I know she killed Andy," a voice drawled, "but she's awful handsome."

Arguments ensued: "Hang her," a testy voice shouted. "She killed our friends."

"She's too handsome to hang!" a miner said as he stared at her stilled body.

"Ain't we forgettin' somethin'?" A deep voice heightened as a miner said, "It was a fair fight. You ain't got no cause to hang her."

"Yep," another miner said, "She's too purty to hang.

A gleam in one miner's eyes grew. He grinned and said, I reckon she's the marrying sort." His hands fidgeted with gold weighing his pockets down.

"You have to pay," James loudly announced.

"What fer?" miners shouted, their anticipation growing.

"Is she alive?" an anxious man asked.

"How much does it cost if she's dead?" a crusty old-timer asked, surveying Kitty's still form.

The men watched as James dragged Kitty toward a nearby stream and then submerged her mud-laden body carefully into the slow-moving water.

The men stared with lust in their eyes as mud disappeared, exposing Kitty's natural attributes.

"Huh?" Kitty came instantly awake. "Get off of me!" she hissed, her brain still foggy.

Everybody stepped back, their eyes widening. A deep silence set in as leering grins formed on each face.

The cold water teased her, offering instant relief, reminding Kitty of simple pleasures. Goose bumps formed on her skin as shivers shot up and down her bony spine.

With deep... long... sighs...Kitty willingly disrobed.

James' eyes darted from her to the gaping men, who seemed lost in her beauty. His eyes, too, settled on Kitty's lovely body.

Refreshed and comfortable and with her eyes half opened, Kitty lightly said, "Thank you." Then she offered James a tiny smile.

With his heart pounding, his thoughts changed. Slowly he asked, "Ma'am, have you ever been to San Francisco?"

Kitty, filling with anger, screamed, "Turn away! Where are your manners! I thought you were a gentleman."

Holding tight to her exposed breasts, she jumped from the water. "Get away!" she screamed. "You're just like the rest."

Men eased back, keeping their distance.

"I'm not a whore!" she insisted, grabbing her soaked clothes and quickly dressing. With her heart racing, her hands fumbled for her hidden gun. "Back off!"

"You heard the lady. Back off!" James eased the triggers on both barrels of his shotgun. "You can't have her!" he shouted. Lifting the rifle, he challenged any man to touch her.

Kitty enjoyed the protection.

"You men need to get!" he said again. "Take that gold dust with you."

Ugly murmurs grew. Men, heads shaking, stepped away.

His eyes steady on the men, protecting her in a way James never thought possible, he said, "Ma'am, you'll like my soft bed."

Kitty's heart raced. Fatigued, but grateful, she threw a glance and a warm smile at James saying, "I'm grateful for your hospitality and I'd love to marry you."

James studied his surroundings. "Can you cook?" he questioned.

"Kitty placed one hand at her waist and calmly said, "Of course."

James nodded. "I got beans and bacon. Can you cook that?"

"Why…" Kitty's heart leaped as she studied James's fancy clothes and soft hands. "When was the last time you had biscuits?"

James' voice softened as he said, "Back in San Francisco last spring."

"You've been there?" Kitty's eyes suddenly filled with emotion, "Is it as pretty as I've heard?"

James studied her petite figure, nodding. "Rooms have spring beds, and there are more cars than horses on the streets."

"I ain't…I've never seen a car," Kitty corrected her words, eyes swollen with wonder.

"You are the prettiest picture I've ever seen. What are you doing way out here?"

"I can't hold a candle to them city women," Kitty teased, smiling brightly.

"You're more beautiful than all of them city folks," James admitted, blushing.

Their eyes met as he lowered his shotgun. "Can I help you inside?" he offered, and Kitty took his arm.

Chapter 5

With a gleam in her eyes as she daydreamed of big-city comforts, Kitty sighed. "I didn't mean that thing about marrying you. I'm just hungry and tired."

James' voice softened. "I know."

James was a newcomer in camp. He had settled in last fall. He minded his own business and stayed out of trouble's way. He trusted no one.

Roads were becoming passable, and after a numbing, backbreaking, fruitless winter he figured that mining was for a different sort. With his supplies almost exhausted, he had planned to move on.

Kitty's slow step along with her golden locks and whisper of a physique sparked ungentlemanly thoughts. A grin grew on his face and James scooped her up.

"Well!" Kitty, heart racing, staring deep into James' widening, lustful eyes, calmly said, "I thought you were a gentleman." Squirming, she barked, "Are you intending to have your way with me? Cuz if you are, then get it over with. I'm tired."

James slowed, catching Kitty's radiance. "I can't protect you here," he reasoned.

The genuine concern in his voice melted Kitty's suspicions. Swinging her arms around his neck, she girlishly admitted, "I knew you were the marrying type. Will you take me to San Francisco?"

Mostly James spoke like an educated man, and he wasn't wearing digging clothes.

James dropped his gaze and simply said, "You need to get out of here. You're not what I figured."

"No...No...." Kitty's embrace tightened, her golden locks falling, covering James' shoulder. She whispered, "I Love you. Take me with you."

An angry miner just outside the tent yelled through the tent flap, "We've got some talking to do." He ripped aside the flap and stared at James, his needs showing in his eyes. "We'll make her feel right t' home. Now hand her over."

Face darkening, James gently dropped Kitty behind his back and loudly announced, "I'm gonna marry her."

"We ain't seen that sort in a long time," a voice called out. "You can marry her after we have our turns with her."

Lifting his shotgun, James dropped to his knees and focused on the growing crowd.

"She's mine!" he hollered. "Nobody's touching her! We're getting married!" he hollered again, his eyes tightening.

"No, I'm marrying her!" Big Jake pushed past the knot of men as though they were flies.

"Oh no!" Kitty cried, watching Big Jake approach. "I didn't say I would marry him!" she exclaimed.

"Go away!" Big Jake demanded of James. "She's my wife."

"Yeah! She's real trouble," someone shouted. "I'd bet she'd marry them both if she could."

"I'll take that bet."

"What bet?" a heavy-pocketed miner shouted. "How much?"

Kitty's back straightened. Face filling with anger and frustration, she barked at Big Jake, "I'm not your wife! And where's my friend?" she screamed.

"I like her." Big Jake's fast response surprised the miners.

"I ain't seen him move that fast, ever," a man whispered, cautiously, stepping back.

"Heck," another man quietly said, "I didn't even know he could talk."

"He must be in love." An old coot laughed. Heads nodded in agreement as the heavy-pocketed miner said, "So who's gonna win this fight?" Hesitating for a second, he scratched his beard and said, "I'm betting on the big guy."

"What fer? He ain't got a gun."

"Cuz he's fast, real fast. I saw him take out Andy's brother."

"I don't care!" Kitty angrily hollered, pushing James aside and stepping outside the tent. "You're stupid," she screamed! "And where is Candice?" she demanded of Big Jake.

Big Jake leaped, grabbing for her waist. "You're my wife!"

Kitty dodged left, stepping fast.

Big Jake fell, sliding in the pooling mud.

Grins formed as quiet chuckles exploded into uncontrollable loud laughter.

"I'm bettin on the whore!" someone roared. "She's a feisty one."

James cautiously removed himself from the situation. This wasn't his fight.

"You ain't gonna catch me!" Kitty hissed, studying Big Jake's every movement while angrily shouting, "Where's my friend? What did you do to her?"

Big Jake lunged again and again, mud thickening and sticking with each fall. Kitty's tiny frame jumped, twisting and dodging his every move. Knowing her small gun couldn't kill him and tiring fast, she threw a quick glance back toward James. He was nowhere in sight. Rows of miners had her circled and she saw the lust growing in their eyes.

She calmly said to Big Jake, "I've got to get out of here. Show me where Candice is and…" she hesitated, catching her breath… "and you can come with us."

"Big Jake, stay here!" several men shouted at once.

He lunged again, this time catching Kitty's left arm. In a single swoop he grabbed her, throwing her on his shoulder.

"Put me down!" she demanded, squirming and slapping his brawny shoulders.

"I won that bet," a miner excitedly hollered. "Pay up."

"I bet you she would marry him. I didn't hear any marryin' words." Gold dust exchanged hands as voices raised and heads nodded.

"Let 'im have 'em both. Them types will just cause us trouble."

"She's sure a feisty one," a stout, dark-bearded miner said out loud, grabbing his pick and shovel. "I'd pay a summer's diggin' on that one."

Most men headed back toward their claims. A few men lingered, grinning, watching Kitty squirm and scream.

"I'm not a piece of meat!" Kitty cried. "Put me down!"

Big Jake's huge arm had her hogtied. "I'll shoot you!" she warned, grabbing at the hidden pocket in her skirt. The miners dispersed, and in a winded, tiny voice Kitty asked, "Where are you taking me?"

"I Big Jake…you my wife." His slow, deep voice demanded attention. Layers of drying mud slowed his movements.

"I hate you!" Kitty screamed. "I'm not your wife."

"Let her go!" Shotgun aimed and cocked, James sprang from behind a crop of huge boulders.

Kitty's head spun awkwardly, following Jame' voice.

"No!" Big Jake's face reddened, filling with anger. "You git… she's my wife."

James wiped sweat from his face as his eyes tightened. "She can't be your wife. She's married to me."

"Huh?" Big Jake abruptly stopped and scratched at his muddy neck. James kept a keen eye on his movements. "Okay," he simply said, releasing Kitty from his iron grip.

"Wait!" Kitty yelled, grabbing at Big Jake's clothes, twisting hard and hoping to land legs first.

"Big Jake don't like you."

Kitty managed to gain her balance and landed feet first.

"You not nice." Big Jake's large hands slapped Kitty's back, throwing her forward, headfirst in the mud.

"I hate you!" she screamed, sitting up, fist raised, swinging at air.

"Big Jake don't like guns." He stared at James, his eyes cold as granite. "Put gun away."

James took a step backwards saying, "I'll put this gun down if you walk away."

Big Jake simply said, "Okay," continuing on his way.

Their eyes following Big Jake's steps, both Kitty and James' movements froze. The musty smell of the gray clay layering Kitty's face brought on a fit of sneezing and coughing. James didn't offer a sympathetic eye or word. His face was cold and distant.

Kitty studied James' pensive features. She liked everything she saw. Clearing her voice, with a feminine ring she said, "I didn't know I married you. When did I do that?"

Blushing, turning away, his shotgun falling, James admitted, "When I saw the need in the miner's eyes."

Back straightening, voice filling with excitement, Kitty exclaimed, "Why, I do declare, you are a gentleman."

"I've got your horses fed and ready," James said. "I'll meet you in Bodie."

"Huh? I thought we were going to San Francisco," Kitty balked. "Where the heck is Bodie?"

James' eyes filled with wonder as he said, "It's where gold and silver are plentiful and for the taking."

"You and I will build the grandest saloon California has ever seen," Kitty said, her eyes widening as he basked in the thought.

"But…Wait!" James gently lifted her out of the mud and tenderly said, "It's not safe here. Get while you can."

"I can't." Grabbing onto James' thin arm, she admitted, "I can't."

"What's wrong with you?" James' disposition quickly changed. "Get out of here while you can!"

"No!" Kitty insisted. "Not without Candice."

"Big Jake has her. Forget about her…and get out of here NOW!" James' eyes tightened. "I won't help you again. Get while you can."

"I don't care." Kitty pushed him aside, stepping in Big Jake's plowed path. Her thin legs shook, pulling hard from the sucking mud. James turned and walked away, glancing back time and time again.

Warmth from the sun slowed Kitty's steps. It tightened the mud on her clothes and face.

"I hate it here!" she screamed carelessly, not noticing all the wondering eyes following her every move. "I ain't marrying any man ever!" Stomping through the guck just added to her fury. "Men are pigs!" Raising her voice, she angrily screamed, "Candice…you're right."

A branch snapped, arresting her wandering thoughts. Laboring for breath, she cautiously whispered, "Is that you, James?"

A long silence ensued. Kitty froze, easing her hand into her skirt. "I'll kill you all!" Without hesitation she cocked her gun and fired.

Someone moaned. "I mean it!" she barked, her voice shaking.

"We ain't gonna hurt you," a miner sneered. "We just want your company."

With only one bullet left, Kitty's heart leaped. She fired again, aiming toward the voice. She bolted forward, flying through the mud.

"Get her!" someone shouted. "She's getting away!"

"I'll wing her." A steady arm rose.

"No!" Slapping the gun aside, a crusty, balding miner growled, "You can't shoot her."

"Why not? It'd slow her!" Shaking his head and strongly disagreeing, he bellowed, "Now look what you done! She's gettin' away."

"Open up!" Kitty cried, her fist pounding on Big Jake's door. Grabbing for air, in a puny voice she demanded, "Let me in!"

"Huh?" Big Jake's rocking chair slowed, surprised at the pounding. "Go away!" he said, settling back into his rocking movements. "I'm Big Jake. Go away."

His huge physique slowed as he studied Candice's sprawled, stilled body.

Chapter 6

"I'm not married!" Kitty yelled. "James lied to you."

Big Jake had built his cabin for his comforts. Kitty's tiny voice fell, ricocheting off his massive wood door.

Pounding feverishly, she screamed, "Let me in!"

"We ain't gonna hurt you," a voice hollered behind her.

"We just want your pleasures," another voice quickly shouted. "We know you're hungry. Our vittles are pretty tasty."

A thick, pocked miner said, "I got a bed…a real bed. We can use that."

"Let me in …now!" Kitty screamed, her voice parched and cracking, her fists still pounding.

Big Jake heard most of the words. He didn't stir. He sat in his rocking chair and rocked.

"She's mine!" an excided voice hollered.

"I say she's mine first," another claimed, his gun raised.

Men stepped back, as a gun cocked.

"You can't out draw me!"

Gunfire exploded. Kitty ducked, still pounding at the door.

"Huh?" Candice stirred.

"I hate you!" Kitty screamed.

Inside, Candice leaped upwards demanding, "Open that door, Big Jake! That's my friend out there!"

"No," Big Jake slowly replied. "I don't like her."

Candice rolled out of bed, grabbing at the locked door.

"You make me laugh." Big Jake chuckled, rocking harder.

"Open this door!" Candice demanded, fist rising.

"No." A wide grin slid onto Big Jakes' flat face.

Gunfire exploded. "That's my friend," she screamed, turning fast.

"Don't care…don't like her." Rocking faster, repeating his words, his laughter grew.

Candice stormed over to the natural pine rocker and grabbed at its arms saying, " I won't stay. "Open this door NOW!"

"Let go!" he demanded, hands flying.

"No!" Candice's heavy body plopped on the left arm of his rocker, slowing its movements.

"You not funny now." Big Jake lifted his arm in a swift movement.

Quivering, remembering her husband's hard hand, Candice's shied.

With his yes following her, Big Jake said, "I want to play a game now."

Frightened, heart racing, understanding the panic in Kitty's voice, Candice quickly replied, "Yes. We should play a game."

"Let's play…." Men's loud grunts were deadly close.

Big Jake stopped rocking, yelling, "Big Jake wants to play a game…we play game now!"

I know how to play hide and seek," Candice recollected, her voice shaking.

"Okay. Big Jake likes games." Hands clapping, he swung his powerful legs up. His rocker jumped, throwing him backwards. Landing with a hard thud, he laughed, kicking his raised legs, roaring, "Big Jake play game now. Is Big Jake it?"

"Yes! Yes, you're it," Candice hurriedly replied, cautiously backing away. "And… you need to hide!" she girlishly hollered, her eyes darting across the room.

"I like this game." A smile grew on his boyish face as Big Jake rolled, slowly rising.

"Open the door," Candice teased, "I'll tag you."

Big Jake tore at the door. The roof moaned as wood exploded. A grin and playful eyes lifted as he hollered, "I it."

His wrath sent men scattering.

"Don't shoot!" Candice hollered, grabbing at Kitty's back.

"What took you so long?" Kitty screamed. "I hate you. You did this on purpose…didn't you? Get out of my way," Kitty yelled, her body flying inside the cabin. Kitty fell, curling.

"I'm sorry," Candice yelled, closing the heavy door as best as she could. "We need to get out of here!" Her voice shook as she said, "We aren't welcome here! We've got to go now!"

"I can't get." Kitty cried. "I'm married."

"What? Who'd you marry?"

Mud laden, her head rose as a spark grew in her eyes. Proudly she said, "The gentleman going to California."

Candice giggled. "Are you sure?"

Eyes rolling, Kitty sighed. "James and I are going to have the grandest saloon in California."

"But we're in Nevada," Candice recollected. Angrily she said, "Are you in love again?"

"I'm coming in," Big Jake hollered. "I know where you're hiddin'."

"We got to get now!" Kitty whispered, listening to Big Jake's voice.

Locking eyes, both women loudly hollered, "You're it!"

"I'll get you both," Big Jake laughed, grabbing the cabin's door.

Hearts racing, opening the thick door, the women peered outside as Big Jake ran in. Bodies scattering, surprising the miners, the two women dodged past them.

Their team of horses stood in a clearing a short distance away.

"They need to eat," Candice cried. "Or we won't get far."

"James fed them," Kitty yelled.

Both women jumped into the wagon.

"I thought you were dead!" Kitty said.

"Where we goin' now?" Candice demanded, grabbing at the reins. "You just use men! I ain't leaving till you tell me why."

Eyes filling as her head fell, Kitty admitted, "I'm tired and I'm hungry…and I need a nice glass of champagne."

Both women nodded sharing a quick glance. "Get up," they both yelled at the horses.

Miners swarmed the buckboard. Kitty laughed loudly, surprising Candice by saying, "I can kill them all…but I won't."

"Huh?" Whipping the reins as men slowed the team, Candice screamed, "Kitty, shoot!"

Kitty's gun exploded without her aiming at anything in particular.

"They're whores...don't let them get away! Shoot 'em!"

"I got 'em," a man announced, jumping onto the wagon and grabbing the reins.

"Don't shoot, she's mine!" one of the miners shouted.

"Kill him!" Candice cried. "He's slowing our horses."

"I hate men!" Kitty barked, quickly reloading her gun.

"He's got the reins!" Candice screamed, kicking.

"Duck!" Kitty screamed, pulling the hammer on her gun.

"Get off of me!" Candice demanded as a body landed in her lap. "Can you shoot the next one somewhere where he won't fall on me?" she yelled, kicking the body off of the wagon.

"So," Kitty screamed, "You're mad at my shootin'?"

"What shootin'?" Candice screamed. "You couldn't shoot a rabbit."

"Why would I shoot a rabbit?" Kitty yelled, glancing over her shoulder, the gun exploding again. "Oh no!" she cried. "I think I hit Big Jake!"

"What did you do that fer? He didn't whore me," Candice quipped. "He fed me and then I heard you screaming at the door."

"I wasn't aiming at him." Kitty's lips tightened. She threw Candice a frown, saying, "And I wasn't screaming."

"You were crying like a baby." Candice laughed, her voice rising. "Look out!"

"Where did he come from?" Kitty screamed as a miner latched onto her flapping skirt. "Let go of me!" she screeched, wildly kicking, hands flying as she reloaded.

"Lean back," Candice yelled, slapping the horses' reins downward at Kitty's legs.

"That hurt," Kitty barked. "Hit him, not me!"

The man's face reddened. "I got 'em!" he shouted in triumph.

Kitty's body flew off the buckboard seat.

"No!" she screamed. Her gun exploded, bloodying the man's face. With his hands still locked on her skirt, he dropped to the ground.

"Hold on," Candice yelled, grabbing at Kitty's falling body.

Throwing the reins to her feet, she leaned sideways, almost lying down on the rocking wooden seat. The man's body dragged Kitty down with his weight.

"Let go of me!" Kitty screamed, her head dangerously close to the racing buckboard's wheel. She lunged, stretching her neck, her teeth tearing flesh from the miner's clenched hand. The salt and dust lay hard on her taste buds, turning her stomach.

The man's hand convulsed, and he slowly released his iron grip.

Twisting thoughts racing, her legs quivering, she kicked at his face screaming, "I hate men!" His body dropped.

Without direction their buckboard turned, falling into a small cropping of river rocks, sending their bodies flying.

"That's not funny!" Kitty barked, her body flying. "Grab the reins!" Regaining her balance, she angrily screamed, "Why did you let them go!"

"I hate you!" Candice snarled, awkwardly releasing her grip on the reins. "And where are we going now?"

"I hate Nevada. Were goin' to California," Kitty hollered. "Oh no!" she cried, her head falling forward.

"Did you shoot yourself?" Candice's screamed, offering sympathy.

Back straightening, Kitty's eyes darkened. Blood flowing, she screamed, "Look what he did to my skirt." Standing up, shooting at shadows, she screamed, "I'll kill him twice next time."

"Why are we going to California?" Candice demanded impatiently.

With a gleam in her eyes Kitty replied, "Gold. Lots of gold."

"What do we need gold for?" Candice teased, looking forward to Kitty's sharp response.

"What?" Kitty's young face twisted as a short smile crept across Candice's face. "I already told you," she barked. "I ain't whoring no more."

Candice hid her smirk, quickly turning away from Kitty.

"You know something I don't?" Kitty inquired. "You're just a pig farmer!" she angrily screamed, her eyes seeking a reaction from Candice.

"You can't even shoot a rabbit." Candice laughed, her muscular arms relaxing as she drove their team hard.

"I already told you…" Kitty loudly said as her head shook in disagreement, her voice rising. "I won't shoot at them cute things."

"Then…you ain't gonna eat tonight." Candice laughed, slowing the horses.

Back straightening, Kitty proudly said, "I don't care. I have all the food I need."

Candice purposely whipped the horses, throwing Kitty's light physique backwards. "You'll never make a rancher," she roared, watching Kitty grab for safety.

"You're doing this on purpose!" Kitty screamed, hands slapping wildly at Candice. Grabbing hard at her lip, she forced a smile. "James love's me," she said.

"I don't care!" Candice yelled. "Get up!" she hollered at the team of horses, again throwing Kitty's body backwards.

"Huh? Where's my bird?" Kitty barked while her eyes studied the safe spot where she had left the bird.

"What bird?" Candice asked, her eyes darting around the buckboard.

"You killed it…didn't you?" Fists rising, Kitty threw a punch, surprising Candice.

"Are you on that stuff those crib whores are on?" Candice angrily replied, quickly protecting herself with her broad forearms.

"No," Kitty slowly replied, remembering the pleasures of her opiate experience, missing the substance. Her voice fell. "All I want is champagne and a clean bed."

"I hate you!" Candice angrily yelled, grabbing the horses' attention. "You've never worked for an honest dollar!"

"I just saved your life!" Kitty spat. And I ain't gonna kill a rabbit."

Candice jerked the reins, stopping their horses, mud flying, bringing their wagon to a sliding halt. Jumping out and surveying the countryside, she calmly said, "The sun's going down and I'm tired and hungry."

"Huh?" Kitty eyed her surroundings, confused. In an uppity voice, standing tall in the buckboard, she loudly said, "Are you catching the rabbit or me?"

"Have you ever shot a shotgun before?" Candice whispered, eying the thick brush.

"Why would I use that big thing?" Kitty's eyes rolled. "If I carried that around I'd never find true love. Loudly sighing, she said, James loves me. Oh!" she hollered, suddenly remembering what James had said about packing the buckboard with food.

"Quiet!" Candice whispered. "I see him. Don't move."

Kitty froze. "You're not really going to kill a rabbit are you?" she whispered.

Candice's arm dropped. Taking aim, she skillfully squeezed the trigger and the rifle exploded, dropping her target. "Got ya!" she broadcasted to her surroundings.

"Is it really dead?" Kitty cried.

Shaking her head at Kitty, Candice hurried over to claim her next meal.

"It's a big one!" she proudly shouted, holding the rabbit up by the ears.

"You'll never be anything better than a farmer," Kitty declared, her face grimacing.

"Then you won't get to eat it!" Candice shouted.

"I don't care!" Kitty shouted back. "Them miners will be coming for us. We should get farther away."

"Look at the horses!" Candice angrily screamed. "We ain't going any farther until they get rested."

Throwing the rabbit at Kitty, she yelled, "And this stupid farmer noticed that none of them miners had horses."

"Huh? Are you sure? Eew! Are you sure it's dead?"

"I'm sure." Candice bent down. In a calm voice she said, "I counted eighteen donkeys and four mules. Gather some wood and go get me a bucket of water from that creek."

"What? Why? Just because you counted those stupid men's animals don't give you the right to tell me what to do," Kitty barked back.

Fed up, Candice said, "Okay, here." She hurled the rabbit directly at Kitty. "You skin it…and cook it."

The rabbit's bleeding body landed directly on Kitty's boots. Kitty jumped backwards saying, "Okay, but I ain't gonna eat it."

Laughing, Candice replied, "Okay." She turned abruptly, heading back toward the buckboard. "And," she roared, "You ain't smart enough to be a rancher!"

Surrounded in a rolling valley overgrown with thickets of dark green grass, Candice unharnessed the horses. Their backs were wet and their chests were still bellowing. "You eat good," she said as she watched their muzzles fall to the lush grass.

Warm sunlight and birds singing slowed Candice's restless thoughts. She yawned hard.

Chapter 7

"I think the rabbit's burning!" Kitty screamed, shattering Candice's calm. "Look at all that smoke!"

Candice lifted her tired eyes and her smile widened. She enjoyed Kitty's panicky voice. "You ain't gonna eat it, so what do you care?" she snarled.

"Well, it smells good," Kitty admitted. "I didn't know it would smell this good."

Candice caught a whiff of the meat as she leaned into the buckboard.

"What are you doing?" Kitty demanded. "I know that meat's burning. Get over here!"

Candice tucked in a smile and calmly replied, "Turn it, then."

"Turn what?" Kitty shrilled, sending Candice into an uncontrollable fit of laughter. "And what are you smilin' at?"

Candice's stomach gurgled loudly. "I told you to turn it!" she snapped, eyes focusing on the burning meat.

"And I told you," Kitty screamed, "I'm not eating it." Her face reddened. "Oh, I don't care!"

"I hate you," Candice cried, grabbing at the smoking spear of wood they'd used as a spit.

"I hate you, too, but I'm in love." Kitty laughed. Then in a humming kind of voice, she looked up at the crescent moon and said, "Who needs food when you have love?" She began a whimsical dance, twirling in the tall grass that grabbed at her boots.

"What do you know about love?" Candice spat as her fingers darkened from the charred spit. "Ow!" she yelled, blowing on her blistered fingers.

Giggling softly, Kitty said, "I sure know more than you."

Kitty gazed into the stars as her movements slowed. "I thought we were heading north."

Candice drew a deep breath in between blowing on her burning fingers. Her frown deepened as she began to turn the meat.

"Skip, skip to my Lou…I love this song," Kitty shouted still laughing and twirling. "Skip to my Lou …my… darlin'," she finished breathlessly.

Head shaking in dismay, Candice kept her eyes on the rabbit.

"No!" Kitty's voice instantly turned girlishly polite."I'm going to eat what James gave me."

"Huh? What are you talking about?"

Kitty's arms flew upwards, and she began to dance again as the twinkle in her eyes grew. Still humming, she announced, "James loves me." She stopped twirling for a few seconds, close to the fire. She stared at Candice's lowered head.

Tired of Kitty, Candice demanded, "When are you gonna eat?"

Kitty snapped back, "Where's my bird?" and began to twirl again.

Candice's chubby cheeks caught the firelight as she slowly lifted her head. She gingerly replied, "I gave it to Big Jake."

"Huh?" Kitty stopped twirling. Her arms dropped and she planted them at her waist. Her back straightened as she barked, "Why in tar nation did you do that?"

"Cuz I hate you," Candice fired back. "And…you can't eat my caught rabbit."

Kitty resumed her humming and twirling, laughing loudly as her head dizzied.

Disgusted with Kitty's odd behavior, Candice shook her head and kept turning the rabbit. "Why did I go with you, anyways?"

"Heck, I don't know," Kitty laughed, still humming and twirling.

"You are too simple," Candice barked. "All you think about is love."

Kitty's movements slowed. She grabbed her spinning head and said, "All I'm thinking about now is food. Ain't it done yet? I'm hungry. And," her voice deepened and slowed, "if you would have schooled me on how to cook that rabbit, I could have had it roasted by now."

"You're trying to make me look stupid, ain't you?" Kitty kicked at the tall grass, then glared at Candice. "You're jealous of my golden hair, ain't you?"

The hard ride had taken its toll on Candice. She yawned. Throwing Kitty a frown, she calmly said, "Men are all whores."

"Huh?" Kitty stared hard into Candice's eyes. "Are you taking that opiate stuff?"

"A little," Candice hesitantly admitted with a slight nod. Eyes darting, she whispered, "I could use some now."

"That meat's getting blacker," Kitty screamed. "Get the rabbit away from the fire, now. You saw what happened to me," Kitty barked. "That stuff will kill you." Her eyes flared. "Why are you doin' a stupid thing like that to yourself?" Not waiting for a response, her face tightened as she screamed, "I ain't goin' any farther with you!"

Candice's head fell and tears pooled in her eyes. "You won't survive out here by yourself." Candice pushed her tears aside and sniffled.

In a tiny voice Kitty asked, "Will you please take the rabbit away from the fire?"

Kitty watched Candice's movements as she tended to the rabbit. She knew what damage the white powder could do.

Candice suddenly fell, curling dangerously close to the fire.

"Hey!" Kitty yelled, lightly kicking Candice's thigh. "If you don't get up this minute I'll have to shoot you."

Candice came around and pulled Kitty down, almost on top of her. "Why don't you just shoot me?" Candice cried, her voice faltering.

"This ain't fair!" Kitty moaned. "Now look at what you've done. You almost got us both burned!"

Candice sniffled. "You're smarter than me about men. I'm just a tease."

"That rabbit sure smells good." Kitty stroked Candice's hair and said excitedly, "I got a surprise for you." Curious about what food James had packed, she jumped up and headed for the buckboard.

Daylight was fading and the high altitude made breathing difficult. Glancing back at Candice, Kitty stepped up her pace. Knowing Big

Jake and the miners would be coming left her mind as she approached the buckboard and the goodies she'd find.

"Huh?" Stopping abruptly, she stared at the metal and wood that had connected the horses to their buckboard.

"Where are the horses?" she screamed.

Chapter 8

"I let them go." Candice laughed.

"I don't get it!" Kitty snarled. "Them men will be after us. You're going to get us both killed."

Candice lifted her portly body out of the thick, moist grass. Calmly she said, "You'll never be good at horses."

Kitty's hands fidgeted, shuffling through everything inside the buckboard. "I got it!" she excitedly hollered.

"Got what?" Candice yawned.

Kitty's face filled with glee. "We have champagne!" she proudly announced.

"Are you sure?" Candice questioned."Maybe it isn't the real thing."

Humming to the heavens, Kitty hurried back. "Are we going to share that rabbit or not? Of course it's real."

Watching carefully for a response, Kitty demanded, "How long have you been takin' it?"

Candice shook her head. "Not as long as you did!"

"Okay." Kitty kept watching Candice. "I ain't ever et a rabbit before. So what part is good to eat?"

Candice jumped up saying, "None of it!" Her body unnaturally shook.

"Okay," Kitty's voice softened. "I ain't good with horses, and I ain't good at cookin'. I just like champagne. So let's pour us some and eat."

Candice's hollow eyes grew wide as she cracked a smile. The women shared a glance, and then studied their surroundings as night fell.

Candice loudly admitted, "I never thought I'd hit this rabbit, you know."

Kitty popped open the bottle of champagne, then gazed up at the stars. They shared the champagne straight from the bottle.

A warm breeze offered comfort as the women settled, ate, and drank.

"I thought we were heading north." Candice yawned after awhile.

"No," Kitty yawned, too. "We need to go southwest."

"No," Candice barked, surprising Kitty. "We need to go north."

"No," Kitty shouted to the heavens. "I'm in love." She slapped at Candice, grabbing the empty bottle of champagne. "Why did you drink it all?" she protested.

Candice jumped to her feet laughing. "So how does that song go?"

"What song?" Kitty studied Candice's face. Voice hardening, she spat, "Oh, get some sleep."

"What for?" Candice giggled. "The night is young."

"Cuz." Kitty laid out her bedroll. Yawning, she said, "I still hate you." Her body stilled as she curled underneath her blanket.

"Skip, skip to my Lou," Candice sang, annoying Kitty.

"Stop it!" Kitty screamed.

"What for?" Candice laughed, her heavy body quivering.

Coyotes howled, and Candice paused.

"Go to sleep!" Kitty screamed.

Chapter 9

Ten years earlier.

"You get now, Katherine. I'm busy." The teasing look in her father's eyes just drove his daughter harder.

"If you school her any more she won't listen," his wife warned, but respectfully.

The spark in Katherine's young eyes grew, as did her sass, which often worried both her parents.

Jason's voice hardened. "Listen to your mother," he spat. "Go get the water."

Sally threw her husband a confused glance and lowered her eyes. "Yes, Katherine, go get the water," she said, her eyes following her husband's as Katherine obeyed.

Studying their surroundings, she whispered to her husband, "Are you sure she ought to go off on her own?" as their only child disappeared into darkness, leaving the safety of the evening fire.

"Yes," Jason nodded. "Now Sally, don't you fret. She'll learn, just like she's learning how to read."

Sally's eyes darted from her husband to the sound of her young daughter's laughter as the girl disappeared into the darkness. Straightening her aching back, she said, "Supper's ready."

Out of nowhere a frigid wind tore through their camp, tossing and toying with everything in its path. As the wind calmed, both parents nervously called out for Katherine. An owl hooted, shooting adrenaline through them both. "Katherine! Where are you? Come back."

A long, dead silence ensued. "My baby!" Sally cried.

"Stay here," Jason demanded, "I'll find her."

Another fierce gust of wind tore through their camp, displacing everything in its path.

"No!" Sally screamed, watching their belongings fly off in different directions.

"Put some more wood on that fire," Jason hollered as he disappeared down a steep embankment.

"I don't want to go west," Sally angrily screamed after him. "I want to go home."

Dark clouds dropped rain as thunder exploded. Heavy, freezing rain began to slap her delicate skin. She ran in circles as she grabbed for her precious possessions.

"Look at this," she cried. "It's ruined. Stop it! Give me my clothes back." She barked at the wind as though she were talking to a person.

"Mom!" Katherine yelled. "I'm cold."

Sally dropped the clothes she had been collecting as she followed the sound of her daughter's trembling voice.

Jason, short of breath, hollered, "I found her. Sally, you need to check on the horses."

Bolts of blinding light pierced the darkened sky. A second later thunder exploded, shaking the limbs of the trees their horses were loosely tied to.

Another loud clap sent the horses into a panic. They bolted in all directions, their own confusion adding to their fright. In a blur they broke free and began running off in different directions.

Reaching the top of the steep embankment, Katherine cried, "Mommy!" as she flew to her mother's skirt.

"My baby!" Sally cried. "Are you hurt?" Sally pulled her daughter tight, and then pushed her a few inches away as she stroked her daughter's thick blonde hair.

Jason hurried back to the fire. With a labored voice he demanded, "Get that dry scrub from under the wagon. I told you to keep this fire going."

Sally hurried Katherine to their covered wagon's warmth. Dropping her empty water bucket, Katherine cried, "I'm hungry. Can I eat now?"

Jason's eyes narrowed. "Where are the horses?" he hollered as he caught a whiff of boiling stew.

"I don't know," Sally admitted as she hurried back to the fire after grabbing her wool shawl from the wagon.

"And, young lady, you need to help your mother," Jason shouted, looking at all of their belongings getting soaked.

"Why?" Katherine cried. "I'm cold and hungry."

Wind tore at the treetops, sending limbs crashing to the ground. A heavy branch dropped, ripping apart the wagon's canvas roof. Their wagon swayed.

"Get underneath the wagon!" Jason yelled, as he grabbed the cast-iron pot off the fire.

"My stew!" Sally cried, as she watched her husband fight wind and rain as his fingers blistered.

"Can I eat now?" Katherine asked petulantly.

Jason ducked for shelter, his body shuddering as Sally used her skirt to grab the hot metal. "Thank you," she said with a smile.

"I don't like Arizona," Katherine complained. "It's too cold here."

"This isn't Arizona." Jason shook his head. His daughter's whine reminded him of children he'd schooled in Maryland.

Heat from the cast-iron pot radiated warmth as the aroma of hot stew offered comfort.

Katherine asked, "I'm still hungry. Can I eat now?"

Both Jason and Sally considered the frightening wind, rain, and noises thrashing their surroundings. Katherine's simple request lightened their worries. Sharing a quick glance, they watched the weather beneath both sides of their covered wagon. "Yes, it's time to eat," they agreed.

"How?" Katherine asked. She looked up at her parents and said, "I don't have a plate."

The confused look on her cherubic face drew a chuckle from her parents.

"Why are you laughing?" Katherine questioned as she huddled closer to her parents.

Sally's fingers curled around her husband's soft hands.

Their young daughter dipped her finger into the boiling pot. "Ow!" Katherine cried. "It's hot."

Jason grabbed her tiny hand and delicately kissed her throbbing finger. Then in a commanding voice he said, "You're a lady. You've been schooled. All ladies use plates and silverware."

He threw a hard glance at his wife.

"I'll be right back." Sally let go of her husband's hand and wiggled backwards, slithering like a snake from beneath the wagon.

"Where is Mom going?" Katherine yawned. "I'm still hungry."

Chapter 10

Ten years earlier.
The early morning's light pierced the darkness, spilling its warmth onto everything it touched.
"Run, Katherine, run!" Katherine's mother shouted.
"Hide her!" his father hollered. Katherine, oblivious to her parents' concerns, yawned and curled tighter beneath her blanket.
Her parents' voices lifted and then dropped.
Yawning, Katherine said, "Can I eat now?"
She looked around for the stew, then smelled an unpleasant aroma.
"Mommy, where are you?" In panic she loudly cried, "Mommy...Daddy...where are you?"
Coyotes howled and small twigs snapped, frightening her. She hid, waiting for her parents to return. But nights turned to days, and days turned back into frightening night.

"If you women even think about crossing me I'll leave you right here!"
"Stop!" a strong voice demanded. "We should burry them folks."
"I'll leave you here if you try!" the older woman shouted. "Don't you ever interrupt me again."
The girls in the wagon lowered their heads. A few lifted an eye for a quick glimpse outside the safety of the wagon.
"These people were killed by savages," the older woman said. "Do you want to be whored by an Indian?"
"What was that?" a young voice asked.
Surprised and a bit uncomfortable with her surroundings, the woman replied, "That's Indians watching us.
The naive young women huddled together, their bodies shaking.

Katherine heard the familiar squeaking of ungreased wheels, an annoying noise she hadn't ever forgotten. Cautiously she rose. Staring through the rims of the wheel, she watched as a wagon neared.

A smile crossed her face as she stood up and waved. "Mommy, Daddy, why did you leave me here?"

The wagon didn't slow.

"Don't leave me here!" Katherine yelled. "Mommy, Daddy, where are you going?"

"What was that?" a frightened voice inside the wagon asked.

"Stay down, ladies!"

"I don't want to die!" a tiny voice cried.

"Samuel, turn this wagon around," the older woman demanded.

"Yes ma'am." Without hesitation Samuel turned the six-horse team.

Katherine jumped out from underneath the wheel and ran as fast as her puny legs would carry her toward the approaching wagon.

"What is that?" the older woman asked, throwing Samuel a quick glance.

"Why, ma'am," he paused as he stared long and hard. "Ma'am I think it's a girl."

A smile lifted the madam's heavy face as her eyes tightened. "Pick her up," she coldly said.

Out of breath, Katherine's pace slowed as she waved wildly toward the wagon. "Why did you leave me?" she shouted. "I didn't mean to try the stew before you. I'm sorry, I was just hungry."

Young ears, still frightened, listened.

"Your parents are dead," the madam callously announced as the wagon slowed.

"You're not my mommy!" Katherine screamed, turning to run away.

"Get back here, you little brat!" The woman's pace was no match for a six-year-old's. "I've got you!" Her eyes tightened as she scooped up Katherine. Eyeing her catch, she coldly said, "Well, well. I do believe you'll make me a handsome profit."

Chapter 11

"Mommy…" Kitty cried, "Where are you?"

"What?" Candice lifted her head, studying her quiet surroundings. "You just told me to get some sleep!" she barked. "So why are you talkin' now?"

"I thought I heard something," Kitty quickly responded.

"You're worse than me," Candice grumbled as she dropped back into her blankets.

"I think it's them," a voice whispered. "I knew them horses we passed looked familiar."

"Are you sure?"

A whiff of foul odor assailed Kitty's senses. Rolling over, she carefully whispered in Candice's ear, "We have to get. Now."

Candice didn't move, so Kitty lightly slapped her.

"I told you!" Candice snarled, annoyed. "I don't have any more of that white stuff."

"Get up!" Kitty demanded as her eyes strained to see into the darkness.

Candice lifted her head. "Why would I want to get up?"

Kitty's hands covered Candice's lips, muting her voice.

Candice squirmed and fought back, biting Kitty's fingers.

Kitty trembled but didn't cry out. No match for Candice, her heart raced as she angrily whispered, "We need to get. Now!"

"You ladies stay right where you are."

Both women froze. Kitty's back straightened.

"Don't move again!" the stranger demanded, "or I'll lay you in your tracks."

Candice curled into a ball while Kitty cautiously stood up and dusted off her skirt. "Why shouldn't we move, sir?" she asked the stranger.

The man's eyes jumped. Kitty fingered her golden locks and gave him a seductive smile. "I'm not going to give you my pleasures without an answer," she said.

She whimsically twirled around to give the stranger a good look at her.

"You are horse thieves!" the man accused, but his voice fell and as his eyes filled with lust as they followed Kitty's movements.

Candice grabbed the shotgun and hollered, "I got him."

"What the...?" The stranger drew fast and sure, aiming at Kitty, but Candice jumped up, aimed, and fired. The man slumped to the ground before he could get off a shot.

"No!" Kitty cried. "You can't kill him."

Candice's eyes tightened. "Kitty, for heaven's sake, shut up or I'll shoot you next."

"So which one of us was he after?" Kitty asked.

"I think you," Candice replied, her shotgun still in hand.

A smile sneaked across Kitty's face. She lifted an eyebrow and said, "What was that song you sang earlier?"

Candice remained vigilant, her eyes searching the darkness, shotgun still raised.

Kitty threw Candice an uppity look and said, "I know I can sing that song prettier than you." She stood tall and added, "And I can dance to it much better then you!"

Her voice fell, as she noticed Candice's raised shotgun.

Familiar noises of frogs croaking and crickets chirping resumed.

"You're wrong," Kitty shouted. "I think he was gunning for you. You told me you borrowed them horses, so why did a man pull a gun on us over borrowin' horses?"

Candice lowered her head. "I didn't have enough money to pay for them," she admitted.

"So you stole them!" Kitty sputtered. "Why would you do that?" Without waiting for Candice's response, she added, "You know...we can get hanged for that."

"I was goin' to give them back," Candice shouted back.

"When?" Kitty demanded.

"I don't know. Maybe when we got to California."

"California?" Kitty blinked. "Yesterday you didn't know where we were goin'."

Both women stood, dusted off their dirty skirts, and eyed each other.

"Okay," Candice admitted. "I borrowed them horses because I knew Jack would be coming."

Kitty shook her head. "Well, there's a big difference between borrowin' and stealin'." Her eyebrows raised. "And I ain't going to get hung for stealing!"

"Then you shouldn't have told me you wanted to leave San Francisco!" Candice hollered.

"Thanks for..." Kitty's voice slowed as she studied the man's still body.

"No, you're right." Candice replied.

Kitty walked over to the man's body and kicked it. He didn't twitch.

"Good night, Kitty," Candice said, crawling into her bedroll again.

"I knew it wasn't me!" Kitty replied with a yawn, following suit. "So what's better?"

"What are you talkin' about now?" Candice grumbled through a yawn.

"Should I marry the marrying type or not? Which do you think's better?"

Candice softly replied, "Just make sure he's a good man, whoever he is."

"But you were married. Is getting married wrong?"

Candice curled and rolled away from the fire as she said, "I'm sure that dead cowboy over there has a brother who will be coming for us. We need to sleep fast and hard while we can."

Surprised at Candice's response, Kitty's thoughts raced. She scooted closer to Candice and curled next to her like a kitten.

A frigid wind howled and a branch snapped. Both women's eyes flew open.

Chapter 12

"What was that?" Kitty whispered, her gun hand fidgeting.

"I think it was only a rabbit," Candice cautiously replied.

"So why are we whispering?" Kitty giggled as her racing heart slowed.

"I think it's time to get out of here," Candice mumbled. "It's a sure thing we ain't gettin' any sleep."

"What fer?" Kitty stretched and yawned.

Still whispering, Candice said, "Because it's almost sunup." She studied their surroundings. The predawn light offered a glimpse of soaring rock croppings paralleling their path. Her voice grew serious as she said, "We could get ambushed here. We need to get, now!"

"Okay, okay," Kitty mumbled, her eyes still closed. She rolled over and tucked in tighter. Giggling, she said, "I'm not the marrying type. But if you promise me I can have your gold mine, yes, I'll marry you."

"What is wrong with you?" Candice barked. "Kitty, get up! I'll get the horses. You pack."

"Sure," Kitty replied as she rolled over and curled away from Candice.

Candice's frown softened as she walked away from Kitty, heading off into the distance where she had left the horses.

She glanced over her shoulder as she walked away, watching Kitty. She stumbled, as shadows hid small rocks strewn in her path.

"There you are." Yawning again, she blinked as she caught a glimpse of the horses in the dim light.

"Did you boys have a good night?" Not expecting a response, she closed in on the horses, and then slowly slipped a rope over their heads. "I'm so glad you boys slept good," she said as her fingers combed their manes. "We have to get going now."

The horses willingly followed Candice. "I'm going to buy you both an entire barrel of oats," she told them, stroking their ears.

Sunlight teased, offering warmth as it danced off of the rocky hillsides above them. "It's going to be a nice day." Candice sighed as she headed back to the wagon.

"I'll shoot!"

Candice stopped in her tracks. Her heart racing, she listened hard.

"I told you!" she heard Kitty scream. "I ain't the marrying type!"

Shaking her head, her heart calmed and she walked the horses forward.

"I ain't never traveling with you again," Candice said, "You're too crazy for me."

Without batting an eye Candice headed toward the buckboard.

"You stay away from me!" Kitty cried, wrenching Candice's heart. The girl was dreaming again.

"Come on, boys," Candice said to the horses her eyes half closed, "We need to go. No, you can't eat this grass." She talked to the horses and they followed her instructions.

In a matter of minutes Candice had the horses hitched to the buckboard.

"What is wrong with you?" Candice yelled at Kitty after taking a few steps away from the horses. "Wake up, Kitty!"

Big Jake threw a familiar shadow, and Candice's heart leaped. Big Jake stood directly in front of Kitty. Kitty was standing and her gun was aimed.

"I already told you!" Kitty hollered. "I ain't goin' to marry you."

Candice slowly stepped backwards and hid in the shadows.

Big Jake lifted his massive arms and said, "I brought your bird back."

Kitty knew Candice was close. She threw her a confused look.

"You need to get back to your cabin," Kitty said as evenly as her racing heart would let her.

"No money," Big Jake said, curling his huge body.

"Why?" Kitty asked, the threat in her voice subsiding.

"I brought you the bird," Big Jake proudly said.

No longer afraid, Kitty approached Big Jake. "You made my bird live!" she said excitedly.

"Me Big Jake." He shook his massive head. "I hungry."

Candice stepped from the shadows.

Kitty yawned. "Me too!" she announced.

Candice was still focused on her husband coming after her. And she was even more worried about the family of the dead man she had shot earlier, who stood before her in full sight.

Big Jake's slow, simple thoughts offered both women comfort.

Kitty yawned again. "Candice says we need to get outa here right know. What do you think?"

"I Big Jake. I hungry."

"Me too!" Kitty grumbled, throwing Candice a scowl.

"But we don't have any food!" Candice yelled.

"I got food!" Big Jake laughed. "I got lots of food."

"Huh?" Both women shared a look as the warmth of the sun and thoughts of food soaked their minds.

"I'm hungry too," Candice spat, "but we have to get out of these hills."

Big Jake surprised both women when he nodded in agreement.

"I'll…" Candice's voice stilled as she watched Big Jake and Kitty pick things up.

"Can I come anyway?" Big Jake asked.

Candice and Kitty grinned at each other. Kitty said, "Sure. You're stronger than us and we could use your help."

Big Jake straightened his back. "I'm married anyways," he said.

Candice and Kitty shot each other a hard glance while Big Jake grabbed his belongings and theirs and threw everything in the back of their buckboard.

"I have two wives, actually," Big Jake laughed.

Chapter 13

"Thank you for your help," Kitty said as she jumped in the wagon as fast as she could. "Go…go now!"

"Where did he come from?" Candice screamed.

"I don't know," Kitty cried, "but I think he'll take care of us."

"I stole his gold," Candice whispered.

"What gold?" Kitty asked.

"Big Jake's gold."

"So why didn't he kill us just now?" Kitty questioned.

"I don't know." Candice's head fell. Quickly lifting it, she said, "I think he loves you, that's why."

Kitty threw Candice an uppity look. "Every man loves me. I know that."

Candice's eyes tightened. She hollered, "Big Jake, which one of us is you goin' to marry first?"

Big Jake simply got back on his horse and said, "We go now."

Kitty screamed, "Wait! Where's my bird Lucky?"

"What are you talking about?" Candice fired back. "If Big Jake's goin' to lead us out of this shootin' trap, he'll get shot first."

Big Jake heard the women and laughed. "I like my wives. You both funny."

"Well I don't like you!" Kitty screamed. "You smell!"

"Hush!" Candice demanded. "We need him. He'll get killed first."

Their buckboard leaped, surprising both women.

Big Jake slowed his horse's pace. "You funny." He laughed as his huge neck twisted to look over his shoulder at the flying buckboard.

"I ain't goin' to marry you!" Kitty screamed as her fingernails dug deep into the rail.

"Why did you say that?" Candice spit.

Big Jake constantly glanced back at the wagon. His head shook and his voice exploded in laughter, time and time again.

Kitty and Candice quit talking.

"Stop or I'll shoot!" a voice demanded.

Big Jake's thick neck lifted as he hollered, "I big Jake....No."

"I ain't after you," the stranger said, "I'm after them whores."

"No," Big Jake replied, "Them are my wives." He watched the man's trigger hand and with a full smile said, "Do you want one of 'em?"

"No." The stranger's gun lifted and aimed.

"I don't need them both," Big Jake hollered.

"I'm here to settle a score," the stranger said.

"I don't need two," Big Jake insisted.

The stranger studied both women as he said, "They're both wanted."

Kitty's heart raced as she jumped up and said, "What fer!" She lifted her gun.

Big Jake laughed, catching the stranger's attention.

Kitty's gun exploded, dropping the stranger in his path.

Big Jake jumped off of his horse and clapped.

"What the heck is he doing that fer?" Candice asked Kitty, then yawned.

"I don't know," Kitty replied, "I think we should let him ride with us."

Candice's thoughts tumbled as she said, "Big Jake, you need to tell us how to get to Bodie."

"Can I eat Bodie?" Big Jake asked.

Both women frowned as they shared a quick glance.

"Like I already told you," Candice whispered, "he'll get killed before us."

Sunlight offered them warmth as they rolled along. Kitty and Candice urged their team on, as Big Jake jumped back on his horse. Both women forced smiles.

"You show us the way, they told Big Jake."

Big Jake kicked his horse's flanks.

"Are you sure about this?" Candice questioned Kitty.

"Yep," Kitty replied.

"Where is Bodie anyway?" Candice asked. "I like the thought of heading south."

Kitty started humming. Big Jake looked up.

"You are the flirting type," Candice laughed. "So where is Bodie?" she asked again.

Kitty began to sing again, louder.

"I ain't going to tell you how to sing that song again!" Candice replied, listening to Kitty's tone.

Heading downhill, they both, willingly, followed Big Jake.

"How far do we have to follow him?" Kitty whispered.

"I don't know," Candice quietly replied."

"But now I have to marry two men!" Kitty complained.

"Huh?" Candice looked up. "What two men?"

"Both of them!" Kitty cried, tears pooling in her eyes she whimpered, "I'm sorry."

"What are you sorry for?" Candice said, looking for an answer.

"I don't know," Kitty laughed. Straightening her back she said, "I still can't trust you."

"I ain't used the white powder since I met you," Candice barked as her eyes tightened.

"You better haven't." Kitty grabbed the horses' reins. "Get up," she demanded

"My husband is still coming for me," Candice's warned.

"I know," Kitty murmured. Her head dropped. "We'll shoot him dead next time."

"You're younger than me," Candice admitted, turning the horses to follow Big Jake.

"What does that mean?"

"I don't know," Candice's slowly replied as she shook her head, working hard at staying awake. Her fingers twitched on the dry, leather reins.

"How much gold did you steal?" Kitty asked as she stretched.

"I didn't steal it!" Candice denied. "I borrowed it."

"Oh. Like you borrowed the horses? I already told you, I'm not getting hanged for horse stealing."

Bodie or Bust

A full smile filled Candice's face.

"So, you're not going to tell me how much gold you have, are you?" Kitty snapped.

"What gold?" Candice laughed.

"If you're still on that opiate stuff and making all this up," Kitty's eyes narrowed, "then I'll just kill you now."

"You're just jealous," Candice teased.

"Jealous about what?" Kitty's back straightened. "I have two men going to marry me."

"Do you really believe James is going to marry you?" Candice laughed.

Kitty exploded. She slapped Candice's arm as she screamed, "I'm prettier and smarter than you'll ever be!"

"I'm richer than you, and I'm not a hog farmer!" Candice fired back.

"You both still funny," Big Jake hollered, laughing. "We go faster now." Big Jake's horse broke into a dead run.

Neither women paid attention. Their horses did. They bolted, following Big Jake's lead.

The reins promptly slipped through Candice's fingers.

"Grab them!" Candice shouted at Kitty as the reins flew into the air.

"I already told you," Kitty replied with her nose in the air. "I don't do horses."

"Then you won't get any of my gold!" Candice screamed.

"So now you're being truthful!" Kitty spat as they raced along.

"Hold on!" Candice shouted, eying the terrain in front of their horses.

"How much gold?" Kitty demanded.

"Grab them reins!" Candice screamed. "The reins are slipping toward you."

"No!" Kitty yelled. "If I'm going to get hung for stealing gold, I need to know." Kitty grabbed for breath. Her eyes filled with dreams, as she angrily demanded, "How much gold?"

"If we get killed it won't matter," Candice screamed as her thick body bumped back and forth on the buckboard.

Kitty started singing, "Jimmy crack corn and I don't care…Jimmy crack corn and I don't care."

"Two pockets full!" Candice cried. "Now grab at them reins!"

Kitty recklessly stood up. Her body swayed as she calmly said, "I hate horses." She dangerously dipped close to the horses' thundering feet as she grabbed for the snaking reins.

In a single swoop her hands latched onto the leather and she pulled the reins but they resisted. Her body flew forward.

"No!" Candice cried, as she bolted forward, grabbing at Kitty's flying body.

"Whoa!" she screamed. "I've got you! Hold on!"

Chapter 14

"What the heck is wrong with these horses?" Kitty calmly asked.

"Nothin'," Candice cried as she grabbed hold of Kitty's skinny body.

"What are you waitin' fer?" Kitty cried. "Stop these critters!"

"Hang on! I'm doing the best I can."

"Well, hurry up!" Kitty screamed. "I don't want to die by way of a horse."

Gunfire exploded.

"Help me out!" Kitty screamed.

"You're not as slim as you think you are," Candice cried as her thick arms reached for Kitty.

"What!" Kitty yelled. "I am too slim. Just let me go, then."

"What the heck are you talking about now?" Candice hollered.

"You!" Kitty yelled as her blonde hair flew in the wind.

"I ain't sure why I'm rescuing you anyways!" Candice screamed. Candice stood up and swayed. "If I die for this, I'll kill you!"

Kitty caught a glimpse of fear in Candice's eyes. She roared, "I already told you, we should just go back to them miners."

Candice studied the thundering horses. Throwing her arms forward, her body wobbling, she said, "Next time I'll let them animals kill you."

Kitty giggled, surprising Candice. "Do you want to die by horses?" she yelled.

"No!" Kitty said. "But if you pull on my arm any harder, yes."

With a strong yank, Kitty flew into the buckboard and Candice kept an iron grip on Kitty's right hand.

Kitty's hips fell hard on the seat. "That hurt!" she screamed. "Why did you do that?"

"We're headed south," Candice told Kitty smoothly.

"Why?" Kitty questioned, offering her friend a short smile.

"Because you told me to," Candice quietly replied, yawning again.

"Give me them reins!" Kitty demanded.

Without any resistance from Candice, Kitty grabbed the reins and slowed the horses.

Daylight fell and a cool breeze settled in. Candice fell asleep on Kitty's shoulder.

"I back!" Big Jake roared, his horse foaming.

"Good for you," Kitty said with a yawn.

"Indians," Big Jake shouted, as he disappeared as fast as he had appeared.

An unfamiliar noise grew and Kitty sensed danger. She slapped Candice on the shoulder. "Wake up! Indians are coming."

Candice didn't stir.

"Turn!" Kitty screamed at the horses in panic. "Go now!"

The horses, not familiar with her commands, kept up their pace--forward.

"You stupid horses!" Kitty cried. "Candice!" She slapped Candice's face. "Wake up!"

Indians flew past her as she toggled the reins and the horses gained speed.

"No!" she cried. "You're supposed to run *away* from the Indians!"

In anger she dropped the reins. "Okay, I don't care. You go wherever you want to."

Candice stirred. "So where did you say Bodie is?"

"I ain't ever going with you again!" Kitty cried.

Tired of Kitty, Candice said, "Thanks for letting me sleep. Hey, what is all that noise?"

"Indians," Kitty replied.

"What!" Candice's back straightened as she said, "Hold on!"

Her hands latched onto the snaking leather reins and she slowed the horses. Eyeing a valley filled with tall, thick shrubs, she screamed, "Get up!"

Kitty fell backwards and her legs shot upward.

Candice saw her and laughed.

"They're only men!" Kitty shouted. "I can handle them."

Bodie or Bust

Candice studied the cliff. She shook her head in disagreement as she said, "Kitty, I ain't goin' to get scalped today. Hold on!"

"What was that?" Kitty cried as an arrow pierced wood only a few inches from hrt back.

Both women glanced behind. The Indians were gaining ground. Hearts pounding, they screamed, "Get up!"

The horses bolted. "Hold on!" Candice cried. The buckboard moaned and slid. "NO!" Candice shouted, as she tried to tighten the reins, but the horses ran until the Indians gave up the chase.

"Why are they lettin' us go?" Kitty shouted as she glanced over her shoulder.

"I don't know," Candice cried. "Maybe this is a trap. But I'm killin' these horses and I've got to slow them." She yanked on the reins and slowed the horses as she turned them and headed into a thicket of overgrown grass.

"Whew, that was a close one," Kitty whispered. "Now, what do we do?"

"We rest the horses and sleep," Candice offered cautiously.

"You know I hate horses," Kitty whispered into the darkness toward Candice. "I ain't ever going to get back into a wagon again." Kitty settled under her blanket.

"I got us away from the Indians, didn't I?" Candice yawned.

"I miss James," Kitty cried. "I really think I'm in love."

"Let's pray the Indians won't be coming at us tonight." Candice turned away from Kitty, hoping for silence.

Chapter 15

Melting snow and constant sunshine dried their once muddied path.

A frown settled on Candice's young face.

"All the champagne I can drink!" Kitty said.

"Hush!" Candice warned. They're still here!"

"Who's still here?"

"The Indians!"

"I already told you." Kitty threw Candice an uppity look. "I can handle men."

"These are Indians," Candice whispered, hoping to still Kitty's loud mouth.

"I know what Indians are!" Kitty hollered, "They're just men."

"Be quiet!" Candice whispered.

Kitty shook her head and cautiously raised her voice. "How long were you on that white powder?"

"They're comin' in from the north," Candice said.

"Who is comin'?" Kitty snapped, her voice jumping.

Candice threw Kitty a glare. "You have blonde hair. They'll scalp you first."

Kitty's eyes grew wide as she whispered, "How did they find us? We just almost got killed falling down that ridge."

"Because they're Indians," Candice said, lifting her head. "They know this country better than us."

"I'll kill them all!" Kitty screamed.

"Stop yelling!" Candice whispered. "They'll follow your voice."

"It's dark." Kitty hollered, "You Indians want me?" Her face reddened as she screamed, "Come get me!"

"Are you crazy?" Candice cried in a tiny voice.

"What was that noise?" Kitty asked, staring into the darkness.

"It sounded like…no it can't be." Candice hesitated.

"It's a baby," Kitty said. "It's crying. I'll save her."

As Kitty stood up, Indians with white paint lining their dark faces, surrounded their fire. She pushed through the thick stand of men and grabbed a crying baby from one of the Indian's arms. The Indians raised and aimed their weapons.

"Are you crazy?" Candice screamed as she ducked to the ground.

Kitty unbuttoned her blouse, and without hesitation, offered her breast to the infant. "What are you crying for? Where's your mommy?" Her voice softened as she rocked the infant and whispered, "Its okay. I have milk." The crying instantly stopped.

Candice cautiously stood up. "Kitty, what the heck are you doing?"

"It's a baby!" Kitty proudly announced. "And it's hungry."

The Indians' threatening voices stilled. Their weapons lowered as their eyes fell onto Kitty's exposed breast.

"I'm feeding a hungry baby," Kitty said, drawing the infant close.

With her mouth agape, Candice watched as Kitty hummed and rocked the baby.

Kitty stepped past the men, her eyes focused on the baby.

"Where are you goin?" Candice whispered. "These are Indians. Give them the baby back."

"I know they're Indians." Kitty glanced at Candice and smiled. "Isn't this baby cute? Her body's cold. I'm going to warm her by the fire."

Candice followed Kitty's every movement. She cautiously asked, "How come you have breast milk?"

"I don't know, "Kitty sighed. "When I marry James I want at least ten kids."

Candice stiffened. "These are Indians," she said. She shook her head, "That's a baby Indian. You can't keep it."

Kitty threw Candice a frown, then grimaced as the infant suckled hard. "Ow!" she cried as she adjusted her nipple. "You're really hungry, aren't you, little one?"

A graying older Indian wearing a colorful headband dotted with dyed feathers spoke to the crowd as the rest of the braves argued.

One rail-thin brave's voice was louder than the rest. He kept pointing toward Kitty.

"What are they sayin'?" Candice asked as she joined Kitty by the fire.

"Rock–a–by-baby." Kitty paid no attention to the men or Candice. "You are the cutest baby in the whole wide world." Her smile faded as the Indians' voices flared. She turned away from them and quietly sang to the baby.

The chief stepped away from the arguing braves and walked toward the fire. His unhurried pace and dark, leathery face made Candice's gun hand jumpy.

Without turning to face Candice, Kitty calmly said, "Don't shoot. I'll give the baby back."

The rest of the braves raised their bows and arrows.

"Are you sure?" Candice whispered as her fingers fidgeted.

Kitty turned and faced the chief. "You be good." She kissed the baby's forehead and wrapped it tight as she tucked her breast back inside her blouse. She offered the baby back to the chief.

His black, hardened eyes never left Kitty's face. He showed no emotion as he grabbed the baby and carried it upside down.

"Be careful!" Kitty shouted. "It's a baby, you know."

An arrow flew, landing inches from Kitty's boots.

"Hush!" Candice cried as she lowered her head submissively.

"It's a baby," Kitty repeated as she stepped past the arrow and approached the chief who was still holding the baby sideways.

The chief glanced over his shoulder and hollered toward the rest of the braves.

"Like this," Kitty said as she gently turned the baby around. She smiled and hummed, and the infant gurgled.

The chief reluctantly swayed the baby in his arms.

"That's it. See? It works." Kitty knew the chief didn't understand her. She just hoped her simple gestures would help keep the baby alive.

The chief shouted something, and a young brave flew to his side. He handed the child to the brave and showed him how to hold the baby and how to rock it. The young brave threw Kitty a killing look. A frown settled on his face as he awkwardly rocked the infant.

Kitty giggled as she watched the brave. "That's it." She nodded. "Just like that."

The chief quietly disappeared into the darkness. His braves followed him.

"Listen," Kitty whispered with a smile. "I think the other braves are teasing the brave who has to carry the baby."

The Indians' voices faded.

"How long have you been pregnant?" Candice asked, staring at Kitty's stomach.

Chapter 16

"Kitty yawned as she stretched. "I ain't pregnant. I'm in love!"

Candice shook her head, strongly disagreeing, "You don't have breast milk unless you've been pregnant."

"I was and now I'm not," Kitty admitted. "Shouldn't we be getting out of here?"

Candice nodded and headed toward the horses.

"The rabbit tasted good," Kitty shouted after Candice. Candice bowed her head and mumbled something under her breath.

"Are you mumbling at me?" Kitty jumped up. "Didn't I just save us from them Indians?"

Candice glanced over her shoulder and calmly said, "Why didn't you tell me you were pregnant?"

When Kitty looked down at the ground, Candice gingerly said, "You're right. Let's just get."

Tears pooled in Kitty's eyes as she said, "I'll pick up camp."

Both women headed off in different directions. An owl hooted, surprising Kitty. Coyotes cried, spooking Candice.

Both women jumped into their buckboard and shared a worried glance. "Get up," Candice snapped at the horses.

"You're not mad at me, are you?" Kitty softly asked.

"Why? Candice teased. "Because you don't know how to shoot a rabbit?" Candice laughed and hollered again, "Get up." After a moment she admitted, "Jack was so hard on me. "And I thought I knew men."

"Me, too." Kitty's back straightened as she offered her friend a mindful eye. "So why did you run from him, anyways?"

"I married too young," Candice slowly admitted.

"Was he handsome?" Kitty asked.

Candice's head dropped then slowly lifted. "No." Tears sprang to her eyes as she said, "All he did was rape me and hit me."

Kitty yawned. "So why did you marry him?"

"Stop asking all them personal questions!" Candice bawled. Her eyes narrowed as she asked again, "Are you or ain't you pregnant?"

"I already told you, I ain't anymore." Kitty replied, exasperated.

Candice's voice softened. "Where did you say Bodie is?"

"It's..." Kitty studied the stars still visible in the early light and said, "That way." Her hand pointed left.

Kitty threw Candice a comforting look and Candice regained her composure.

"Okay. So how much gold do you have?" Kitty asked, her eyes widening at the thought of riches.

"What gold?" Candice teased as she watched Kitty for a reaction.

"Don't lie to me!" Kitty spat. "You told me you stole gold from Big Jake."

"No, I didn't," Candice calmly replied, enjoying Kitty's frustration.

"I told you..." Candice turned abruptly away from Kitty, catching her laughter before it spilled, "I told you," she composed herself, "you'll never be smart enough to be a farmer."

"I hate you!" Kitty screamed as she slapped wildly at Candice. "I just saved us from them Indians!" Stiffening, she said, "Stop the horses. I can fend for myself."

Candice pulled back on the reins and the buckboard came to a jarring stop. Kitty jumped from the buckboard and slapped dust off of her skirt.

"You won't survive a day out here without me," Candice shouted.

Kitty paid no mind to Candice and walked away.

Candice watched Kitty disappear into a thick cropping of mature pine trees. "I ain't coming back for you!" Candice warned.

"I don't care," Kitty shouted as she disappeared from Candice's view.

"What is wrong with you?" Candice screamed. "You're pregnant, for Gawd's sake. Get back here."

"No I ain't," Kitty angrily shouted back.

The early morning light offered Candice a glimpse of her surroundings. They were in a narrow canyon that snaked miles in both directions. "Kitty," Candice shouted, "we'll get picked off from here." A rabbit jumped. It startled her. "I'm not kidding," Candice, shouted, "I'll leave you now!"

"I'll shoot!" Kitty screamed at someone Candice couldn't see. Her high shrill echoed around the steep canyon walls.

Candice grabbed for her gun.

Chapter 17

A gun fired. A second shot exploded. Candice jumped out of the buckboard and crawled beneath it. She cautiously whispered, "Kitty, are you alive?"

A long, dead silence set in. A crow landed on the buckboard and cawed.

Candice's heart leaped as she cautiously left the safety of the buckboard. Her voice shook as she shouted, "I've got a gun. I'm coming in."

Kitty ran straight toward Candice, leaving the shadows of the tall trees. She spooked Candice and Candice fired.

"What did you do that for?" Kitty barked. "You could have killed me!"

"You're alive." Candice said, relieved. She shook her head and said, "I don't know why I ever went with you, anyways."

"I found Big Jake," Kitty proudly announced.

"What are you talking about?"

"He's hurt." Kitty's eyes dropped. "I don't think he'll be helping us much more."

"I heard you screaming," Candice said as she followed Kitty into the shadows of the forest.

"That's not Big Jake." Candice bent down to get a better look at a sprawled, lifeless man.

"Oh, not him," Kitty simply replied. "I killed him." Shaking her head, Kitty said, "He pulled his gun first."

"This place is creepy. Is it much farther?" Both women hurried. "There he is." Kitty pointed down an incline.

"Are you sure that's Big Jake?" Candice studied the bloody man's huge physique.

"It's him," Kitty cried. "He's dying."

"How do you know?" Candice questioned.

"Look at all that blood. Nobody can live with that much blood gone."

"So now what do we do?" Candice asked.

"Why are you askin' me?" Kitty said. "Should we shoot him?"

"What for?" Candice threw Kitty a confused frown.

"So the bears don't eat him alive," Kitty said in her annoying uppity tone. "For being a farmer you sure don't know much about the great outdoors."

"I think we should leave him be and get," Candice whispered. "This place is creepy." A second later, changing her mind, she said, "No, I take it back. We can't just leave him here."

"Yes we can. Besides," Kitty added, "the two of us couldn't pull him to the buckboard even if he was alive."

"You just said Big Jake was alive," Candice fumed. "So which is it? Is he dead or alive?"

"I saw his hand move a few minutes ago. So I guess he's alive."

"You didn't go down there and look at his face?"

"No. It's steep. I didn't want to climb back up."

"We've got to go down there," Candice said, talking mainly to herself.

"What was that?" Both women grabbed for their guns, their eyes darting. A faint rustling noise came from the general area of Big Jake's lifeless body.

"He's alive," Candice whispered. "Let's go help him."

"I tell you, he's dead." Kitty shook her head, disagreeing. "I already told you, even if he's alive, we can't lift him."

A soft chirping sound grabbed their attention. "Is that you, Lucky?" Kitty called into the trees. A smile crept onto her face, "Where are you? I saved you some crumbs."

Candice studied Kitty's pale face and said, "Maybe you should sit down. I'll go down there and see if he's dead or alive." Candice drew her gun and cautiously slid, boots first, down the steep embankment.

"Where are you, Lucky?" Kitty repeated.

"I don't like this," Candice said out loud. A musty odor sent her stomach turning. "It smells down here!" she shouted.

"You're a hog farmer," Kitty laughed. "You should be used to bad smells by now." Her voice turned serious as she asked, "Is he dead?"

"Sh... I hear something," Candice whispered as she tucked low to the ground and raised her gun.

"What is it?" Kitty shouted.

"It's...no it can't be. Candice fell silent, piquing Kitty's curiosity.

"It's what!" Kitty demanded. "Is he dead?"

"It's that baby bird." Mumbling, she slowly added, "I think it's your baby bird."

"It's Lucky!" Kitty shouted. "Big Jake has Lucky. What are you waiting for?" she demanded." Bring him up here."

"Yep," Candice replied in a drawn voice. "Big Jake's dead."

"Bring me my bird!" Kitty demanded again.

"What is wrong with you?" Candice barked. "We've got to bury him. Go back to the buckboard and fetch me the shovel."

"Not until you bring me my bird," Kitty shouted.

"I'm not climbing this hill twice!" Candice hollered. "If you want this bird," her voice shook as she screamed, "then go get me the shovel, now!"

The small bird was curled in the palm of Big Jake's left hand. "You're a funny one," Candice quietly said. "Why didn't you fly away?" She scooped the bird up and carried it a few feet away from Big Jake's body, then gently set the bird down in a pile of brown leaves. "You stay here until I bury Big Jake."

"How does Lucky look?" Kitty asked as she threw Candice the shovel. It slid downwards and landed dangerously close to Candice's boots.

"I'll bury Big Jake. You just go check on the horses," Candice shouted. She grimaced as she kicked Big Jake's heavy body into a shallow grave. "I'm sorry, Big Jake." She grabbed a breath, and as she buried him said, "You didn't deserve this. I'll kill them Indians for you."

She picked up the bird and dropped it into her skirt pocket. "Let's get out of here!" she shouted as she scurried on hands and knees up the hill.

"Drop the gun," a man's deep voice demanded as Candice reached level ground. Grabbing for breath, Candice nodded and dropped her gun.

"Did you kill my brother?" a thin, worn man asked as he took aim.

Candice shook her head, and with a labored breath, said, "No."

"I don't believe you," he angrily spat as his face tightened. He cocked his gun.

"I killed him!" Kitty hollered from behind him. He spun around and fired at her. Gunfire again exploded. Kitty beat him to the draw.

The man sank to his knees. His hand shook as his gun lifted. Kitty fired again. He fell to the ground and stilled.

"Why is everyone trying to kill us?" Kitty barked. "Where did he come from?"

Chapter 18

Still grabbing for air, Candice shook her head and said, "I don't know. Let's get out of here."

"Wait!" Kitty stopped halfway back to the buckboard. "Where's my bird, Lucky?"

"He's in my pocket. Keep walking," Candice demanded.

Kitty threw her hands around her hips, "No. I'm not moving until you give me my bird."

"There they are!" a familiar man's voice shouted. A rifle exploded from the cliffs above.

"I'm not dying over some stupid bird!" Candice cried as she ran back to the buckboard.

"Give me my bird!" Kitty screamed, chasing Candice. Both women jumped into the buckboard and yelled, "Get up," to the horses.

"It's Jack!" Candice shouted, "I heard him."

"You should have killed him back in Reno," Kitty yelled. "I'll kill him for you!"

"You're real fast with a gun. Where did you learn to shoot like that? Hold on!" Candice shouted. "Maybe we can outrun him." Both women ducked as their buckboard flew down the narrow canyon.

Gunfire exploded, echoing and ricocheting off of the steep canyon walls.

"I hate men!" Kitty screamed, looking up.

"Do you want to get killed?" Candice cried as she slapped Kitty's head, forcing her downwards.

"Why is Jack still following me?" Candice hollered as her trained hands pushed the team of horses to their limit.

The sun peeked above the cliffs. "Stay in the shade," Kitty hollered. "The shadows will slow his aim."

"I only heard one gun." Candice threw Kitty a quick glance and asked, "Do you think he's alone?"

"I want my bird back!" Kitty calmly replied.

"*What is wrong with you?*" Candice screamed. "We're being shot at and all you can think about is your stupid bird."

Chapter 19

Kitty glanced up at the cliffs. Her body swayed as she said, "Do you have a gun as far ranged as his?"

"No!" Candice cried as she slapped at the reins, driving the horses to an even greater speed.

"Then just stop," Kitty calmly said. "I'll fetch him myself...and I'll kill him myself."

"You're crazy!" But then she curiously asked, "What do you have in mind?"

Kitty's back straightened, and with a raised eyebrow she said, "He's a man."

"Huh?" Candice urged the horses faster. "You're sick," she cried. "And you're gonna' get me killed!"

Kitty casually fluffed her blonde locks as a spark grew in her eyes. With confidence she said, "He's just a man. Slow the horses."

Confused yet happy for a solution, Candice slowed the horses.

Bullets ripped their surroundings. "I don't like this idea!" Candice cried, jumping off the buckboard and ducking for cover.

Kitty boldly stood up, calmly disrobed, and hummed.

"What the heck are you doing now?" Candice cried as she curled into a tight ball.

In a calm, melodious voice Kitty sang, "Skip...skip to my Lou...skip, skip, skip to my Lou."

"Are you crazy!" Candice shouted as she cautiously studied the countryside.

"He may kill me," Kitty admitted, "but he's coming for you, so get your gun ready."

"No!" Candice screamed. "This is not your fight."

Kitty jumped from the buckboard and kept singing.

The gunfire eased up. Kitty enjoyed the freedom of her body and giggled as she sang.

Confused, her heart racing, Candice grabbed for her gun. A flutter in her pocket startled her. "Our bird is alive!" she hollered at Kitty from the shadows underneath the buckboard.

Kitty in a trance, sang and twirled.

Candice crawled from the safety of the buckboard and slid into a shaded thicket of tall grass, her gun ready.

In the blazing full sun Kitty's fair skin reddened. She stopped dancing and put her clothes back on, then calmly said, "I thought he would come for me." Her head drooped as she said, "It's hot here. I could sure use a glass of champagne."

"Where's my wife?" The tone of Jack's voice sent her heart racing. Kitty calmed herself, then raised her head. With feminine charm she slowly turned to face him.

"Where's my wife?" Jack demanded again. "If you don't tell me, I'll shoot you first!" he sneered. "She's here somewhere. Come out!" he hollered. "Or I'll shoot your friend."

Kitty's eyes lowered as she sniveled, "You killed her! She ain't here cuz you killed her! And I hate you for it."

Jack's face tightened. "No girl will ever make me feel this bad again!"

"Well, she won't cuz she's dead. Why did you kill her!" Kitty cried, tears flowing down her cheeks.

Candice's shotgun remained aimed. She grinned listening to Kitty lie to Jack. What a priceless performance.

Jack kept his gun trained on Kitty, but his eyes darted. "Where's her body?" he demanded.

Kitty lowered her eyes and said submissively, "Over there. We need to bury her," she bawled.

When Kitty dropped to her knees, Jack smoothly asked again, "Where's her body? I don't see it." Jack cautiously lowered his gun, then an instant later raised it again. "You best not be lyin' to me! Where's her body?"

"I'm right here!" Candice screamed as she jumped from the tall grass and fired both barrels.

Jack's eyes widened, his neck dropped, then his bloodied chest slammed to the ground.

"You got him!" Kitty excitedly shouted.

Candice dropped the gun and stared.

"You killed him!" Kitty shouted again.

Candice walked over to Jack's lifeless body and dropped to her knees.

Kitty caught a glimpse of tears pooling in Candice's eyes. "It's not your fault. He would have killed you," she said.

"He was my husband," Candice cried. She bent down and stroked the back of his shirt. Tears ran down her cheeks.

"I know he was your husband." Kitty walked over to Candice and tenderly said, "He was no good. He beat you! He deserved to die."

Her words weren't comforting. Crying, Candice curled up next to Jack.

Not sure what to do or say, Kitty softly murmured, "You keep Lucky. She'll take care of you."

"Oh." Candice sat up and fumbled in her pocket. She sniffled and wiped the tears from her face as she said to the bird, "I hope that loud gun didn't frighten you." She stood up and wiped her face dry, then stared at Jack's body for a minute. Then she dusted off her skirt and took a deep breath.

"I'll get the shovel." Kitty choked up when she saw the pain in Candice's eyes. "And I'll bury him."

"No!" Candice protested.

Candice's tone surprised Kitty. She froze and glanced over her shoulder.

"Let the wolves eat him!" Candice pushed past Kitty. Her swollen reddened eyes tightened as she callously said, "You're right. He raped and beat me. Let's get."

As Kitty hurried to the buckboard, she threw her friend a short smile.

"Get up!" Candice shouted at the horses. "He wasn't all bad," she whimpered.

"I know," Kitty consoled. "Men aren't all bad, just some of them."

The women rode in silence all morning long. Steep canyon walls disappeared by early afternoon. Candice drove the horses until their bodies were thick with sweat. Then she walked them.

Kitty complained that she was thirsty and hungry. When Candice hushed her, she remained silent, only occasionally glancing at her friend.

Candice showed no emotion. She just stared ahead and drove the horses hard.

The sun rose and fell. Kitty curled next to Candice and slept. By nightfall the horses' pace slowed to a crawl. When Candice let go of the reins, the horses stopped and their necks dropped. Candice helped Kitty into the back of the buckboard, then curled next to her and slept.

Neither woman noticed the flicker of a campfire in the distance.

Chapter 20

"I love the smell of bacon." Kitty yawned as she sat up and blinked into the blinding sunlight. "Where did you get it?"

Candice was nowhere in sight. Kitty grabbed her gun. "Candice?" she whispered. "Where are you?"

She stood up in the back of the buckboard and studied the land. Mature pine trees as far as she could see dotted the countryside. A winding river gurgled through the woods and emptied into a massive lake in the valley below.

"This must be the lake James was talking about," she said as she stretched.

Candice appeared from the shadows of a cluster of overgrown trees.

"Where did you get the bacon from?" Kitty hollered, yawning again.

"Quiet!" Candice hushed her. "There's a camp right over that next ridge."

"Good. I'm starved." Kitty dusted off her clothes and climbed back into the front of the buckboard. "Get some of your gold out," she demanded, "I want to buy as much food as they'll sell us."

"I think they're mountain men. I'm not tangling with those sorts."

"I'm starving!" Kitty shouted. "We're buying supplies."

Candice shook her head in disagreement. "I'm hungry, too, but it's too risky."

"Don't worry," Kitty said with a long yawn. "They're only men. I can handle them."

A frown settled on Candice's face as she reluctantly turned the horses to head toward the camp.

"That's the lake James told me about," Kitty said as she fussed with her hair.

"So, is that Bodie?" Candice asked.

"No, it's...." She yawned again. "I think he called it Tahoe Lake."

"So how much farther is Bodie?" Candice's frown lifted into a smile as she studied the dark blue lake and endless greenery surrounding it. "It's beautiful. I bet it's got good eatin' fish."

"Who cares about stinky fish?" Kitty raised her eyebrows. "I want tables with linen, fine china, and champagne."

Candice shook her head and chuckled. "The gold wouldn't last long in your hands."

"Well, I'm glad to see a smile return to your face," Kitty said. "Can we at least buy bacon?"

"How far did you say Bodie was?" Candice asked again.

"I'm not sure." A pensive look filled Kitty's face. She mumbled, "I know he said past the lake we need to head southwest to California." She glanced at Candice. "Why do you keep asking me? I've never been there. I don't know."

"If we're going to buy supplies, I would like to know how many we need." Candice threw Kitty an uppity look. "I bet you've never bought supplies before, have you?"

Kitty crossed her arms and straightened her back. "Why should I pay for supplies? I've always got them for free."

"We're not stealing from mountain men," Candice insisted. "They're real mean. I've heard they scalp Indians."

"They're just men," Kitty replied in a snotty tone. "I want to save the gold for champagne. I'll distract them, you grab their food."

'No!" Candice insisted. "We're not stealing from mountain men! And," her tone lightened, "the gold is for a ranch, not champagne. Quiet, the camp's just around the bend."

Candice slowed the horses. "Hello to the camp! Can we come in?" she shouted.

Two tattered, makeshift tents about ten feet apart sat inbetween a smoldering fire pit surrounded with blackened rocks.

"Hello camp," Candice raised her voice again. "Can we come in?" She pulled the horses to a halt.

"Maybe they're out setting traps," Kitty whispered, pointing to a line of drying beaver pelts. "Let's get their supplies while they're gone."

A gun cocked. Kitty caught a flash of the gun's shiny metal. "Don't shoot!" she shouted in a girly voice. "We're lost and hungry. Can we buy some supplies from you?"

"No! Get!" a burly voice hollered. "Get, now or I'll shoot you dead."

"But we're hungry and we're girls." Kitty stood up in the buckboard and rocked her hips.

He fired the gun, spooking the horses.

"I warned you Kitty!" Candice screamed, pulling hard on the horses' reins, turning the animals as best she could.

Before they could get away the mountain man fired his gun again.

"That's not very neighborly!" Kitty shouted at him as she drew her gun and fired back.

"No!" Candice yelled. "Don't shoot at him! He and his friends'll track us all the way to California. Stop!"

But Kitty shot again as she shouted, "Let them!" A frown settled on her face, as she barked, "No man shoots at me!"

Candice guided the running horses into the forest and slowed them.

"Let's go back and kill them!" Kitty insisted angrily.

"No! They're too dangerous. They can out track an Indian and they eat raw meat." Glancing over her shoulder, Candice added, "We're gettin' as far from here as we can." She lightly whipped the reins and whistled at the horses. They broke into a slow trot.

"Keep your gun ready and a keen eye open," she whispered to Kitty. "I've got my hands full with all these trees. They know we can't get away fast, so they'll be commin' for us for sure."

"What fer?" Kitty complained. "We didn't steal anything. And they shot first."

"Because they can," Candice replied bitterly. "What they got is theirs. What *you* got is theirs. And they'll track you till you're dead for it."

"Why didn't you tell me that before?" Kitty's eyes darted toward their back trail and her gun hand fidgeted.

"I did," Candice barked as she snaked the team of horses around trees.

"What am I lookin' for?" Kitty asked as she trained her gun on the shadows flying by.

"I don't know," Candice whispered. "Just keep your eyes open.

Gunfire exploded and both women ducked.

"Where's it comin' from?" Kitty asked as her gun jumped.

"Get up!" Candice shouted at the horses. "Hold on, Kitty!" I'm not sure I can control the team in these trees."

Gunfire exploded again.

"Give me that shotgun of yours, Kitty shouted. "No man is going to shoot at me for doing no wrong!"

"Hold on!" Candice warned as she pulled back her left arm with all of her strength.

"No!" Kitty screamed, flying out of the buckboard with a shotgun in her right hand and her pistol in her left.

Candice, catching a glimpse of Kitty's flying body, slowed the horses just as gunfire exploded again.

"I hate you, Kitty!" she angrily screamed as she led the horses to thicker cover.

Dizzy, Kitty shook her head, clearing her blurred vision.

"Hold on girly!"

A man's voice set her grabbing for her guns. Pain shot through her right arm as a boot stomped on it.

A man whose face was covered in thick whiskers chuckled. "Hank, look it here. I trapped me a whore."

The man stomped harder, twisting his boot. "That hurts!" Kitty cried, "Let me go!"

"She's a lively one," he chuckled, scratching his face.

"Where's the other one?" Hank cautiously asked, coming up beside them.

"She can't be far. I don't hear the horses, but that don't mean nothin'." His blackened tongue licked his lips as he said, "You go track her. I get this one."

"Don't you touch me!" Kitty hissed. "I'll kill you if you try."

He grabbed Kitty's hair.

"Stop it!" she shouted, and he punched her in the face.

"Hank!" he shouted after his companion. "Since she's got golden hair, will you trade me a pelt or two for her favors?"

Chapter 21

Candice eased out of the buckboard and studied her shadowy surroundings, then cautiously headed downhill. Every crack of a branch sent her heart racing. She knew the men knew every inch of these mountains. Kitty's blood-curdling cries fueled her anger.

"I got the other one!" Hank shouted as he leaped from a tree, surprising Candice. Candice fired her gun as Hank's weight knocked her to the ground. Her gun hand shook as she lifted it to his face.

"Ya shot me!" Hank's face went dark with angry blood. He lunged for Candice and she shot again, hitting him directly between the eyes. He shook his head, moaned, and fell to the ground.

Heart racing, Candice reloaded. She stared at the man's twitching body for a moment, then kicked it. Swallowing hard, she coldly said, "That's for Kitty."

"I'll kill you twice next time!" Candice heard Kitty scream. "Get off me!"

Candice hurried down the hill and slowed as she neared the tents. Gun raised, she demanded, "Let her go!" then charged the tent. She abruptly stopped as a hidden bear-trap snapped around her ankle, tearing into her boot. Flying forward, pain shot through her body.

"Kill him!" Kitty cried. "Kill him now! What are you waiting for?"

The mountain man laughed and slapped Kitty as he clawed and ripped her clothes.

Candice howled in pain as she fell to the ground.

"Caught me another one," he growled as he glanced over his shoulder at Candice.

"No!" Candice spat back. "No man is ever goin' to hit me again."

She aimed her gun at the heavy metal encasing her boot. As she fired she ducked her head and turned away. "You're right, Kitty!" she cried. Her face reddened with rage as she screamed, "Men are all bad!"

The mountain man leaped from the tent and fired a shotgun in the direction of the trap. But Candice surprised him. She was free and already ten feet away. He reloaded, cussing under his breath. Candice aimed her gun and fired, hitting him in the chest.

Unfazed, he cocked his shotgun and sneered. Candice leaped for the safety of a fallen tree. The pain in her ankle slowed her.

Kitty ran from the tent, half naked, and fired both barrels of Candice's shotgun at the man's back. "I'll kill you twice next time!" she screamed again as she tried to shoot the empty weapon again.

The man's body flew forward and fell to the ground. Candice cautiously rose from the safety of the downed tree.

Kitty screamed, "I hate men!"

Candice limped over to Kitty and cried, "I told you we shouldn't have mixed with mountain men."

"How bad are you hurt?" Kitty asked, watching Candice gimp along.

"Not as bad as you are," Candice replied. "Your face is a mess."

Kitty pulled her torn clothes tight and simply said, "You're right. We should stay away from mountain men."

"You don't understand." Candice threw a hard look at Kitty. "Mountain men have friends." Her voice grew with fear. "Lots of friends."

"But we did nothin' wrong!" Kitty spat as she kicked the ground.

"It don't matter!" Candice barked. "They're mountain men!"

"Well, I'm not dying on an empty stomach," Kitty snarled, disappearing inside the tent. Her voice softened as she reappeared with both hands full of grub. "I told you," she teased. "I ain't ever paid for food."

"We need to get out of here!" Candice shouted nervously as Kitty disappeared inside the second tent.

"Not without food!" Kitty shot back as she reappeared with more supplies. "I think this will keep us fed all the way to California, don't you? I'll put this stuff in the buckboard and come back to get you." She hurried to the buckboard.

When she returned, she helped Candice onto the buckboard. "Can you handle the horses?" she questioned. She touched her swollen face."I hate men! And I hate what they were about to do to us."

"Me, too," Candice sighed. "So let's go to California and buy a ranch."

"No!" Kitty quickly replied. "I love James." Then she chuckled in that girlish way of hers.

"But you don't even know him!" Candice said. "And you just told me for the hundredth time you hate men."

A smile grew on Kitty's face, her eyes widened, and she raised an eyebrow as she said, "Oh, I know him, all right."

A frown settled onto Candice's face. "I ain't ever gettin' married again. You might want to, but I sure don't."

Kitty sighed and said, "I sure could use a glass of champagne."

Candice flicked the reins to get the horses moving. "What did you say that lake's name was?" she asked, urging the horses forward.

"I think it's called Tahoe Lake." Kitty yawned. "Oh," her voice jumped. "James said to stay clear of the south shore."

"Candice threw Kitty a curious look. "Why?"

"I'm not sure. Indians, I think. But never mind that now. I'm starved. Let's eat."

"No," Candice groaned. "We've got to get out of these mountains before we can stop to eat."Eying Kitty's torn clothes, she carefully said, "And you need to get yourself into a different blouse."

Kitty nodded and crawled over the seat into the back of the buckboard. On her knees, she swayed with each turn of the wagon.

"You're not goin' to throw me out again, are you?" she barked at Candice as the buckboard picked up speed.

"I'm doin' the best I can," Candice shouted. "It's hard steering this thing around these trees."

"Let's see now. We've got flour, coffee, cans of beans, and three satchels of dried meat." Kitty untied one of the burlap bags and held it close to her nose. "I think this one's venison. If you stop I'll make us some biscuits and stew."

"Hand me a piece of that dried meat." Candice reached over her shoulder. Kitty obliged and slapped a thick piece of dried meat into Candice's hand.

"It's really salty," Kitty complained, taking a bite of meat herself. "We should have taken their drinking water, too."

"What fer?" Candice chuckled. "We're following a stream downhill. Can't you hear it?"

"I'm not drinking from anythin' unless it's a champagne bottle!" Kitty exclaimed.

With a full grin Candice said, "Then you're goin' to get mighty thirsty."

"What's this?" Kitty said, her voice jumping. "Eew. It looks like a piece of animal." She cautiously lifted it to her nose. "It *smells* like a piece of animal."

Her curiosity growing, Candice threw a quick glance over her shoulder. "Let me see it."

Kitty, being overly cautious, used only two fingers to pick up the dried animal's skin, careful not to let the skin touch any part of her body. She gingerly handed it to Candice. "I've never seen anything so dead before." She grimaced as she gnawed on the salty jerky.

Candice roared.

"What's so funny?" Kitty snapped. "I know it's dead. It *smells* dead."

"You'll never make a rancher." Candice hid a grin as she calmly said, "It's a goat's bladder."

Kitty abruptly stopped chewing on the dried jerky as she cried, "Eew, throw it away!"

Candice exploded in laughter, then quickly regained her composure. "How much gold would you pay for champagne right now?"

"That's a stupid question! Now throw that smelly thing away!"

"No," Candice simply replied. "I think I'll have a taste of it."

Kitty gawked at Candice as she watched her friend lift the bladder and awkwardly squirt liquid into her mouth. Candice dropped the skin and went into a coughing fit. "That's bad stuff," she hoarsely spat.

"Are you crazy?" Kitty slapped Candice's swaying back. "What are you doing?"

"With a full grin, Candice scooped up the bladder and squirted more moonshine into her mouth.

Her head shook and she gasped for air as she howled, "Oh… that's bad stuff."

The horses veered left. "Watch that tree!" Kitty screamed as she crawled back into the buckboard seat.

"It's champagne," Candice roared as she handed Kitty the bladder.

"Champagne?" Kitty quipped. "That ain't champagne. That's a dead animal."

"Then I'll drink it all myself," Candice roared as her body weaved heavily.

"Give me them reins," Kitty barked. "I don't know what's wrong with you." She hesitated as she watched Candice squirt more liquid into her mouth. "I'm not going to die because of your bad drivin'," she warned.

Candice causally threw the snaking reins in Kitty's general direction as she squirted more moonshine into her mouth.

"I don't know why I came with you!" Kitty whined as her eyes darted from Candice to the horses and back again.

Chapter 22

Years earlier

"Candice, I'm tired of your spat." A broad-shouldered man raised his hand, demanding his daughter's attention. Candice froze and her eyes fell. She'd been exposed to her impatient father's hard hand often.

His angry, demanding voice suddenly changed. It softened as he said, "Jack asked for your hand in marriage." With a sad look on his eyes, his voice turning suddenly bitter, he added, "I can't feed all of yous anymore. It's time for you to move out."

"But I don't want to marry him," Candice nervously replied in a respectful yet serious voice.

"He's goin' to take care of you." Her father's eyes turned cold as he stared at his oldest daughter's trembling body. He growled, "You're just like your mother...worthless." Candice fell to the dirt floor and curled into a tight ball. The fury in her father's voice gave her a warning of what to expect from him that night.

"Yes, Daddy," she tearfully mumbled as he slapped the side of her head with his meaty hand. "Yes, Daddy!" she cried. "I'll marry Jack." Candice knew she was getting too old to stay with her parents, but she wanted nothing to do with Jack. She calmed her racing heart and forced a smile to her bruised face. Lifting her head, in the calmest voice she could find, she repeated much louder, "Yes, Daddy, I'll marry Jack." Her father abruptly stopped his slapping. He turned and slammed the creaking wooden door as he walked outside into the night.

Jack had been the only man who had offered Candice a second look. She knew her short, stout body and masculine facial features kept men away.

Around sunset the next day Jack showed up at Candice's rickety shack, dressed in church clothes and driving a rented buggy.

Candice was outside folding dried clothes from a clothesline. "What are you doing here?" she asked him, though she knew by his attire what was coming next. "My parents and the three youngest are in town. My pa will get mad if you stay here, what with me being all alone."

"I knew you would marry me!" Jack told her, his voice full of excitement. "I'm goin' to be the best husband this side of the Missouri river!" he exclaimed. His genuine sincerity and excitement sent Candice's heart racing. Maybe the rumors about his short temper were wrong. Maybe she *would* find a good husband. She threw Jack a short smile as she said, "I didn't say I'd marry you."

"Your pa said you would." He threw Candice a hard stare and drew his six-shooter. Aiming widely into the sky, he fired. "Yahoo!" he hollered.

"What you wastin' bullets for?" Candice asked, watching Jacks wild eyes.

"Don't question me!" His eyes darkened as he jumped off of the wagon, walked over to Candice, and grabbed her waist. "A woman never questions her man! I ain't marryin' a girl that doesn't trust me!" he spat as his hand slapped her young, delicate face. "You're just a girl!"

Candice caught a glimpse of the fire in his eyes. Her head lowered.

"Get me that bucket of water," he demanded. "That is, if you want to marry me," he said, his voice hardening. When she didn't move fast enough, he kicked Candice on her butt and roared, "You need to move that fat butt of yours faster."

Heavy bucket in hand, Candice fell to the ground, spilling the water.

Jack laughed. "If you want to be my wife," he sneered, "you'll also need to understand pigs."

Candice nodded. She wanted to get up out of the mud the spilled water had made in the dust, but she didn't dare move.

"Get used to the mud!" he howled. He kicked her and grabbed her fiery red hair.

"No! she cried. "I love you." Her words didn't make sense in her own mind, but she had to do something to diffuse his anger.

Jack immediately let go of her hair. He helped her off of the ground and gently brushed dust off of Candice's blouse as he asked with a keen eye focused on her frightened face, "Can you cook? I get mighty hungry. You ain't the purtiest thing in these parts...but I reckon' I could live with you if you know how to cook."

Candice's heart pounded as her thoughts turned to marriage. She surprised herself as she blushed and said, "I'll make you the best stew and biscuits you've ever et." Her back straightened as she threw Jack a girlish grin and hastened her pace to the kitchen stove.

Thoughts of freedom and a man offering her marriage sent her heart into a patter. "Supper's ready," she proudly shouted an hour and a half later as she straightened her skirt and double checked the checkered tableclothed table.

Jack poured on his charm, entering the house with the air of a prince. His thick black hair was neatly combed, and he removed his hat in a gentlemanly fashion as he wiped his boots outside before entering.

Candice blushed and giggled as her heart raced and feelings she had never felt before bubbled inside her. Not sure of what to say or how to say it, she began, "I know I'm not the prettiest girl around, but I'm the smartest." She gulped hard and her voice trembled. "And I'm a good cook and I'll be a good wife."

"Prove it," Jack said, his voice deepening. "Feed me."

Candice grabbed his plate and quickly filled it, then walked away from the table heading back toward the stove.

"Where are you going?" Jack's voice changed again to a lighter tone.

"I don't understand." Candice turned around and lowered her head submissively.

"Well, I ain't eatin' alone!" Jack remarked, surprising Candice. She was used to her father eating first, and it had become a habit to her.

"You mean," her head lifted and a smile big enough to fill the room filled her face, "I'm to eat with you?" She quickly filled a plate and rushed back to the table. She sat and watched Jack inhale the meal. She didn't start to eat because he hadn't given her permission to yet.

He abruptly stopped, and with food falling from his mouth he threw Candice a hard stare, as he said, "Ain't you hungry?"

"You didn't tell me I could begin," she respectfully replied.

Jack choked on his meal as he remarked, "Your father's trained you well. I guess I'll *have* to marry you." Coughing and catching his manners, he straightened his back and cleared his throat. As his eyes fell to Candice's he warmly said, "Woman, do you want to get hitched to me?"

Candice's face went pale because this was the first formal proposal of marriage she'd ever gotten. She couldn't help it, she dropped her spoon. It fell in the stew and hot gravy splashed. Jack roared as a blob of gravy slapped onto Candice's cheek.

After a moment, he cleared his throat again, his eyes following Candice. "Well?"

Overwhelmed with emotions, Candice simply replied, "Yes."

Chapter 23

"Oh…" Candice groaned. "Where am I?" She tried to stand. Pain split through her brain, forcing her to the ground. "Oh…" she slowly groaned again. "My head hurts."

"I ain't caring much about your head hurtin'," Kitty remarked. "I'm worried you might lose that leg." Kitty grimaced as she glared at Candice's blackened, swollen leg.

"How did that happen?" Candice moaned again.

"Well, at least you killed him, and I'm glad for that," Kitty whispered, offering Candice comfort.

"Killed Who?" Candice murmured, rubbing her forehead.

"Jack," Kitty remarked. "Don't you remember killing your husband?"

Candice sat up, her head spinning. "What? Are you sure?"

"Are you telling me you don't remember?" Kitty demanded.

"My leg is numb," Candice whined. "Ow," she cried. "And my head hurts awful bad, too."

Kitty stood, and without complaint picked up their camp while Candice complained like a baby.

"This isn't fair." Kitty remarked. "Now you sound like me!"

"I'll never sound like you," Candice said, still rubbing her forehead. "I'm smarter than you."

Kitty threw an empty bucket and a shovel on the ground as she huffed, "See…you're complaining like I do." She shook her head and stomped her foot, then quickened her pace to load their belongings into the buckboard.

She distanced herself from Candice and cautiously approached the grazing horses. "We got to get now," she calmly said as she threw a rope over their necks and urged them forward.

She'd unhitched the horses in total darkness the night before, and her eyes widened as she stared at the lines of leather she was supposed to know what to do with now.

"You ain't smarter than me," Candice pointed out, catching a glimpse of Kitty's confusion.

Kitty threw Candice a heavy frown and hitched them up as best she could. With the horses hitched up and Kitty unsure about what she had just done, she urged them slowly forward, then proudly circled their campsite.

"Just because you know how to hitch up horses don't mean nothin'," Candice said, having a hard time raising her voice. When her voice rose her head screamed in pain.

Kitty enjoyed watching Candice's long stares and deep frowns. She circled the horses tighter and carefully stopped them inches away from Candice.

Gloating, she said in an uppity tone, "I know how to read and write." She clutched her tiny waist and quipped, "So I reckon I'm smarter than you."

Candice's eyes filled with anger. Her numb leg throbbed as she tried to stand.

Kitty wrapped the reins around the brake and jumped out of the buckboard to offer Candice her shoulder.

"I don't need your help," Candice barked, her voice full of vinegar.

Kitty took a step backwards. "Don't look like you can climb into the buckboard alone," she said with fire in her voice.

Candice's weight pulled on her swollen leg and she cried out. Kitty ran to her friend.

"Get away from me!" Candice spat. "I can do this myself."

Though her feelings were hurt, Kitty patiently resisted helping her injured friend. Candice threw a few dagger glances back at Kitty as her body refused to stand.

"You're takin' to long," Kitty said. In a commanding voice Candice hadn't heard before she said, "We got to get, and you're gonna let me help you into that buckboard."

Candice didn't say another word. Her leg and head hurt too much to argue anymore.

Without another word, Kitty strained every muscle she had in her body helping Candice into the buckboard.

Candice went a little limp, frightening Kitty. She couldn't be sure about Candice's immediate situation, and she didn't know what to do.

She had studied the valley below last night and had seen the dotted fires and had heard an occasional spatter of men's laughter. She knew it wasn't a mountain man's camp. She was hoping it was a big enough settlement to have a doctor.

She had never driven a team of horses before, let alone straight downward. She drew a deep breath. "Get up," she said, flicking the reins.

The reins ripped at her delicate fingers as she struggled to manage the team. She kept glancing at Candice for support, but she found no help there. Candice's heavy body fell forward.

"No!" Kitty cried, scrambling to keep Candice from flying out of the wagon.

"I hate you, Jack!" Candice mumbled as a bump jarred her awake. "What the?" She shook her head and blinked. Her head still smarted a mite. "Give me the reins," she ordered to Kitty, still half awake.

"Hold on!" Kitty screamed, her body frozen stiff.

With little energy to offer her terrified friend, Candice pointed out, "You need to put the brake on." But then she fainted and went limp.

"Do you think this is easy?" Kitty screamed at Candice.

But Candice curled up like a fat kitten, and her body stilled on the buckboard's seat.

The horses fumbled on down the slope, and for one alarming instant the buckboard came dangerously close to flying forward. A second later it leaned dangerously to the left, almost flipping over.

Kitty knew that without the help of a doctor, her friend would die. Gulping hard, she released the tight grip she had on the reins and surprised herself when she shouted with more confidence than she had ever felt before, "Come on, horses! We can do this!"

Chapter 24

Given full rein, the horses slowed and stopped. "Kitty shouted, "Get up!" whipping wildly at the reins. The horses refused to budge on the steep ledge.

Releasing the brake, Kitty slapped their bodies with a whip. Her hands shook, as did her voice. The horses leaped, unwillingly sliding downwards.

"Oh no!" Kitty screamed as the buckboard lurched straight up and a second later leaned dangerously to the right. Grabbing for the brake, she screamed, "Candice hold on!"

Candice's limp body bounced as the buckboard plowed downwards.

Kitty's fears grew. As she repeatedly shouted at the horses, whipping them, her voice could be heard for miles. The ground beneath the horses gave way, spilling down the hillside. Rocks flew everywhere.

"I've got to get you to a doctor fast!" Kitty screamed as the buckboard jumped again. Her fingernails dug into the soft wood of the buckboard's rails. The horses slid, and a second later leaped over a cropping of uneven rocks, adding to the buckboard's speed.

They swayed dangerously left, their heads almost slamming into the seat. A second later the buckboard leaped, sending them soaring. Kitty closed her eyes and ducked, protecting Candice with everything her tiny body could offer.

The buckboard picked up even more speed, then a few seconds later abruptly slowed.

Kitty opened her eyes and cautiously sat up. She heard a whisper of piano music and studied the wide fertile valley in front of her. The horses resumed walking and veered left. The buckboard had landed a few hundred feet from a bustling camp. Men's demanding voices and women's laughter brought back a flood of memories. "No," Kitty whispered at the horses.

The horses' foaming backs caught a stranger's eye. "Where you headin'?" he huffed as he grabbed the horses' leather, stopping their movement.

"We need a doctor!" Kitty said, picking up the whip and throwing the man a hard look.

He studied their buckboard. "We ain't got one here." A grin crept on his face as he pointed out, "But we got a saloon."

Kitty slapped the whip, hitting the man directly in the face. Sputtering, he stepped a distance from the buckboard and shouted, "No whore whips me! Draw!"

Kitty's eyes hardened. The only thing she drew was a long yawn. But she cocked her hidden gun and coolly said, "What does *draw* mean? Do you mean like drawing a picture?"

A puzzled expression settled on the stranger's face, buying Kitty the seconds she needed. She whipped the gun from her skirt, aimed, and fired. The stranger's eyes widened as he dropped.

Picking up the reins, Kitty calmly said, "Get up," to the horses.

The town stretched out over a block long. Recently built one- and two-story buildings lined the wide street. She knew she could find champagne and a warm bed here. Her thoughts stayed focused on Candice.

She walked the horses through town, cautiously glancing at the shadows in the alleys. Her scowl lifted as she saw a small sign with black lettering that said: Doctor.

She led the team into an alley adjacent to the doctor's office, jumped out of the buckboard, and while her eyes darted, she softly knocked at the door. When nobody answered right away she got impatient and pounded her fist.

"My friend's real sick!" she cried, pounding harder.

"Why does everybody beat up my door?" a calm, collected voice asked as the door opened.

Kitty gulped hard. His hair was thin and white and his manner was light. She froze as he stared at her bruised and swollen face.

"Who did this to you?" he demanded.

"It's not me," Kitty explained. "I need you to help my friend."

The well-dressed man followed Kitty to the buckboard and peered inside. His eyes tightened. "Come with me," he softly commanded.

Back inside his office he closed the front door and hollered, "Jeremy, come here this instant." A boy half the size of Kitty jumped from nowhere. "Yes, pa?"

He glanced over his shoulder, offering Kitty a comforting glance as he locked the front door behind him. "You stay put." Kitty heard the click of the lock.

She nervously glanced around the room, counting the minutes. Her gun hand fidgeted.

When a door groaned behind her, she dropped to the floor and aimed her weapon.

"Your friend's hurt bad," the doctor said, stopping in his tracks.

Kitty heard the doctor but wasn't sure if he had set her up for a trap. "I don't see her," she said, cocking her gun.

"Put down that gun," the doctor demanded lightly. "If you shoot me, I can't help her." His voice deepened as he said, "Or you."

Kitty jumped up, expecting a fight. To her surprise her body buckled like a wet noodle. "I have money," she whispered as she went down, but her voice faded dead away.

Two days passed, and neither woman stirred. Jeremy obediently followed his father's instructions while the doctor tended his patients.

Candice awoke first. She kept her eyes closed as she listened to her surroundings. She grasped lightly at her skirt, hopping to feel cold metal.

"I see you're awake." The doctor picked up her wrist and gently squeezed it.

"What are you doing?" Candice opened her eyes and stared at him.

"Well," he exclaimed, "you're not goin' to lose that leg."

"Where's Kitty?" she whispered, sensing she could trust this man.

"She's had a few complications." The doctor lowered his head and shook it as he said, "Losing a baby is hard on a woman. She's lost a lot of blood." The doctor's voice showed his worry. "You ladies need to stay put and rest."

Candice sat up. "Where is she?"

"She's in the bed in that dark corner over there. If you need anything, Jeremy will fetch it for you."

"We can pay you," Candice offered. But he doctor just shook his head as he closed the door behind him.

Chapter 25

Days passed. Jeremy followed the young women's demands, hiding a grin each time he entered the room, stealing glimpses of the scantily dressed women.

"Jeremy," Kitty whispered from the shadows, "can you get me a bottle of champagne?"

"I don't know," he honestly replied. "What's champagne?"

Kitty sat up for the first time in a long time and drew a deep breath. Candice rolled over, dragging her hurt leg as she listened to Kitty's coy tone. Both women sighed.

Kitty mumbled, "I think you're right, Candice."

"Right about what?" Candice whined.

"Men." Kitty raised her head off the pillow.

"Men?" Candice laughed. "I just killed the only man who ever loved me. What do I know about men?"

Both women sat up. Kitty started giggling.

"What's so funny?" Candice whispered.

"The young boy." A grin crept onto Kitty's face.

"Yeah, he was staring at my breasts, too." Candice held back her laughter.

Just then, the doctor entered the small room, surprising them. "Well, I see you two ladies are feeling much better." Turning up the lantern, he said, "The sheriff wants to talk to both of you. I gave him my word he could speak to you when you were well enough to talk. I've got to go fetch him now."

Candice's back straightened. "Doc, we have gold and we need to know how much we owe you."

The doctor shook his head. "Two dollars and fifty cents, but you're not well enough to travel." He turned and closed the door behind him. A second door closed.

"We've got to get!" Candice grabbed her clothes. Limping, she got dressed. Throwing Kitty a quick glance, she said, "The doc told me everything. Can you walk?"

Kitty jumped from the bed, and in a teasing voice said, "I could break into a full trot if I had a glass of champagne." But then her face went pale. Her legs buckled and her bottom dropped back onto the bed. "My head's spinning just the same as when I drink two bottles of champagne." She shook her head and inhaled a deep breath as she quickly dressed, still seated on the bed.

"We got to get!" Candice said again, worried. "I ain't much at helping you. This leg smarts something bad."

Their ailing bodies slowed them as they hurried to the back door. Candice tried to hide her limp. Kitty found her gun and kept it ready.

"We got to get to the stables," Kitty whispered as she offered Candice her thin shoulder.

"I can do this," Candice assured herself aloud. She grimaced with each painful step.

Outside the townsfolk casually strolled up and down the hard clay street. Most of the women were using umbrellas to ward off the midday's blinding sunlight.

"Where's the stable?" Candice asked, walking as straight as her body would let her.

"Must be just up ahead," Kitty replied.

"If we get to Bodie," Candice exclaimed, "I want a fine linen dress just like that woman's wearing. I love purple. Look at that cute bonnet. I want one of them, too. Where is the stable?" She huffed again. "I don't know how much farther I can walk."

"My head's not spinnin' as bad," Kitty said. "I think walkin' is good for me. Oh!" Kitty's voice filled with excitement as she exclaimed, "I want that dress, too!"

"Lower your voice," Candice spat. *"How much farther?"*

Kitty nodded and helped steady Candice's limp. "There it is," she said.

They edged inside the stable, deep shadows impairing their vision. "It's dark in here," Kitty whispered. "I think we're here alone. Let's find our horses."

From the shadows a man's voice called out, "Can I help ya?" Shaken, both women abruptly turned.

Kitty stroked her blonde locks, and in a girly voice replied, "Why, yes. We're here to fetch our horses and buckboard. How much do we owe you?"

A tall, slinky man stepped from the shadows and studied the women. "Are them two horses over there your horses?"

Candice shook her head. "No, ours are over there."

"What are you talkin' about?" Kitty snapped. "You know those are our horses." She threw Candice an uppity look as she pointed out, "I know you think I don't know nothin' about horses. But I remember one of our horses had three white stockings. It's that one."

The man stiffened. "Stay where you are!" He drew his Peacemaker Colt and swallowed hard. "You two stole these horses from my brother, didn't you? So now I'm gonna collect."

"You told me you borrowed those horses!" Kitty angrily shouted at Candice.

"As I told you, mister," Candice's tone hardened as she insisted, "them ain't our horses."

"Them horses got my brother's brand on them, and you two...." He shot a glance at Kitty's pale, bruised face. With hesitation he said, "And you two fit his description, I reckon."

Kitty's voice tightened as she threw the stranger a mean look. "You listen up!" Her body swayed. Surprised, she shook her head as her knees buckled. She clutched her hidden pistol as her eyes closed and her body crashed to the floor.

The stranger glanced down at his gun.

"What did you do that fer?" Candice cried. "Can't you see she's sick?"

The stranger took a step backward, eyeing the situation.

"What's all the ruckus about?" A chubby, balding man demanded as he walked with a hard limp into the stable. Looking the situation over, he said, "Why did you shoot that woman?"

Concerned, the man said, "I didn't shoot her. I think she fainted."

"Then why do you have a gun still aimed!" the older fellow hollered.

"Them two stole my brother's horses and buckboard," the man hollered back. "And I aim to take these women back and have them hanged!"

The older man's face tightened. "Can you prove it?"

"I don't need proof!" the man shouted. "Those horses have my brother's brand and I've been tracking these whores for a long time."

"We need the law to settle this," the older man remarked out loud to himself.

The stranger nodded. "That's why I'm taking them back."

"I'll go get the sheriff," the older man said. "And if ya'll ain't here when I get back, I'll hunt you down myself and kill you."

Kitty stirred. Candice raced to her side. "You're too weak to travel," she told Kitty in a hushed voice. I think we should turn ourselves in."

In a puny voice Kitty murmured, "Why? We ain't done nothin' wrong."

"Don't pull any tricks on me," the man quipped. "I ain't ever killed a girl before, but there's always a first time."

The horses were in a stall too far away, and unhitched. Candice could barely walk. Kitty couldn't stay conscious. Candice lowered her head, sat next to Kitty, and gingerly lifted Kitty's head onto her lap.

"I guess our luck just ran out," she softly whispered to her friend as she stroked Kitty's thick blonde hair.

The tone in the man's voice softened as he saw the dismay in Candice's eyes. "When were you plannin' on bringin' the horses back?" he asked.

"I wasn't," Candice replied, shaking her head. "We just wanted to stop whoring."

A deep scowl filled the man's face. "I ain't ever met an honest whore before. Where were you headed?"

"I want to buy ranch in California. Kitty here wants a saloon in…Barley? No it's not Barley. It's a mining town in California."

"Are you talking about Bodie?"

"Yeah, that's the name."

"So why are you traveling together?" he asked.

"You sure ask a lot of questions!" Candice barked as she closed her eyes and tried to ignore him.

"It's awful cold in Reno," the stranger offered. "I thought about headin' to California myself. I've heard gold and silver claims are as easy to find as running water. By the way, my name is Sam."

Candice opened her eyes. She lifted her head and threw the stranger a short smile. "My name is Candice. My friend's called Kitty."

"That's them!" The stable hand pointed out to the sheriff as he limped back inside the stable. "I tried to figure it out for ya, but when girls are involved, I get confused."

The sheriff was all business. His thick black eyebrows narrowed as he demanded, "Where you ladies headin'?"

"To California," Candice mumbled.

A scowl settled on his face as he asked, his words fast and hard, "Where did you get them horses from?"

"I borrowed them from Sam's brother," Candice insisted.

"Can you prove it?" the sheriff questioned.

"No," Candice admitted, "but I have gold and I can pay for them now."

The sheriff abruptly turned and left the stables. The stable owner followed on the sheriff's heels and asked, "So what are you goin' to do?"

"I'll wire the sheriff in Reno."

"Then what?"

"If they stole them horses, we'll hang "em." The sheriff headed across the street toward the hotel. But then he swung around and said, "Tell my deputy I'm havin' lunch." His voice hardened. "Tell him to put them whores in jail and to stop tearing down the gallows."

The livery stable owner's face lit up. "Another hangin'! Hot dang, that'll be two this month." He slowly counted on his fingers and howled, "No, that'll be three."

Chapter 26

"Are you sure I've got to arrest those girls?" the deputy whined.

"Yep, that's what the sheriff said. They're sure a purty bunch, ain't they?"

The deputy followed behind the stable hand and shook his head. "I don't like this," he complained.

"That's them," the stable man snickered as he pointed at Candice. A grin crept over his face.

The deputy studied the shadows in the stable, then glanced at Sam and his raised gun. He cautiously circled Kitty and Candice and admitted, "I don't know what you women did, but my job is to put you in jail." He lifted his gun from the holster and commanded, "Get up."

Sam stepped back a few feet into the shadows and slowly lowered his gun.

The deputy shot a fast glance at Sam and said, "If they stole your horses we'll hang 'em by week's end."

Sam's eyes widened and he eased farther into the shadows.

Candice and Kitty remained curled on the ground. "Get up!" the deputy demanded. "I ain't ever shot a girl before, but I will!"

Candice moaned and leaned on a thick support beam, dragging her leg upward. She offered her hand to Kitty and insisted lightly, "It's time to get you to a bed, Kitty. You need to stand up."

Kitty moved slowly and Candice did her best to help her to her feet.

"Don't play with me!" the deputy impatiently called out. "You two made me miss my lunch."

Kitty lifted her pale, bruised face. The deputy caught a glimpse of her battered face and surprised himself by saying, "Ma'am, who did this to you? I'll kill the beast."

As best as her swollen lips would allow, she mumbled, "A bear."

Sam, still in the shadows, watched and listened, his trigger hand still readied.

"I might get fired for this," the deputy said out loud, "but I ain't goin' let a girl as sick as you walk to the jail." He swooped Kitty up in his arms. Her head lifted for an instant. With her eyes partially open she whispered, "Thank you."

Sam's proper upbringing got the best of him. He put his gun away, stepped from the shadows, and said, "I ain't gonna let you fall and hurt your leg worse gettin' across the street." He blushed as Candice's deep blue eyes studied his face. He swooped Candice up, just as the deputy had with Kitty, her weight surprising him. His arms and back strained. His knees shook and buckled, landing him and Candice back onto the floor. His face reddened.

Candice softly giggled. "I'm not as small as Kitty."

Sam regained his composure. Taking a deep breath he lifted Candice as gentlemanly as his strained body would let him.

Candice tucked herself into his arms. Neither women offered resistance.

Townsfolk gathered and whispered. Some came for the amusement. Others wanted a glance at the whores. And a few came to get a glimpse of who would be hung on the gallows next.

The men carefully laid the women down on weathered jail cots. Both women snuggled deep into the blankets, whispering their thanks.

Sam and the deputy stared. "If I was wrong," Sam asked, "what would happen?"

"Don't know," the deputy replied. "I'm just a deputy. You need to ask the sheriff."

Sam nodded. "I'll do that. By the way, anywhere around here I can eat?"

"Yep...." The deputy scratched his head, then warned Sam, "But it'll cost you a purty penny."

Sam threw the deputy a hard glance, grinned and said, "Is there a good saloon around these parts?"

The deputy nodded as a grin trickled across his face. "What you lookin' for... whiskey or women?"

"Both," Sam replied. "And in that order."

"I shouldn't say this," the deputy glanced around the room and whispered as best as any man could whisper. "The Red Bucket Saloon on the edge of town."

Sam nodded his thanks and left the jail.

The deputy, deep in thought, casually walked over to the two cell doors and locked them. His feelings stirred at the sight of the women. He studied their bodies.

"Did we get a telegraph back yet?" the sheriff questioned as he came through the door.

The deputy jumped. "No, sir." He hesitated. Clearing his throat, he said, "I got 'em."

"When did you send out the telegraph?" the sheriff asked, his eyes cold.

"I don't remember." The deputy scratched his head.

Angry, the sheriff shouted, "You forgot to send it, didn't you!"

"Well, I got the girls in jail, didn't I?" the deputy pointed out.

The sheriff's face reddened. "Don't let them whores talk to you about nothin'. Especially about lettin' them go." His scowl deepened as he left the jail.

Sunlight pierced through the metal bars on the jail cell's small window. Kitty's cot was set up perfectly to catch it. The warmth heated her swollen face and offered comfort for a short time. "Stop it!" she screamed. "Let go of me!"

The deputy jumped up, his pistol ready, aiming at shadows. He cautiously approached the jail cell. Kitty was still curled up in the cot.

"Ma'am, you all right?" he whispered. His eyes darted around her cell. Kitty yawned and slowly sat up. He caught a glimpse of the sun dancing off of her golden locks. "I thought you screamed," he offered, concerned.

Kitty' body melted, falling back onto the cot. She whimpered, "I need a doctor."

The deputy getting a full view of her battered face, replied, "Don't you go nowheres ma'am. I'll go get the doc."

He shook the thick metal door on Kitty's cell, checking the lock. Grabbing the keys, the deputy hurried out the jail's reinforced front door.

Candice sat up and giggled. "What are you trying to do to that young man?"

Kitty sat up, throwing Candice a frown. "I'm trying to get us out of here."

Candice shook her head. "Kitty, sometimes men are smarter than us. This is one of them times."

Kitty's back straightened, as she said, "No man is smarter than me." But her head felt dizzy and she fell back into the cot.

Chapter 27

"I got a reply from the telegraph I sent," the sheriff announced as he sauntered through the jail's front door. He stopped dead and drew his gun. "Where the heck is my deputy?" He crouched and his face tightened. Aiming the gun at shadows around the room, he demanded, "Did you whores put him up to something?"

Candice's ankle was throbbing, her face wet with fever. She sat up as best as her aching body would allow, and focused on the sheriff's loud voice and fast movements.

"Sam's brother says he never rented you them horses. He says you stole them." The sheriff threw Candice a hard look. "I wired the judge. He'll be here in a day or two."

"We didn't steal them horses!" Candice insisted in a puny voice, "We paid for them."

"Tell it to the judge." The sheriff checked the locks on the women's cell doors, his gun still raised and aimed. "Where's my deputy?" he demanded.

"I don't know." Candice shook her head and whimpered, "My leg hurts real bad. I need a doctor."

"You're goin' to get hung soon. I ain't givin' up taxpayers' money for a doctor to fix a whore who's goin' to be hung."

Candice dropped to the filthy cot and let her throbbing leg settle.

"Why did you whores come to my town?" the sheriff growled. "All your kind brings is trouble." The sheriff's voice rose dangerously. "If you did anythin' to my deputy, I'll hang you both right now."

The heavy front door creaked as it opened. "I brought the doctor," the deputy shouted out.

The sheriff turned sharply and aimed at the door, his trigger finger itchy. "I told you to stay in this jail!" he spat as the deputy entered.

"But--" the deputy froze at the sight of the marshal's aimed gun.

The doctor pushed past the deputy. Blustering, he demanded, "What are my two patients doing in jail?"

"They ain't your patients anymore," the sheriff replied. "They're goin' to get hanged by week's end." The sheriff shot a frown at his deputy. "And I told you to stay put!"

The deputy swallowed hard. Glancing around the room, he slowly replied, "They didn't escape. They're still here."

The doctor walked over to the locked jail cells. Peering through the bars at the women's curled, still bodies, he grew concerned. "Sheriff, if these women die before the hangin' what do you think the townsfolk will say?"

"Die?" The sheriff's eyes flared wide. "These are whores. They've suffered worse."

The doctor got a glimpse of the hatred in the sheriff's eyes. "That one just lost a baby, and if I don't take of her, I'm tellin' ya… she'll die. If you're goin' to hang her, you better do it today. I don't believe she'll be alive tomorrow." Tired of the sheriff's demands, the doctor shook his head and headed out the door.

The sheriff thought hard about what the doctor had said. He was up for reelection next month. "Wait!" he hollered. "You take them, doc." He unlocked the cell doors. "But if they get away," he threatened, "you'll have me to reckon with."

The doctor returned and shouted, "I can't carry these women by myself. Get over here and help me."

The deputy flew to his side. The sheriff kept his distance and watched the men lift the women from the cots.

Chapter 28

"Are we still alive?" Kitty whispered. Candice and Kitty sat in total darkness in the doctor's back room.

"Don't care," Candice yawned. "I'm tired, and I like this bed better than that filthy cot over at the jail." She glanced toward the door. The doctor had heeded the sheriff's warning and locked his back room each time he left it.

Days turned to weeks. The judge didn't show, but in the meantime the women's bodies healed.

Townsfolk's curiosity grew with each passing day. Some folks even made up excuses to visit the doctor, hoping to get a glimpse of the two women who were going to be hung.

"Doc," Kitty sighed, "will I ever be as pretty as I once was?"

The doctor gingerly touched her healing face and remarked, "I have never seen a woman's bone structure this perfect."

The confidence in his reply offered Kitty comfort. "Is that good?" she asked curiously.

The doctor replied with a nod. "Young lady, you're healing faster than I thought nature could help you. So, yes, that's good."

A tiny smile lifted the corners of Kitty's lips, replacing the scornful frown which had permeated her face for weeks.

"Yes," the doctor nodded with a grin. "It's very good," he said again.

"Doc, are you in there?" The sheriff pounded on the door. "The judge just got here on the afternoon stage. We're havin' a hearin' in the saloon as soon as he gets settled. Look alive now, cuz I'm sendin' two deputies back to fetch them whores."

When Kitty heard the sheriff her face went pale.

"You'll hang purty," the doctor offered.

Kitty's shoulders sank. Head lowered, she moped back to her guarded room and took to her bed.

"Are you just goin' to lie there and let 'em hang us?" Candice angrily whispered.

"The doctor said I'm gonna hang pretty." Kitty sighed, but Candice saw the sparkle in her eyes.

"There's a deputy guarding the back door," Candice said.

"Do you have a plan?" Kitty asked, grinning. "I'm too pretty to get hung." She studied Candice, her blue eyes filled with vinegar.

Drawing a deep breath, she admitted, "I missed you." Then, after a moment she said, "I don't want the doctor to get hurt." A wild look filled her face. She found and loaded her hidden gun.

Candice shot Kitty a quick glance and giggled. "I think Sam's waiting for us."

A scowl bloomed on Kitty's face. "Who the heck is Sam?"

"Don't know…" Candice giggled again. "But he's the one who got us into this mess."

"Are you crazy?" Catching herself, Kitty said in a quieter tone, "Then he's most likely goin' to draw us out there first, and shoot us before they can hang us."

"Why would he do that?" Candice barked, her smile falling.

Kitty hissed, "Because you're only a hog farmer! You don't know men."

Candice stood up and put pressure on her injured leg. There was no pain. Her back straightened and she walked around the room, then bent and lifted the mattress of her cot. Pulling two six shooters out, her eyebrows lifted. "So how do you think I got these?"

Kitty stared at the guns, her mouth agape. "Are they loaded? Give me one."

Candice pulled them from Kitty's reach. "He's gonna to marry me and we're goin' to California together."

"How are we gonna do that?" Kitty laughed. "We're goin' to get hanged today."

Candice handed Kitty a six-shooter. Its weight pulled on her fingers and she nearly dropped it.

Candice teased, "On a pig farm you have to carry real guns."

Kitty scowled and steadied the heavy gun. "I'm ready," she said. "And I can certainly handle this puny gun!"

Kitty put on a theatrical performance of a lifetime. She stomped around the room and screamed, "Don't hurt me! Stop it!"

Candice grinned and hid in the shadows behind the locked door, her arms raised, holding a porcelain water pitcher.

Kitty slammed her fist into the back door and screamed, "Stop! You can't have my favors!"

The deputy guarding the back door unlocked it and kicked it open. "Let go of her!" He demanded, his eyes darting around the room, looking for a man.

Candice slammed the water pitcher down on his head. His gun dropped and he fell to his knees, his hand reaching for his gun. Kitty grabbed the washbowl and slammed it down on the deputy's head. He fell flat out on the floor.

"You sure were convincin', "Candice whispered. "Sam said he'd have our team of horses waitin' at the stables."

"How do we get back to the stables unnoticed?" Kitty questioned.

"We just walk," Candice replied with a smile. "No one here knows us. We ain't limping or hiding our faces as we did before. We're just two ordinary women."

Kitty sashayed down the street with confidence. After awhile she asked, "so how is Sam gonna keep us from bein' hanged?"

"I don't know," Candice replied lightly. "All I know is the buckboard should be ready and the horses should be willing."

They kept to the shadows until they reached the livery.

Kitty caught sight of a familiar walk. She stopped, her heart racing.

"What the heck are you doin'?" Candice questioned.

"I think that's James!" Kitty shouted, "James, I'm over here!"

Candice's heart leaped as she hastened her pace. Her eyes turned cold as she grabbed Kitty's arm and hissed, "I ain't gettin' hung over a fool man."

When Kitty shoved Candice away it surprised Candice. "I already told you! Kitty, Men will get us both killed!"

The townsfolk paused from their chores to listen and stare.

Candice bit her lip. She saw the men and women staring and she knew their curiosity would lead to questions and suspicions.

"If you talk to him," Candice mumbled under her breath, "I'll never speak to you again."

Kitty threw Candice a frown and an instant later raised an eyebrow. "So, is Sam comin' with us?"

Candice replied, "I told you he was. Now let's just get goin'."

Familiar with the stable, both women stepped cautiously as they walked into the livery, their guns raised.

"It seems pretty quiet," Kitty whispered. "Where did you say the horses would be?"

Candice's eyes darted around the interior.

"You ain't goin' nowheres," a man snarled from the shadows. "I'll kill the both of you with a single shot. Now throw them guns down."

"What fer?" Kitty demanded as she froze.

"It don't matter what fer," the stranger sneered. "The sheriff offered me a chance to make two dollars, and I aim to collect."

"Drop your gun," Sam demanded from behind the stranger.

The stranger turned, gun ready. Sam got off a shot. The stranger, slammed back by the force of the bullet, crumpled to the ground.

Candice's heart leaped as she threw Sam a short smile.

"I hid the team north of the town," he said. "Everyone here's suspicious. You need to get as far away from here as you can. Folks from miles away are gathering for the hangin'."

Kitty's back straightened as she spat, "You're the one that got us almost hanged. So why are you helping us now?"

Sam scowled at Kitty and shook his head. "I don't know. I just am."

"We can't trust him," Kitty huffed as she threw Candice a hard look.

Candice watched Sam. A wide smile filled her face as she gushed, "Yes we can."

An angry roar rose from the streets. Both women kept to the shadows as they hurried their pace. The team of horses was right where Sam had said they would be.

Candice threw Kitty an uppity look as she whispered, "See, it's not a trap. I told you we could trust Sam."

"Lower your voice," Kitty spat, slowly circling the empty buckboard.

I know you're more schooled than me," Candice remarked, heavy in thought, "but I do believe Sam loves me and will take good care of me."

"Kitty cautiously emerged from shadows and simply said, "Let's just get."

They jumped into the buckboard and Candice hollered, "Get up" to the horses.

"I'm goin' to shoot every mountain man I see!" Kitty shouted in anger only a short distance away from town.

"Keep your voice down," Candice demanded, lowering her voice. "I don't want to get hung today."

They drove the team hard, heading south. Both kept a watchful eye out on their own side of the buckboard, their guns heavy in their hands.

Determined and rested, they drove the horses all night, helping each other whenever one or the other tired. By morning they had comfortably distanced themselves from Tahoe Lake. Kitty didn't argue or question Candice. Their occasional glances spoke for themselves.

Long days turned into long nights. They slept light and covered each other's backs. The terrain changed daily. They followed scrub pine out of the mountains, then croppings of thick junipers as the trees faded. Grassy fields eventually melted into endless, steep, rocky hillsides.

"You're different," Candice stated flatly. "I miss the old you. Are you sick or something? The doc gave you a lot of medicine. One minute you would be awake and a second later you'd be still, like you drank too much champagne." Candice giggled. "It was kind of funny to see you so quiet."

"I can't believe you're in love," Kitty spat back. "How the heck did you say you got them guns?"

"Sam brought 'em to me."

A twinkle that Kitty had never seen before sparked in Candice's eyes. Candice bowed her head and said, "I know you're educated. And I've seen the things you can do to men." She quickly lifted her head. "I never thought I could trust a man again. Sam's a good man."

"But that don't explain about the guns." Kitty's smile widened. "How the heck did you get 'em?"

Candice's eyes danced. "I told you, Sam brought them to me."

Kitty's impatience returned. "I know that, and I know I slept a lot." Her voice jumped as she screamed, "All I wanted to know was how you got them guns!"

The fire in Kitty's eyes sent Candice into a fit of laughter. "You snore!" she cried. "Sam snuck in one night and thought a man was lying next to me."

A frown wrinkled Kitty's forehead. "Humph," she huffed. "I know how to get to Bodie and you don't."

Candice checked her laughter, and in a proper tone replied, "I have food and champagne."

Kitty's eyes widened. "You wouldn't be trying to bluff me, would you?"

"Get up," Candice hollered to the horses.

"I'm real tired," Kitty cried. "And I'm real hungry. When are we goin' to stop?"

"When we get to Bodie," Candice smiled.

"I can't go much farther without food!" Kitty griped. "Give me them reins." She slapped Candice's shoulder and grabbed for the reins.

Candice leaned dangerously left, distancing herself from Kitty, holding tight to the reins. The wagon jumped. Candice's body jumped and flew off the wagon, landing hard on the dirt trail.

"What the heck are you doin'?" Kitty shouted as she watched Candice land. Kitty snatched the reins and tried to slow the horses. "Stop," she shouted, looking over her shoulder at Candice's stilling body.

But Kitty's light yank on the reins didn't work. The horses picked up speed. "I hate horses!" she screamed. "And I hate mountain men!" She wrapped the reins around her thin arms, and putting her back into it, she screamed, "Whoa!" The horses eased to a stop.

"I'm sorry!" she cried as she jumped out of the buckboard and ran to Candice. "You're right, I have a temper."

Candice's body lay curled and still. Kitty nervously approached it.

"That hurt!" Candice moaned.

"What can I do?" Kitty asked, concerned.

Candice choked on a giggle. "Get me that bottle of champagne."

Kitty grabbed her hips as she circled Candice's still body. "That's not funny," she barked. "I don't want to go back to a doctor, ever."

"If you do that again," Candice sprang up, "I'll throw you out of the buckboard and you can tell me how good you feel afterwards!"

Kitty rolled her eyes and walked away, heading back toward the horses.

Candice shouted, "You're not the only one that can get a man!"

Kitty kicked the ground with her boots, raising dust. Over her shoulder she shouted, "James loves me."

Candice hollered back, "Sam loves me more!"

When she reached the buckboard, Kitty circled the horses and stopped them in front of Candice. "I reckon we're both gettin' married."

Candice, still wearing a wide smile said, "I reckon." Candice resumed the driving position and urged the horses on.

"I'm still really hungry," Kitty whined. "And that champagne might help your ailments."

"What was that noise?" Candice strained to listen.

"I don't hear anything," Kitty replied, but she kept her trigger hand alive.

"I'm not sure," Candice whispered. "But I heard something."

"It might be a posse," Kitty warned.

"I know. Hold on. We've got to get outa here fast."

"Get up!" they both shouted at the horses. They ducked for safety, guns raised, as the buckboard tore through the countryside.

Chapter 29

"Can we slow down soon?" Kitty shouted. She glanced over her shoulder. "I haven't seen or heard nothin'. I don't think it's a posse."

"They'll all be comin' for us," Candice yelled. "We're goin' to get to Bodie tonight."

Kitty threw Candice an angry glare. "How the heck are we goin' to do that?"

"We just are, and I'm leavin' you there and I'm goin' on even farther to California with Sam."

Kitty pulled lightly on her golden hair and snapped, "Bodie is in California, you dumb hog farmer!"

Candice shouted at the horses and mumbled under her breath.

"And," Kitty laughed, "you don't know men."

"Yes I do!" Candice snarled. "You're a pain. I should have just let you get hung."

"Why do you trust Sam?" Kitty shouted. "You're makin' a big mistake with him."

"Because he visited me every day," Candice snapped. But then she admitted, "I didn't trust him at first. His eyes were hard and cold."

"But," Kitty questioned, "Didn't you think about him being the reason we were goin' to be hung?"

"No," Candice admitted. "I just enjoyed his attention, so I let it pass."

Kitty yawned and said again, "Candice, you don't know anythin' about men."

Candice whipped the horses and they bolted forward. "I'm goin' to marry Sam!"

"I don't believe he'll be waitin' for you in Bodie!" Kitty said. "Now slow these horses down…and open that bottle of champagne."

The frown on Candice's face disappeared as she gave her friend a short smile and abruptly stopped the horses.

"Kitty said, "So how did Sam get those guns to you?"

Candice blushed and simply said, "I never met a man that worried about me before. Sam went back to the sheriff and changed his story. The sheriff didn't believe him. Then Sam offered to pay for the horses. He even wired his brother askin' him to change his story. That sheriff is a mean one. He has fire in his eyes and his mind was set for a hangin'."

Kitty's head lifted. She shared a smile with Candice and said, "You're right. We need to get farther away."

Candice whipped the reins. "Kitty, I thought all men were born angry. Sam's not like that. He's kind and gentle."

"It took me a long time to figure them out," Kitty exclaimed. "Some men are born angry. Some have a score to settle and so they become angry. Others just want our pleasures and act tough and angry for no good reason."

"Jack was always angry." Candice sniffled. "No matter what I did to please him…." Her eyes pooled with tears.

"Well, he's dead now and you don't need to waste any more tears on him." Kitty watched as Candice wiped tears off her cheeks.

"I'm tired of eatin' jerky," Kitty mumbled. "If we're gonna be up all night again it'll go faster if we're drunk."

"No! I said no champagne until we get to Bodie. Besides, if we're drunk, we'll get caught easier. I don't want to see a man's gun aimed at me ever again."

"Are you losin' your nerve?"

"I'm fed up with runnin'." Candice stared into the heavens and with a long sigh said, "I want babies and a man to cook for who won't hurt me."

"That's boring!" Kitty scoffed. "You'll age overnight. I've seen the sadness in them ranchers' wives' eyes. You should stay with my plan. You can always get a ranch when you're old. Right now it's time to live." She took a deep breath and exhaled adding, "I want a fancy saloon with fancy champagne and fine silk dresses."

Their voices settled and they leaned into each other, seeking warmth. Their horses slowed and stopped as early morning light drew up against the eastern rim of a downhill descent.

Gunfire exploded, tearing through the silence. Birds took to flight, spooking the horses. They bolted forward.

"Huh?" Kitty awoke and calmly stretched, eyes still half closed. "Hey! It's not funny. I already told you I was sorry about you being thrown from the buckboard. Slow these horses down!" she demanded.

Eyes closed in sleep, Candice mumbled, "Kitty, if I get thrown out of this buckboard again I'm goin' to kill you."

The buckboard leaned dangerously to the right. Candice slid into Kitty. Fully awake now, adrenaline flowed as they frantically assessed the situation.

"Where are the reins?" Candice cried.

"I thought you had them," Kitty shouted. Both women leaned over the front end of the buckboard.

"Hold my waist," Kitty shouted. "I think I can reach them."

"Be careful! Watch the horses' legs."

"Stop jumping so much!" Kitty screamed.

"I'm not!" Candice shouted back. "Hurry up. You're getting heavy!"

"You ladies need a hand?" Men dressed in military uniforms and at full gallop flanked both sides of the buckboard.

Surprised, Candice sat up straight, almost releasing her grip on Kitty.

"What's wrong with you?" Kitty cried, "Hold me steady!"

A soldier leaped off of his horse, landing on the back of one of their horses. Kitty, almost upside down, caught a glimpse of his boots.

"Whoa!" he commanded in a strong voice. Still on a steep incline, the horses scrambled to slow their dangerous downhill drop.

"Hold on, ladies," the soldier hollered. "This is goin' to get a little rough."

"Pull me up!" Kitty screamed as she slid downward.

"I can'," Candice shouted. "You're too heavy!"

Another soldier jumped off of his horse and landed next to Candice in the wagon seat. "Ma'am, you hold on. I've got your friend."

Bodie or Bust

The wagon moaned and creaked as their descent sharpened. With reins in hand, the soldier riding the horse shouted, "This might be a bad jump." His voice showed fear, catching the other soldier's attention.

Hearts leaped as the wagon flew off the side of a cliff. The soldier in the wagon grabbed Kitty around the waist and pulled her tight. Candice ducked and held on. The soldier on the horse yelled, "You stupid horses!" as his body flew off the horse in a freefall.

The buckboard slapped the river. The horses plunged deep into the raging water. They panicked as they resurfaced and grabbed for air. Kitty and Candice clung to the buckboard for dear life.

The soldier still in the buckboard, shouted to the horses. Picking up the whip, he smacked wildly at the horses' bobbing backs.

"Private, are you alive?" he hollered as his eyes darted around the fast-moving waters. He honed his aim and whipped the horse to his left. "You can do it, turn!" he shouted. The horses' heads disappeared under the water. The wagon started to turn. "That's it!" the soldier shouted as he wiped water from his brow. He called out again to the private.

A voice weakly sputtered and coughed. "Over here, sir."

The soldier in the buckboard shouted, "What are you waitin' fer? Help me get these women to safety."

Water churned as the private swam with all his might and crawled up on one of the horse's backs. "Get up!" he shouted, choking and spiting water. The horses turned and found shallow footing. Their panicky movements slowed as they pulled the buckboard out of the frigid water.

"Ladies," the young soldier coughed. He proudly announced, "You're safe now." Kitty and Candice's hearts were racing so fast they didn't look up. Both trembled, their soaked clothes stealing their warmth.

"What do I do, sir?" the young private asked as a look of confusion filled his face.

"Light a fire," his commanding officer, the sergeant, barked. "Can't you see they're cold?"

"Yes, sir," The youthful private, paying no mind to his chilled body, ran to find anything dry that would burn. In a matter of minutes he gathered and carefully piled the wood. Using a flint and dry grass, his shivering hands whisked back and forth, then when the sparks caught, he blew softly into the dry grass.

"Hurry up!" the sergeant demanded. In a matter of minutes the fire was roaring.

Kitty rose as she caught a whiff of smoke. "Who are you?" she asked through chattering teeth. "I ain't seen men dressed like you since the war ended."

Both men stared at Kitty.

Candice readied her hidden gun.

The men laughed as they dried themselves by the fire. "Where we're from, women thank us and offer us a hot meal when we help them out. Where are you ladies from?"

Kitty paused, looked at the sergeant with a smile of apology, and with feminine charm replied, "Where are my manners? We don't have much, but you're welcome to what we've got."

The Southern men were drawn to Kitty's golden hair. "Ma'am," the boyish man said, "I just shot a large buck. I'll go fetch it if you're hungry."

"I thought the war was over," Candice interrupted, her voice filled with alarm. She eased the hidden gun from her pocket. Both men's backs tightened as they turned to face her.

"Put your gun away," Kitty said. "These gents just saved our lives. And they've got fresh meat." She jumped out of the buckboard and hurried to the crackling fire. The men slowed their trigger hands.

Enjoying Kitty's feminine charms, both men studied her with interest, paying little mind to Candice.

Candice shook her head and bit her lip. "Kitty, come back here. What the heck are you doin' now? The war ended a long time ago. These men are trouble."

Kitty frowned at Candice, and pouring on more charm said, "I know that." Lifting one eyebrow she said, "They're just men and they have fresh meat. I'm staying. I'm hungry."

Candice stood up in the buckboard. A scowl settled on her forehead. Kitty rolled her eyes and walked toward the fire. Candice's scowl deepened as she jumped off the buckboard and cautiously followed Kitty. She kept her trigger hand ready.

"Can I go now, Sergeant?" the young soldier impatiently asked. The sergeant kept a keen eye on Candice. As she approached the fire he commanded, "Don't be gone long."

"Yes, sir!" The rail-thin soldier snuck a glance at Kitty's breasts. Her wet clothes offered a fine view of her womanhood. She caught his eyes and threw him a short smile as she turned to face the fire. He blushed and ran to his horse like his back was on fire. Kitty giggled, fussing with her wet blonde locks of hair.

"How is he gettin' across that river?" Candice questioned with a suspicious tone.

"There's a bridge about a quarter mile from here. We crossed it earlier today. Where are you headin'?"

Candice studied the unshaven man's face.

Kitty hastily replied, "We're goin' to Bodie. We're gettin' married."

Candice's frown deepened. "My friend gets a little anxious and trusting-- like your private," she said. "We're headed down river. Our family is waiting for us."

The sergeant grinned. Candice abruptly said, "We've got the law heading our way."

The sergeant's grin widened. "So do we." A puzzled expression filled his face. "What can a woman do to get the law after her?" he asked.

Candice simply replied, "We stole some horses and killed some men who deserved it."

The sergeant chuckled so deep he lost his breath.

"It's not funny," Candice cried. "We're just tryin' to keep alive."

The sergeant's grin faded. "Why don't you come with us? We're just tryin' to keep alive, too."

"We've got plans," Candice sharply replied.

"So do we!" The sergeant's grin returned, "And we'd welcome you in 'em."

"No!" Kitty insisted. "We're goin' to Bodie. Have you been there? How much farther is it? Do they have champagne there? " Kitty's annoying questions hindered the sergeant's thoughts. His face hardened.

"I told you I could ride faster than lightnin'," the private shouted as his horse galloped into sight. "The buck's not as big as I thought it was," he remarked, "but it'll feed us for a week or two."

Kitty stared at the carcass draped over the horse's shoulders. She grimaced. In a girly voice she shrieked, "You killed a deer."

The soldier halted his horse, confused by her high shrill.

Candice and the sergeant caught the fright in the private's eyes and roared.

"What's so funny?" the private asked as his face filled with confusion.

"You killed it!" Kitty shouted. "Why?"

The young soldier scratched his head as he flung the buck off of his horse.

Candice and the sergeant held in their laughter until their breath exploded.

Kitty added to the hilarity. Stomping angrily as she approached the soldier's horse, she screamed, "I could have killed us a rabbit. I ain't helping cook this big thing."

"What?" The young soldier looked up, trying to grab his sergeant's attention.

"Daniel," the sergeant said, "you killed it. You and her can cook it."

A puzzled expression crept onto the private's face as he listened to Kitty's nonsense.

Candice and the sergeant sat down and watched the show.

Chapter 30

"She's got her mind set," Candice smirked.

"He's determined," the sergeant chuckled.

"I killed my husband," Candice informed the sergeant as her trigger hand twitched.

"I ain't ever been married," the sergeant informed her. "You ain't a thing like a Southern girl."

"What do you mean?" Candice curiously asked.

"Southern girls don't talk like you." He grinned. "They're short on words and long on smiles."

Candice's head drooped.

"Did I say somethin' wrong?" The sergeant's grin faded.

"Where are you headin'?" Candice asked, raising her head back up.

"Don't know." The sergeant's eyes tightened. "You're whores, ain't you?" he sneered. "I haven't had a woman in a long time."

Candice's stomach turned as she stood up and distanced herself from the man. Her eyes flared as her voice raised. "Kitty, we need to get away from here, now!"

"This thing is full of blood," Kitty hollered back. "Eew."

"Remember the mountain men!" Candice screamed, her voice shaking.

Kitty dropped the neck of the deer. She swallowed hard as she thought about what Candice had just shouted. "Thank you," she quietly said to the private as her heart raced. "This is much bigger than a rabbit. Would you show me how to skin it?"

"Yes, ma'am," the young soldier offered. "I know it's bigger than a rabbit, but pullin' the skin off is the same." He pulled the skin down off the deer's back, peeling it as though it were a piece of fruit. "He

proudly said, "See?" Kitty's face went pale. "You've never seen this done before, have you?" He grinned.

Kitty's stomach turned as she caught Candice's alarmed voice, again. "No." she murmured, her voice quivering.

"It's easy." The young soldier exhibited his talents.

Kitty drew a soft breath. The blood and creamy color of the exposed carcass nearly made her faint.

Tired, hungry, and out of patience, the private raised his voice and yelled at Kitty, "We're hungry and I'm tired of your spat. Are you or ain't you goin' to help me cook this?"

"We ain't," Candice announced, her voice alarmingly loud.

"Then why the heck did I wear my horse out gettin' it?" the soldier barked.

"Don't know," Candice offered in a calm voice. "But Kitty and I need to get, now."

The sergeant stood up and pointed out, "You women are tired and hungry. We're tired and hungry...." Lust grew in his eyes as he calmly said, "You help out with the cookin' and we'll help out with them lawmen comin' after you."

"No!" Candice shouted. "You ain't goin' to have our pleasures. And if you're thinkin' about stealing them, well, these canyon walls carry noise a long distance."

Kitty stomped the hard ground and screamed, "Snake!"

Both men turned abruptly, going for their guns. "Don't shoot!" the sergeant ordered. "She's right. These canyons will carry a gunshot for miles. It's only a snake."

Kitty, as white as a ghost, was dancing in her boots. Both men lowered their pistols. Their eyes filled with lust.

Candice whipped her gun out of her pocket and raised her eyebrows as she insisted, "We're leavin'. Get out of our way!"

"You won't get five feet from us," the sergeant sneered. "I get the dancing one first," he smirked as he threw a quick glance at the private. "Watch the other one. Don't let her get away."

"Yes, sir." the private nodded.

"Ease them guns out of your holsters," a familiar deep voice demanded.

"Sam?" Candice excitedly shouted. "Is that you?"

"I don't know you, and I don't want to fight you," Sam hollered from the safety of the side of the buckboard, closely watching both men.

"This ain't your business!" the sergeant warned.

"I'm making it mine," Sam shouted, his face dark with worry.

Both Kitty and Candice flew to the ground.

"Show yourself!" the sergeant demanded.

Sam began to reply impatiently, and then corrected his tone. "Ain't goin' to do that."

"You're a coward, ain't you?" the sergeant sneered. "Is you one of them yellow Yanks that's been followin' us?"

"No. I'm here for the women." Sam's voice tightened. "They're family, and they're leavin' here with me." Sam stepped out into the open. "Like I said, stranger, I ain't got a fight with you. I'm here to collect my family."

The sergeant nervously cracked his knuckles. His fingers twitched. He went for his gun.

Sam drew his. It came up unbelievably fast and fired.

The sergeant moaned, falling to his knees. Though seriously wounded, he stood back up. His face darkened as he aimed and pulled hard on the hammer of his six-shooter. Bullets flew. Sam leaped, covering Candice, and fired back.

"No!" the private shouted, reaching for his gun.

"Drop it!" Kitty shouted as she aimed her small gun.

"The young soldier's eyes fell to Kitty's small gun. He smirked as he said, "That won't even kill a rabbit." Amused, he slowed his actions.

"It'll drop you in your tracks," Kitty warned. "Put your gun down." Her face reddened, which wasn't becoming to her feminine features.

"The soldier laughed. His eyes flared as he went for his gun. Kitty's gun exploded, throwing her hand back. The soldier cocked his gun. "This one's for the union!" she screamed as her gun exploded again, hitting the private directly between the eyes. His gun hand lifted with difficulty. His eyes fell to his gun hand. He dropped and stilled.

Sam, still protecting Candice, quipped, "Remind me never to draw on your friend."

Face still flushed, Kitty kicked the private's body as she spat, "I was hungry. Now what am I goin' to do?" She threw Sam a hard look. "I still don't trust you. Why are you followin' us?"

Sam kept a cautious eye on Kitty as he helped Candice to her feet. "I came bringin' good news." Both women turned and listened. "My brother dropped the charges. You ain't goin' to be hung."

Still suspicious, Kitty asked, "Why'd he go and do that?"

"Because I asked him to," Sam unwillingly admitted. "Now, put that pea shooter down!"

Candice, fed up with Kitty, leaped at her, surprising both Sam and Kitty. "Leave Sam alone!" Candice shouted as she grabbed Kitty's gun.

Sam scrambled toward safety.

"Get off of me, Candice!" Kitty shouted. "What the heck are you doin'?"

"You two will take some time to get used to," Sam quipped with a grin.

"We're still goin' to Bodie!" Kitty spat as she slapped Candice away.

"No, we're goin' to California!" Candice growled.

Kitty laughed out loud as she said, "I already told you…you pig farmer, Bodie is in California."

"I hate you!" Candice cried as she stood up and dusted off her clothes.

Sam stared gloomily at his boots. Candice's head turned. Concerned, she lightly said, "What's the matter, Sam?"

"My brother's wife died in childbirth." Sam tried to hide his disappointment. "I've got to go home and help my kin."

Candice's face went pale. Kitty stood up. They threw each other puzzled expressions.

"I'll go with you," Candice offered.

"No." Sam swallowed hard. "It's my concern, not yours. You go to Bodie, and when I can, I'll follow you." Head lowered, he jumped on his horse.

Bodie or Bust

"Don't go!" Candice cried. "I love you!"

Sam kicked his horse into a run, not looking back. Candice fell to the ground.

"I'm havin' that champagne!" Kitty shouted. "I hate men!"

Candice curled into a ball and wept.

Kitty dragged the two men's bloodied bodies to the river's edge and pushed them in, then studied her surroundings as she kicked the hard ground. The dead men's horses grazed close by. "We're staying here till tomorrow. I ain't ever cooked a deer before," Kitty mumbled as she threw wood into the fire. "But tonight we're goin' to have fresh meat and champagne."

"When I get to Bodie, I'm goin' to shoot any man that wants my favors," Kitty shouted to the skies. She dragged the dressed carcass to the fire, and with caution, placed it across the open flames.

The meat sizzled. Candice caught a whiff. She looked up and warned, "It's burning!"

Kitty stomped the ground. "It's bigger than a rabbit. What do I do?"

Candice wiped her tears and stood up. Her mind still focused on Sam, she didn't reply.

"It's too big to cook!" Kitty cried. "How do I turn it?"

Candice put a hand to her waist as a grin replaced a deep-set frown. She raised an eyebrow. In an uppity voice she calmly said, "It's a deer, not a rabbit."

Kitty threw Candice a mean glare. "I know that. How do I keep it from burnin'?"

Candice's head fell as she whimpered, "I love him. Why did he leave me?"

Kitty's back straightened as she growled, "Because he's a man! Now I don't know how to cook this big thing. Can you help?"

Candice, her head still lowered, nodded. She sat closer to the fire.

"That ain't helping!" Kitty grumbled. "Helping is...." Candice's face lifted and Kitty saw the pain in her eyes. Her tone softened. "Helping is...." she shook her head, confused. "I'm gettin' that bottle of champagne now!"

"I don't want to be around men ever again," Candice sniffled.

Kitty walked over to Candice, and in a comforting tone said, "It's not you. It's them." She hugged her friend. Smoke caught her nose. "So what do I do now with the meat?"

"Turn it," Candice mumbled.

"I ain't strong enough to do that," Kitty spat. "Help me!"

Candice slowly stood up and studied the burning meat. She cracked a grin. "You're right."

"What am I right about?" Kitty questioned nervously.

"Everythin'," Candice sniffled. "Men, Sam, the sheriff… everythin'."

"What the heck are you talkin' about?" Kitty shouted. "You're the one that saved me from them mountain men." Her voice erupted even louder as she said, "And you saved me from being hanged."

Candice looked up at Kitty. Standing up, she quietly said, "The bears around here will be comin' for food. They smell it."

"Huh?" Kitty's face filled with a puzzled expression. When Candice caught a glimpse of it she burst out in laughter.

"Are you joshin' me?" Kitty cautiously asked.

"Nope. Bears can smell meat from miles away." Candice dried her tears and turned the huge piece of meat with her bare hands. "This will take about two more hours before we can eat it," she announced.

Kitty studied Candice for a moment, then asked, "How do you know that?"

Candice's smile widened. "Because I'm a pig farmer."

Kitty threw Candice a frown as she kicked the hard dirt.

"Stop kicking the dirt," Candice demanded.

"What for?" Kitty spat.

"Because the dirt will get into the cooked meat." Candice shook her head in disappointment.

Kitty's tone suddenly changed. "I'm goin' to have the grandest saloon in Bodie." She studied the lay of the land then whimsically said, "If this was Bodie, I would put my saloon…" her eyes darted, "right over there."

Drawn in, Candice said, "Why?"

Kitty rolled her eyes. "Because it's pretty there."

Candice roared. "That's too close to the riverbank."

Kitty, upset with Candice's remark, said, "So do you know somethin' I should know?"

A spark flared in Candice's eyes. She teased, "No. Remember, I'm just a pig farmer."

"I'm opening that bottle of champagne if it's the last thing I do," Kitty shouted.

Candice agreed, admitting, "I wasn't sure if I could trust you."

"What? Trust me?" Kitty shook her head in confusion. She stopped walking. "I already told you, I still don't trust Sam."

Candice jumped up. "Why not?"

"Don't know," Kitty simply replied. "Somethin's just not right with him."

Candice's eyes hardened. "Right for who?"

Kitty glanced over her shoulder and said lightly, "I don't know. If you turn that big thing over again I'll get the bottle of champagne."

Candice, and with the help of a branch, turned the thick piece of meat.

"How far is Bodie?" Kitty yawned as she reappeared at the fire.

"Huh?" Candice's face tightened. "Why are you asking me?"

"I don't know," Kitty slowly replied. "I ain't hungry anymore. I'm dead tired."

Candice nodded. Kitty plopped next to Candice. The afternoon's sunshine slowly faded.

Unattended, the fire burnt down to coals. The venison slowly cooked. Its strong gamey smell lifted on the breeze, wafting down river.

Chapter 31

"What was that noise?" Kitty cautiously whispered as she grabbed for her gun.

"It was you snoring," Candice mumbled.

"I don't snore." Kitty sat up and stretched her arms as she yawned. The sun had set and shadows blanketed their campsite. The embers of their fire silhouetted the blackened meat.

Catching a whiff of the sizzling meat, Kitty's nose followed the aroma to the fire. She said, "That meat smells and looks good. Is it cooked?"

Candice stirred. "The bears will be here soon," she mumbled.

Kitty gave Candice a slap. "What do you mean? What bears? That's not funny."

"Candice yawned and sat up. "Where's my shotgun?"

"What was that?" Kitty asked again as a high-pitched scream echoed above them.

Candice jumped. Both women grabbed their guns. A red-tail hawk dove from the sky and landed on the buckboard seat. Two crows dove after it, cawing loudly, and the hawk took to flight. The crows followed it and pecked at it, in midflight.

Two larger crows landed on the buckboard and cawed. In a matter of minutes crows blanketed their campsite.

"Where did all of these birds come from?" Kitty asked as she caught her racing heart.

One of the crows flew over to the meat and landed on the top of it. It grabbed a chunk of the cooked meat and took to flight.

"Get away from our meat!" Kitty shouted.

Other crows followed its lead. Kitty jumped up and aimed her gun at one of the birds landing on the meat.

"Don't shoot!" Candice screamed. "You'll ruin the meat."

Kitty threw Candice a frown and growled, "Then what do we do, just let them eat our meat!"

Candice stood up and aimed her shotgun toward the sky. She fired off a round and the explosion sent the birds into flight. "That will hold them off for awhile," she remarked as she approached the fire.

Kitty studied Candice's face as she approached. "Were you just tryin' to scare me?" She pinched at the meat. "Ow! That's hot!" she yelped. She blew on her fingers. "How do we eat this thing?"

"Do you ever stop talking?" Candice huffed.

"What does that mean?" Kitty licked her fingers and pinched another piece of hot meat. "This is really good. I never ate a deer before. What did I do with that bottle of champagne?"

Candice glanced at the meat, abruptly turned, and headed for the buckboard.

"Aren't you hungry?" Kitty's voice softened as she said, "I'm sorry about Sam."

Candice reappeared from shadows with metal plates and silverware.

"Where the heck did you get those?" Kitty asked excitedly.

Candice grinned as she handed Kitty a plate. "I borrowed them from the doctor."

"You're borrowin' is gonna get me killed," Kitty giggled. "Does it matter what part I eat?"

Candice giggled too. "You're the only person in this entire state that would ask a question like that.

"Well, it's an important question," Kitty spat. "I don't like certain parts of chicken, so I'm sure there are certain parts of this big hunk of venison I won't like, either."

"Where I'm from..." Candice shook her head, "we eat whatever is on our plates."

"Even if you don't like it?" Kitty balked. "Well, then, I sure don't want to go to--" She paused but finally said, "Where did you say *you're* from?"

"I didn't!" Candice grinned. "Where did you say you're from?"

"I already told you, I don't know." Kitty's face tightened. "I don't remember much about my family. All I remember is that woman

Charlotte. She made me learn schoolin' and bossed me around somethin' fierce."

Candice noticed a mustache forming, from the charred meat on Kitty's upper lip. She giggled and said, "Let's open that champagne."

"This is really good," Kitty remarked. "I think I can eat the whole thing." Kitty forgot her proper manners and pulled at the meat with both hands. Grease dripped off her chin.

Candice frowned. "I got you a fork, you know."

"Yes, I know, but I'm really hungry and my fingers are doin' just fine."

Candice hid a grin. "I reckon all that schoolin' was for nothin'."

Kitty raised an eyebrow. Glancing up at Candice, she said, "I'm a lady."

Candice's plate fell from her hand. "You look like a man to me," she roared, pointing at Kitty's darkened upper lip.

"What the heck are you talkin' about?" Kitty demanded. "Give me some of that champagne."

Grease dripped from Kitty's chin. Wiping it off with her blouse, she reached for the opened bottle of champagne.

Kitty's crude manners set Candice into a fit of laughter. "You ain't goin' to eat the horses next, are you?" she cried, tears running down her cheeks.

"You've had too much of that champagne," Kitty snarled. "Give it back to me."

Birds retuned, landing farther away. "Are you goin' to waste another shot?" Kitty asked.

Candice wiped her tears away. With a deadpan face she said, "Are you gonna eat them too?"

Kitty shook her head. When they finished gorging themselves, they both curled up next to the dying fire.

"Is the champagne gone?" Candice whispered with a giggle.

"Get some sleep," Kitty yawned.

"What's that smell?" Candice mumbled, as a putrid stench filled her nose. Eyes heavy with sleep she said, "You need to jump in the river."

"I'm not snorin'," Kitty mumbled back. "What is that terrible smell?" She yawned, then burped.

"You really need to bathe," Candice murmured with a hiccup.

An earth-shattering roar tore through their campground. Both women, eyes still closed, jumped up. Dizzied, they both fell back down.

"I told you bears would be comin'," Candice shouted, slurring her words. "Where's my shotgun?" She blinked. Her blurred vision worsened. She shook her head and blinked again. She saw two black bears, then one, and then two and a half.

"I'll kill it," Kitty laughed. She picked up the empty champagne bottle and threw it. "Darn, I missed," she roared.

"I ain't as drunk as you!" Candice hastily replied. "And I ain't goin' to die by a bear." She jumped up. Her body weaved and stumbled dangerously close to the fire.

"You're drunker than me!" Kitty shouted. "*I'll* kill the bear."

When Kitty jumped up, she saw three bears.

"Which one do I kill!" she shouted as her body swayed.

"The black one," Candice screamed.

Kitty's gun hand lifted and drooped numerous times. Her gun exploded. "I got one," she hiccupped. "Now I'll get another one." Her surroundings spun as she tried to focus. Her gun exploded again. "You get the third one," she shouted to Candice with a hiccup. "I'm a little woozy." Kitty hiccupped again as she dropped and curled next to the fire.

"There you are!" Candice cried, staring at the shotgun. "Duck!" she screamed, not noticing Kitty already had. "Stop moving!" she screamed as her body swayed.

A huge black bear's front legs were stomping on the venison. His gaping mouth and long sharp teeth tore into the meat.

Candice's eyes dropped to Kitty's stilled, tucked body. "You killed my friend!" she screamed at the bear. "I'll kill you with my own two hands!" she cried. Her shotgun exploded, lifting her right shoulder. The bear stood to his hind legs and roared. Candice fired again. He dropped to all fours, and with a quick swoop grabbed the meat and disappeared into the darkness.

Body still swaying, Candice dropped the shotgun and ran to Kitty's side. "How bad are you hurt?" she cried, her head spinning.

Kitty yawned. "Did you get the third bear?" she asked calmly.

A puzzled expression settled on Candice's face. She slapped wildly at Kitty.

"What the heck are you doin' that for?" Kitty squealed. "I'm havin' these awful dreams about bears." She hiccupped again. "I think you're right. We should get. The bears seem mighty hungry here."

Kitty's calm manner slowed Candice's racing heart. Her face was white as a ghost. She reloaded her gun, then her swaying body dropped and curled next to Kitty's. "I think I'm goin' to be sick." she warned Kitty.

"Me too," Kitty mumbled between hiccups.

Chapter 32

"I got ya'!" a gruff voice bellowed.

Kitty and Candice shook their pounding heads as they grabbed for their guns.

"I'll shoot you before them purty eyes open! Drop them guns!"

Kitty opened her heavy eyes to see a tall, thick man standing before her. Daylight pierced her vision so she shielded her eyes with her hand. "Who are you?" she asked carefully.

"I've been following you all night," the stranger sneered. "You're goin' to get hanged one way or another. And you, too!" he shouted at Candice as he watched her right hand slip into her skirt. "I'll kill both of you dead if you don't drop them hidden guns."

To his surprise, Candice chuckled. "This gun ain't hidden. How blind are you?" She eased her hand away from the shotgun.

"I'm gettin' paid handsomely for bringin' you back, dead or alive." The stranger's upper lip tightened. "I prefer dead." His gun darted back and forth, aiming at the women's chests.

Kitty stood up and stretched, surprising him. "I'll shoot," he warned.

"Okay, shoot," Kitty simply replied. "Candice, did you kill that last bear?"

The stranger took a few steps back and studied the area. He saw the heavy footprints of a bear and the rut of a dragged animal.

He raised his six-shooter off the women and flashed it widely in all directions. "Them tracks are big." His gun trained on Kitty, he shouted, "How come you both ain't dead?"

Candice threw a wink at Kitty, and as her back straightened her shooting hand slid into her hidden gun pocket. She simply said, "Because we fed it. It was just hungry."

The stranger's eyes dropped for an instant, and when they did, Candice lifted her small gun and fired.

"Huh?" The stranger fired his gun. His gun hand twitched and grew heavy. "No woman can kill me...." He dropped to one knee and fired from the dirt. His left hand touched his bloody chest and his head shook as Candice got off another shot. He dropped, face first to the ground and stilled.

"I ain't ever havin' champagne again," Candice moaned in pain.

"Why is he after us?" Kitty mumbled, holding her head and drawing a deep breath.

"Let's get outa here," Candice mumbled in a short voice.

"I reckon that's a good idea," Kitty agreed. Both women unwillingly stood up.

"I'll get the horses," Candice murmured in a tiny voice.

"Okay, I'll get the other horse." Kitty's body swayed.

Candice's eyes widened as she glanced over her shoulder at Kitty."What other horses?"

"The ones them two rebels owned," Kitty said.

"No!" Candice's voice jumped. "The brand on them horses will get us killed for sure. We're leavin' them horses here."

"They're strong and young," Kitty shouted. "Someone'll pay good money for 'em."

"That brand will get us hung twice. That's the government's brand. We'll get hung for stealin' them from the government and again for stealin' them from those rebels. No, they stay right where they are."

Kitty dusted off her skirt and picked up the dirty metal plates by the fire pit. "Grinning she said, "When I have the grandest saloon in Bodie, I won't ever have to wash a dish again."

Candice threw Kitty a fast glance, then studied the lay of the land. She calmly said, "Get in. We're not safe here."

Kitty sat tight on the left side of the buckboard. Candice urged the horses forward. "Are you goin' to be sick again?" she asked Kitty.

"No." Kitty leaned her head closer toward Candice and cautiously sniffed at her.

"What the heck are you doin'?" Candice snapped.

"Seein' how bad you smell!" Kitty mumbled.

"Me?" Candice stared at Kitty's face. The charcoal from the charred meat was still painted above her lip. It still looked like a man's mustache. Candice held back laughter. Throwing Kitty another glance, she roared as she grabbed her throbbing head. "I wish I had a looking glass," she cried. "You look a mess."

"Well, at least I don't smell," Kitty said. "I almost tore the blanket off of you and moved somewhere else last night because *you* smelled so bad."

"Me?" Candice raised her voice. "You're the one that smells. I rolled you farther away from me last night because you smelled so bad." They both sniffed at each other.

"You don't smell as bad as you did last night," Kitty quietly admitted.

"Neither do you," Candice mumbled.

Candice shook her head and laughed out loud. "It was the bear who smelled."

Kitty studied Candice's face. "Are you sure?" Candice's smile was a mile wide. Kitty's face was blackened and dragging. "I didn't know bears smelled so bad," she remarked as she sniffed her own body.

"Neither did I," Candice admitted. "I don't ever want to get that close to a bear again." The women shared a quick glance and a nod.

The early showers of spring eased up and the roads hardened as they headed south. "I don't think you should have killed that bounty hunter," Kitty finally said after a long day of silence.

"He wasn't goin' to bring us back alive," Candice coolly remarked. "I saw the hatred in his eyes. He was goin' to force our pleasures and laugh at us as he killed us." A deep frown settled on her face as she spat, "No man is ever goin' to take his pleasure on me again, unless I'm willin'."

"Why was he talkin' about hangin' us?" Kitty said, concerned. "Sam said we weren't goin' to be hung. He drove his horse hard to tell us that. The stranger said we were goin' to be hung, and that there was a bounty on us. I've been pondering them thoughts all day long. They just don't add up."

Candice nodded in agreement. "Sam wouldn't have come that far without a purpose. I know he loves me."

"That's the part that don't make any sense." Kitty shook her head. In her lightest tone of voice she said, "It's Sam who lied."

Candice's face reddened and she screamed, "You want him, don't you!" She slapped at Kitty and burped as the buckboard leaned hard, first in one direction, then the other. "I'm goin' to be sick," she cried as her face turned pale.

"Eew," Kitty cried. "Get away from me."

Candice, reins still in hand, leaned over the right side of the buckboard and vomited. She shook her head, cleared her throat, and said, "It's not Sam. I believe him."

Kitty grimaced and turned pale, too. "Oh no," she cried as she dipped low to the left wheel and vomited. "What kind of champagne was that?" she coughed. "I ain't ever havin' that kind again."

Both women hung their heads over the buckboard.

"I think it was the venison," Candice sniffled, wiping her face.

"Then I ain't ever eatin' that again," Kitty coughed, struggling to regain her composure.

Birds filled the sky shadowing the sun and both women looked up. "We don't have any food!" Kitty angrily yelled at them. "You go eat the venison and get sick. I don't care."

Candice let go of her throbbing head. Her frown lifted as she said, "They're birds. I don't think they understand you."

"Well, they understood you last night," Kitty replied, watching the birds glide side by side above her. She let out a deep sigh. "Wouldn't it be nice to be that free?"

Candice threw Kitty a comforting smile and nodded in agreement.

Kitty's voice changed. She spoke fast and loud as she said, "I've figured it out!"

"Figured what out?"

"Sam got the good news from the sheriff. The sheriff had already posted a reward sign. Townsfolk knew Sam was smitten with you and the bounty hunter followed Sam."

Kitty's words made Candice's head spin. "What are you talkin' about?" She shook her head. "Can you repeat that? So does that mean we're goin' to get hung or not?" Candice cried, grabbing her throbbing head again.

"I don't know," Kitty said with a smug smile. "But I figured it out."

"*What* did you figure out?" Candice said impatiently. "Are or ain't we gettin' hung?"

"I told you," Kitty shook the champagne out of her brain. She began again slowly. "I told you, I don't know."

Frustrated, Candice groaned. "You ain't helpin' us out much."

Kitty changed the subject. "I think we'll be in Bodie by nightfall," she predicted.

Candice, driving the horses hard, shouted above the noise, "Are you sure?"

"Yes," Kitty shouted back as she readied her gun and nervously glanced over her shoulder. She sensed men were close. Something about Sam still didn't make sense in her mind. Yawning, Kitty stretched and said, "I can't keep my eyes open much longer."

Candice watched Kitty's neck droop. "You rest. I'll wake you up when we get to Bodie. You were right!"

Night had fallen and Kitty awoke to a light darkness. "How long have I been asleep?" she asked, glancing over her shoulder.

"Since noon," Candice replied. "We did it!" she cried, excitement filling her.

Kitty, surprised at the vision of lights as far as she could see in any direction, shouted, "We're goin' to have good champagne tonight."

Candice nodded as she pushed the horses downhill.

"What are you doin'?" Kitty asked.

"Goin' to Bodie. Do you think you can control these horses better than me?" She shook her head and calmly raised an eyebrow. "I've had enough of you. I'll walk there. The horses are all yours."

"What do you mean?" Kitty's eyes followed Candice. Her heart jumped. Candice leaped from the buckboard. "What the heck are you doin'?" she screamed. "Are you crazy!"

Kitty grabbed for the snaking reins and caught them. When she got the horses slowed, a smug smile lifted the corners of her lips.

"You just walk then," she hollered. "I'm goin' to have a bath and a good bottle of champagne before you."

Candice let out a deep sigh as she studied her surroundings. The lights of the town were clearly visible. She watched Kitty as the horses sped away.

"You'll never be more than a hog farmer!" Kitty shouted and laughed as the wagon disappeared down the hill.

Candice slowly followed the downhill path mostly used by horses. Halfway down the hill her frown lifted and a smile grew, long and wide. Touching her hidden pocket, she squeezed the heavy pouch of gold dust.

Chapter 33

Kitty slowed the team to a stop next to a saloon and took a deep breath.

"Sir, the stables is over there," a youngster pointed out, his hand outstretched.

Kitty listened to the laughter and piano music coming from inside the saloon and her eyes danced. "Young man, I'll pay you a dollar if you take my team to the stables," she said.

The young boy's voice sailed upward as he shouted, "Yes, sir!"

Sir? Kitty, surprised by the boy's response, regained her composure.

The young man waited a second for the money, lowered his head, and said, "I'll make sure they get fed well, sir." He patiently waited as a skirt jumped from the buckboard. He scratched his head and neck as he said, "Sir, um, ma'am, is there anythin' else I can help you with?"

"I need a tub," Kitty told him, annoyed. "And a bottle of this town's best champagne."

"Yes, sir." His voice cracked as he eyed the thin figure of woman wearing a mustache. "The hotel will take care of you," he replied as he headed the worn-out horses to the livery.

Kitty slapped the dust off of her clothes as she looked around the bustling town. Her back straightened, and with girlish charm she headed toward the hotel.

"I apologize for the wear on my clothes," she said in proper English as she approached the hotel's registry. "I've been through a lot, what with all the Indians and mountain men."

A young lady behind the desk took a cautious step backwards. Blinking hard, she stammered, "What can I do for you?"

Kitty, filled with embarrassment, said, "I need a bath and a room."

The hotel clerk quickly said, "Tim, help this woman to a room."

Kitty's eyes fell as a wide-shouldered man with a hard limp approached.

"The room and bath will be…." The young woman's voice implied worry as she stared at the mustache on Kitty's face. "Fifty cents."

Kitty smiled. "Okay," she said, then closed her eyes and faked a faint. Tim grabbed her and helped her up to the room. "I apologize for my appearance," she said in a flirtatious tone as Tim unlocked the door and handed her the key.

"Ma'am," Tim respectfully lowered his head. "This country is cruel on women. That bath that you'll be wantin' is down the hall. If you need anythin' else, my name is Tim. I'll get it for you." He gently closed the door behind Kitty.

Kitty studied the room and sighed softly as she drew in the room's comforts. She plopped hard on the spring bed. It jumped back, and her eyes lit up.

Someone knocked at the door. "Ma'am?" a quiet voice whispered on the other side. "How many nights will you be stayin'?"

The wimpy, tiny voice annoyed Kitty. "I don't know." she barked. "I'm tired and I need a bath!"

"I understand that, ma'am," the feminine voice replied. "I'll get fired if you don't pay me for tonight."

Kitty jumped out of bed and grabbed her hidden gun, waiting for a fight.

"Ma'am," the young woman continued, "you sleep. I'll just talk to my boss in the mornin'."

Kitty took a deep breath and sat back down on the comfortable bed. Her frown lifted. Another soft knock on her door persisted and she resisted raising her gun.

"Ma'am, your bath is ready." Kitty rolled over and over on the bed. Stifling a giggle, she lifted her legs and let them drop, which sent her body jumping.

"Thank you," she softly replied. "I'll be right there."

Feet swollen, Candice walked gingerly as she approached the hotel.

"Ma'am," Can I help you?" A boy asked.

Her back straightened. Candice saw the need in his eyes and threw him a short smile. "Yes, you can. Did you happen to see a girl with a buckboard and two tired horses pass by this way?"

"He was a girl?" Disgusted, the boy shouted, "That's why I didn't get paid!"

"How old are you?" Candice asked as she stifled her laughter.

"I'm nine," he proudly stated. "Ma'am, you look like I should help you to the hotel." Candice offered him a short smile and nodded in agreement.

"He was a she," the young boy mumbled as he helped Candice into the hotel lobby.

The clerk, employing her best manners, but clearly vexed with distaste, said, "Ma'am, how long will you be stayin'?"

Candice's eyes fell as she whispered, "I'd like a bottle of champagne, and a hot bath to go along with it."

The clerk's face turned pale. "Yes, ma'am. That will be a dollar and a half." She stepped backwards as Candice stepped a little closer.

Candice drew a hard breath and glanced at her surroundings. "Can I give it to you in gold dust?"

"Yes, ma'am." The clerk pushed a metal scale in front of Candice.

Glancing cautiously around the lobby, Candice lifted the heavy bag of gold dust from her hidden pocket and poured some out on the scale.

"That's enough," the hotel clerk said. "I'll have Tim help you to your room."

Candice nodded. Her eyes still darting she said, "I'm glad we made it to Bodie."

A puzzled expression filled the clerk's face. "Um, ma'am, this isn't Bodie. This here town's called Aurora."

Candice winced as Tim offered her help to a room. She threw a fast glance over her shoulder and said, "What did you say?"

The hotel clerk swallowed hard, then quickly replied, "This here town is called Aurora."

Candice shook her head. Tim helped her and her throbbing feet up the steps to her room. She smiled lightly at Tim as she said, "I'm sorry, I know I look a mess. Thank you for your help."

"Ma'am," Tim gushed, "I'd help a lady like you in a heartbeat. Is there anything else I can do for you?"

Candice moaned as her aching legs cramped. She drew a deep breath, then said, "No, thank you."

Tim limped closer as he hurried to unlock the hotel room door. He threw Candice a quick look, and she caught his eyes to make sure she was right about his intentions.

"Good night," she whispered as Tim handed her the room key and softly closed the door behind her.

Feet throbbing, Candice sat down on the spring bed and unlaced her boots. Heavy eyed, she let her head fall to the pillow. Her body curled in the luxury of clean linen.

"I already told you," Kitty's loud voice tore through the room's thin wood-paneled walls. "I'll pay you in the mornin'. Now give me that bottle of champagne."

Hearing Kitty's patter brought a grin to Candice's face. She covered her head with a pillow.

"I'll get the sheriff," Tim warned, his voice raised. "There's people tryin' to get some sleep in this hotel. I'd appreciate you keepin' your voice down. I had to pay for this bottle myself, and I ain't givin' it to you until you pay me."

"I don't pay for champagne," Kitty spat in an uppity voice. "I will get my own bottle from the saloon." Kitty stomped hard on the wood floor and a door slammed.

"I ain't ever goin' figure women out," Tim said out loud. "But she sure cleaned up purty."

Candice rose from the bed and peeked out her door. She caught a glance of Kitty as Kitty stormed down the stairs to the lobby.

"Tim," Candice whispered. "I'll buy that champagne off of you, if you don't mind."

Tim turned and followed the voice. "Oh, it's you. I'm sorry I woke you. I shouldn't have put you in a room next to that polecat." Candice threw Tim a short smile. "I would be greatly relieved if you bought this bottle. I can't return it, and I can't drink it. I shouldn't have trusted her."

"Thank you," Candice whispered. "Do you think I can have a bath now?"

Tim's face brightened as Candice poured gold dust in his hand, "Yes, ma'am!" He swallowed hard, then lowered his voice. "The tub's empty, and I'm gonna make sure you get as many hot buckets of water as you need."

"Thank you." Candice winked at Tim, surprising herself. Tim blushed and limped away. With bottle in hand, Candice's smile widened as she headed down the hall. A door creaked, She glanced over her shoulder and it closed.

The bathtub was made of solid porcelain and featured a feminine lip on one end. Its legs flared out like a claw, handsomely fashioned from metal. A lantern adorned in pink roses was hung from the short ceiling in full blaze. Two skillfully carved wooden shelves etched with roses offered neatly folded towels of three sizes. A short, round wooden table dotted with bars of soap sat to the left of the tub. Candice looked at the clear steaming water and sighed.

"You need more...." A short Chinese woman entered the room with her head lowered. "I get." She stopped and stepped back lightly as she closed the door behind her.

Candice disrobed, and with eyes glazed over, dipped her big toe into the water. She drew a long breath and sighed as she slipped into the tub. Picking up a bar of soap, she lightly sniffed it. Its delicate scent reminded her of summer roses. Her eyes grew heavy as the soap melted and its sweet bouquet filled the room.

"Ma'am," a voice softly asked. "Do you need more hot water?"

Candice peacefully replied, "No, thank you." She sat up in the tub, and with heavy eyes, popped open the bottle of champagne. With toes curled, she drank without a worry in the world.

"I so sorry," the Chinese woman said as she entered the room with her head lowered. "I help you dress."

Candice blinked hard. "Why would you want to do that?" she asked gently, sitting up in the tub.

"Sheriff outside," the woman said in broken English.

Panicked, Candice scrambled from the water and hid the bottle of champagne underneath the tub. She then wrapped a thick white towel around her dripping body.

"Ma'am," a gruff voice demanded. "I'm sorry to interrupt you, but I've got a problem."

Without too much worry left in her mind, Candice lightly replied, "I'll be right out." She inched open the door.

"That's her!" Kitty screamed, shattering Candice's calm.

The sheriff glanced at Candice wrapped in the skimpy towel and lowered his eyes. "Ma'am, this woman said you stole her gold dust. Is this true?"

Candice inched the door open farther. Staring at Kitty, she calmly said, "Sheriff, I ain't ever seen this woman before. May I get back to my tub now?"

"I'm very sorry to have disturbed you, ma'am." The sheriff went to close the door.

"That's her!" Kitty cried. "And she has my gold dust!"

The sheriff shook his head and commanded, "Keep your voice down. I don't know who you are. I don't care what you done...." Taking a deep breath, his hands tightened around Kitty's right arm. He coolly said, "This is a hotel. Respectable folks are trying to sleep. You're commin' with me."

Candice slid back into the tub's comforts and sighed. To the Chinese woman she said, "I know I've been in here a long time, but would you mind bringin' me more hot water?"

The Chinese woman opened the door carrying a steaming pail of water and slowly added it to the tub. Her back straightened as she lightly offered, "You know her? She rotten."

Candice nodded. "I understand. Thank you." Her eyes closed. She soaked away layers of trail dust as the warm water and scented soap soothed every inch of her tired body. Without a worry, she dressed and unhurriedly headed back to her room. A door creaked and opened an inch as she passed it. Candice sighed, not giving it a second thought.

Tim was waiting in front of her door with her room key, "Ma'am, is their anythin' else I can get you?"

Embarrassed because she was robed in a flimsy nightgown, Candice stammered, "No, thank you."

Tim unlocked the door and handed her the room key. Candice threw him a short smile and in a tiny voice said, "You need to get home to your wife. It's very late."

Tim's head fell. "Ma'am, my wife is gone. I work and live here now."

Candice didn't know what to say to that, so she simply said good night and closed the door.

"Why did you believe her and not me!" Kitty spat at the Sheriff. "I'm the one that can read and write. Why, I bet *you* can't read and write."

The sheriff shook his head and bit his upper lip as he led Kitty down the steps and into the hotel lobby.

"Goodnight," he offered the desk clerk. "I won't release her 'til she makes good on her debts."

The night clerk glanced up at the sheriff and nodded as he watched him escort Kitty out the hotel's front door.

"You'll be sorry," Kitty cried. "I have enough gold to buy this town!"

"You sure are a loud one," the sheriff remarked. "I've never had to lock up a girl before."

"What?" Kitty stopped. "What did you say?"

"Keep movin'," the sheriff growled. "I'm tired of your spat!"

"No!" Kitty shouted. "I'm goin' back to my soft bed." She turned abruptly, surprising the sheriff. His grip failed. She lifted her clean skirt and hastened her pace back to the hotel.

"Darn women!" the sheriff bellowed, his face reddening. "If you don't stop I'll shoot!" he angrily warned.

To Kitty's surprise, he fired. She stopped in her tracks and threw her hands on her hips, turning abruptly back toward the sheriff.

"What kind of a sheriff are you?" she screamed. "I don't have a gun on me! Do you shoot people in cold blood around here?"

Her high-pitched shrill grabbed everybody's attention. Piano music stopped. The shuffle of worn boots and clicking spurs drew the sheriff up short.

"He tried to shoot me in cold blood!" Kitty screamed, kicking the hard clay beneath her boots. Grins formed as men from the saloon watched her blonde locks jump and fall in the moonlight.

"I ain't the betin' sort," a weasel of a man said. "But I bet she shoots the sheriff dead."

Another man who was swaying drunk slurred, "I bet…I bet…." He leaned heavily to the right and dropped. Men roared.

"I might have taken his bet," another man chuckled. "Kick 'em."

"What fer?" a white haired, poorly dressed miner said. "He's out of gold dust." The men sneered and watched.

"Lady, I shot over your head," the sheriff told Kitty. "But I'm losin' my patience."

"She ain't a lady!" some deep voice shouted.

The sheriff glanced at the men and saw the lust growing in their eyes. "You men go have another drink," he shouted.

"Are you payin'?" the white-haired miner shouted back. The men's laughter grew.

"I told you," Kitty pouted angrily, "I'm goin' back to the hotel."

"I'll pay for her room!" a drunken man shouted and everybody cheered.

A deep scowl darkened the sheriff's face. The men had seen that warning sign many a time. They cautiously backed up.

"I think he's goin' to shoot her," one of the men predicted, keeping his voice low.

"I think you're right," another man observed, scratching his four-day-old beard.

Kitty abruptly turned again and headed back toward the hotel. The sheriff whipped his gun out and shot.

A bullet creased Kitty's ear. The men froze. Nobody moved, and nobody spoke another word.

Chapter 34

"What did you that for?" Kitty screeched, shaking her head. Blood dripped from her ear. Her eyes filled with fire as she turned and ran as fast as her thin legs would carry her, back toward the sheriff.

"She's got nerve enough for two men," the white-haired miner whispered out loud. Men around him nodded in agreement.

The sheriff's eyes widened as Kitty rushed toward him, shaking her fist. His face turned dark with worry as he anxiously shouted, "You damn' fool."

Kitty slammed her fist into his face. His weapon dropped. His head shook. The men roared.

"You can't kill her at close range," a gruff voice guffawed. "That wouldn't be sportin'."

The sheriff's eyes tightened as he growled, "No woman hits me and gits away with it."

He leaped toward Kitty's swinging arms, landing on top of her, toppling them both. The men cheered.

"You men get back to your business," the sheriff angrily shouted. "This ain't your business."

The hard, deep-set frown on the sheriff's face dampened the men's excitement. As piano music started up again, the men meandered back inside the saloon.

"I don't know where you've been, and I don't care where you're headin'," the sheriff snarled, his weight keeping Kitty pinned to the ground. "But next time you run away from me, I'll shoot you."

"I hate you!" Kitty howled as she fought for freedom like a trapped, wild animal.

The sheriff's eyes darted at shadows as he slapped Kitty across the face and lifted her from the ground by her hair, pulling hard as he dragged her to jail. Kitty fought him, slapping and kicking wildly.

"If you ain't the feistiest thing I've ever seen," the sheriff commented, huffing and puffing. "I have a notion to shoot you right here, right now."

His face darkened with anger, and pooling in sweat, he swung open the unlocked heavy metal cell door.

"You get some sleep," he demanded as he pushed her inside the cell. He watched her fall to the floor, then locked the door with a set of jangling keys.

"That hurt!" Kitty screamed, immediately jumping up. "Are you a real sheriff?"

Confused by Kitty's sharp tongue and fast movements, the sheriff took a step back from the jail cell and grumbled, "You'd better believe I am." He shook his head hard and a deep scowl settled over his face. "You ain't leavin' this jail until you pay for everythin' you owe."

Kitty daintily slapped the dust off of her clean dress and calmly lifted her head. Throwing the sheriff a teasing wink, and with proper manners she said, "I'm sorry, I just lost my husband, and my family said they'd be coming for me. I'm lost."

The sheriff's frown melted at the sight of her natural beauty and feminine movements. She limped hard and coughed with alarm, then fell onto the smelly small cot, hiding a grin and a raised eyebrow.

The sheriff asked in a more solicitous tone, "Ma'am, why did you come here?"

Kitty slowly replied," I'm here to get married."

"You just told me you were lost!" he spit. "Don't you think I can remember anythin'?"

She threw the sheriff an uppity look. "I'm hungry! And I'm thirsty. And I know that if I'm hungry and thirsty, you have to oblige."

The sheriff's face filled with a puzzled expression. He started to shake his head. Before he could speak, Kitty barked, "And I still don't think you know how to read or write, do you?"

The sheriff's face turned bright red. "I ain't had a woman in here before, and as soon as you make good on them debts, I'm escorting you out of my town."

Noticing the anger in the sheriff's voice, Kitty teasingly said, "I think I might stay here. This looks like a great place to live."

The sheriff's face reddened some more. "You ain't welcome ever again in this town. By sundown tomorrow, I want you gone."

Kitty started humming. "I love music, don't you?" she nonchalantly said. "What's your favorite song?"

"If you ain't the...." The sheriff held his tongue and sat back down at his desk.

"I'm goin' to Bodie, and I'm gettin' married," Kitty hummed over and over.

Annoyed, the sheriff turned abruptly and stared long and hard at Her. He stood up and said, "Bodie is a lawless town." He let her young, playful eyes hold his and he growled, "I don't know you, and I'm sick of you. The only thin' I know for sure is that no lawman ever sent to Bodie has come back. Don't know any woman who's ever headed that way either. I reckon you've been lyin' to me all night."

Kitty tucked herself into the uncomfortable cot and said, "I'm gettin' married to James. And he's waitin' for me in Bodie."

The lawman just shook his head, turned the lantern low, then began to leave.

"I'm still hungry!" Kitty hissed after him.

"I'll bring you a hot breakfast in the mornin'," the sheriff quietly replied as he locked the jail's front door.

Chapter 35

"I brung you a hot cup of coffee," Tim whispered with a soft knock on Candice's hotel room door.

Candice's eyes jumped awake as adrenaline flowed through her veins. She reached for the gun underneath her pillow.

Tim tapped on the door again. Candice stretched and yawned, got out of bed, then plodded to the door. Not having a robe, she shyly inched the door open.

"I'm sorry if it's not perfect." Tim's head lowered as he caught a whiff of Candice's sweet smell.

"I didn't ask for any coffee," Candice quickly replied.

"Oh, its okay," Tim whispered. "You ain't gettin' charged for it." His eyes darted up and down the hall as he threw Candice a tiny grin. But then his back straightened and his grin faded as he said, "I'm sorry about that nasty woman who took away your sleep last night."

Candice yawned and gave Tim a short smile. "Thank you. I'll be leavin' today."

"Yes, ma'am." Tim's voice turned serious. "Can I fetch your buggy?"

Candice blinked and gathered her thoughts. Her smile faded. "No, thank you. I'll get it."

Tim eased her door closed. Sun pierced the hotel's window. It danced and jumped around the room. Candice sat down on the comfortable bed and let out a deep sigh as she sipped the hot cup of coffee.

Her smile widened as she lifted the mattress and picked up the hidden gold dust.

Morning noises filled the quiet. Doors creaked and slammed. Candice slowly dressed. Strutting to a mirror, she glared at her wide hips.

A soft knock at her door interrupted her thoughts. "Ma'am," Tim quietly said. "I checked the stables and you don't have any horses. Would you like to hire a team?"

Candice paced a little. She lightly answered through the closed door. "No, I wouldn't, thanks."

Tim, hearing her answer said, "The stage will be commin' late this afternoon."

Candice, clean and rested, grabbed her belongings, and with a sparkle in her eyes, left the hotel. She headed toward the stables and past a mercantile store's window where a ruffled, fancy red dress caught her eye. She slowed, staring through the storefront window.

"Please, come in," a pleasant voice offered, as a sharply dressed woman opened the door. "I know the sign says 'closed on Sunday' but you're welcome, so please come in."

Candice hesitated, admiring the dress. It was impeccably sewn and had layers of fancy lace and silk. Buttons adorned the bodice. She nodded to the store clerk as she fingered the heavy gold dust in her pocket.

"Can I pour you a cup of tea?" the clerk asked with a smile.

"No," Candice bluntly replied. With a heightened voice she said, "I need to collect my horses."

"That dress came all the ways from France. Isn't it beautiful?" The clerk turned the dress around to give Candice a better look. "Why, if I didn't know any better, I would have thought this dress was made just for you."

Candice glanced around the store. Her eyes fell back to the dress.

"Please try it on," the storekeeper insisted, "It's just too pretty to be sitting in the window. It needs to be shown off."

A smile crept onto Candice's face. She nodded and stepped behind a thick changing curtain.

"Are you sure I can't fix you a cup of tea?" Not waiting for an answer the clerk said through the curtain, "It might be a little baggy on you. It was made for a much larger woman. Did I mention that it's one of a kind and it came all the way from France?"

Candice felt the soft material and delicately pulled the dress over her head. The dress fit like a glove. She wiggled her hips. The silk danced. She tried to hide her excitement as she asked, "It looks expensive. How much is it?"

The clerk hesitated. "They make the most elegant clothes in France. Why, that dress could be welcomed at the finest dance anywhere in the world."

Candice spun, touching the material from top to bottom. With a girlish voice that surprised her she asked again, "How much is it?"

The clerk's voice contained a hint of doubt. "It's only four dollars," she said as Candice stepped out from behind the curtain.

"Do you take gold dust?" Candice excitedly asked.

The clerk's eyes widened. She set down her cup of tea and said, "Why, yes we do."

"Do you have a matchin' hat?" Candice asked.

The clerk, not expecting a sale by the looks of Candice, pulled a very expensive hat down from a high shelf. Swallowing hard, she regained her composure as she handed Candice the hat. "This hat was made by the finest hat maker in Europe. It's one of a kind and it will go perfectly with that exquisite dress." She took a step back from Candice and with excitement growing in her voice said, "It fits you perfectly. I have never seen a dress fit a lady so perfectly."

Candice blushed and delicately slipped the hat over her fiery red locks.

The clerk smiled nervously as she said, "If you want them both it will be six dollars."

Candice sashayed around the store a bit, feeling like a grand lady. Finally, she said, "I'll take them."

The clerk carefully asked, "Did your husband strike it rich?"

Candice's smile widened as she simply replied, "Yes."

The clerk eyed Candice for a minute, then with a squeak in her voice said, "I think this would look wonderful on you!" She handed Candice a scarf. "And this would accent your red hair perfectly." She tried to hand Candice a hand-carved ivory hair clip.

"No, this is all I need." Candice lifted her faded cotton dress from the floor. Handing it to the clerk, she said, "It offered me comfort. It ain't much, but it will cover a needy woman."

The clerk nodded. Softly she said, "Thank you. We have many needy women in this town. I'll wash it, mend it, and pass it along."

The clerk looked on as Candice carefully poured gold dust into a scale bowl that lowered as it filled. The clerk nodded when to stop pouring the gold dust, then gleefully announced, "You are now, by far, the best dressed woman in this town!"

Candice's face lit up. Catching her smile, she calmly said, "Thank you for opening up on a church day."

The clerk giggled as she admitted in a soft voice, "I'm not fond of the church here. Thank you for comin' inside."

Candice held a giggle as she strutted out the door.

Townsfolk followed Candice's every move like a magnet. Decent women's heads lifted and they offered her a short smile. Not expecting the attention but thoroughly enjoying it, Candice slowed her pace.

"Ma'am, may I help you?" Men flocked to her like bees to honey. Never having been in this position before, Candice's heart raced. She wasn't sure of any of the men's true intentions.

"I wouldn't walk too close to the jail," a man twice her age offered. "Your type shouldn't be exposed to her type."

Forgetting her manners, Candice spat, "And just what type is that?"

The man stopped walking and scratched his head.

As she approached the jail her curiosity grew. Without a worry she lightly knocked on the thick wooden door.

"You better have brought me breakfast!" Kitty screamed from her jail cell. "Did you forget I could read and write?" Her voice sliced through the door and exploded outside.

Candice's face fell. She knocked harder on the door.

"Ma'am, can I help you?" a man hollered from the other side of the street.

Candice turned and recognized the man's face. It was the sheriff from last night.

"Yes," she called, feeling a tad uneasy.

He hurried across the street, tipping his hat as he approached. "I'm truly sorry about last night." He shook his head and said, "I should have waited until mornin'."

"If you don't get me food soon," Kitty demanded, "I'll have *you* arrested!"

"Ma'am," he offered, "that one's a mean one. I don't want to go back in there until the hotel brings her breakfast. She's plumb made me deaf."

Candice choked on a giggle and exhaled. Delighted, she said, "Sheriff, I might have been mistaken."

"About what, ma'am?" He took a step backwards, eyeing Candice's fine clothing. "You're the most proper lady we've ever had in these parts. Can I buy you breakfast?"

Candice blushed, surprised again by all the attention. "No, I need to tell you somethin'."

"Oh, yeah? What is it?" he asked, regaining his composure.

"That woman inside? I do know her," Candice admitted, lowering her head.

"But why did you tell me you didn't?" the sheriff asked, his voice hardening.

"Because...." Candice sighed and her voice softened. "Because...I just wanted a good night's sleep."

A frown settled on the sheriff's face. "I ain't sure if you broke the law or not," he stated. "All I know for sure is I want her out of my jail." His eyes grew cold as he grumbled, "I ain't had this bad a night's sleep since the last hangin'."

"I will pay for everything she owes," Candice offered.

"Fair enough." The sheriff unlocked the jail door and escorted Candice inside. He sat down on a hard wooden chair and scooted it close to a small, splintery desk. "She didn't pay the hotel, and she owes for a bottle of champagne and a tub." The sheriff used his fingers to add things up and finally announced, "That will be two dollars even."

Candice lifted her skirt. The sheriff gaped and his head turned as he cleared his throat. "Where are you headed?"

Lowering her skirt, Candice calmly said, "Bodie. Can you give me directions?"

"Don't trust her!" Kitty shouted through the iron bars. "I told you last night she has my gold dust!"

The sheriff's eyes tightened. His voice hardened as he demanded, "Where'd you get all that gold dust from?"

Candice forced a tear to her eyes. "My husband is dead," she wept. I trusted his word about the mine bein' safe." Tears dripped down her cheeks.

"I'm sorry, ma'am." The sheriff's voice softened along with his expression. "It's my job to ask."

Kitty's eyes widened as she stared at Candice's fancy clothes.

The sheriff escorted Candice away from Kitty's jail cell and whispered, "I think I can keep her locked up for another twenty-four hours. There's a noon stage headed north. You don't want to go to Bodie. It's lawless."

"Sheriff," a young man shouted as he threw the front door open. "The women at the hotel won't bring a girl prisoner's food over." His manners abruptly changed, as did his panicky voice when he spied Candice. "Hello, ma'am. How do you do?"

Candice blushed.

The sheriff drew his gun. "Andy, how many times have I told you not to spook me like that! One of these days I'm gonna accidently kill you!"

"Stop payin' her all the attention!" Kitty groused. "I'm far prettier than her."

Both men threw her a hateful glare. The Sheriff fumed, "You hush, or I ain't gonna *ever* feed you."

Candice was basking in the moment, a bit afraid of what Kitty would say next. She said, "Thank you again, but I promised my sister I would escort her to Bodie. I'll pay you what she owes and I'd be obliged if you gave us directions."

"Bodie?" Andy questioned. "You can't go there. It's the town from the devil."

"I promised her," Candice said as a frown settled on her face. " And ladies keep their promises."

Her words set the men's minds racing. "Sheriff, can you deputize me and let me guide them?"

The sheriff shook his head. "No, you'll come back in a wood box if I do."

"Shouldn't we try?" the man eagerly asked.

"No." The sheriff's voice hardened. "It's not the law's business."

He unlocked Kitty's cell door and warned, "If you come back to my town, I'll shoot you dead." He glanced over his shoulder at Candice and in a lighter, calmer tone said, "If you're goin' to Bodie, you need to buy guns, ammo, and warm clothes."

"But we're in the dead of spring?" Kitty cried. "What would we do that for?"

Candice saw the pain in the sheriff's eyes as he said, "Them hills are wicked. Nature will play with you till she kills you. Let your horses rest before the climb, or they won't make it."

Not paying any mind to the sheriff's warnings, Kitty stormed over to Candice and said, "You're the one who said we couldn't spend the gold." Her nose flared as she growled, "Give me that dress. I'd look better in it than you!"

The sheriff opened the jail's door and threw Candice a worried glance as he shook his head.

Candice offered him a short smile and sashayed out the door with style as both men watched.

"What the heck are you walkin' like that for?" Kitty snapped. "That's how I walk. Are you on that opiate stuff again?"

Both men shook their heads, glad to close the door behind them.

"I mean it," Kitty barked. "Are you on that opiate stuff?"

Candice shook her hips, and in a sarcastic tone said, "No, this is much more fun."

"Fun?" Kitty shouted. "I've been in that stinkin' jail all night. I want that gold, and I want it now!"

Candice slowed her pace as they ambled to the stables. Holding in her laughter, she said, "Do you want to go back to jail?"

"I hate you!" Kitty snapped as she noticed people throwing her hard looks. "So," she studied the town's surroundings, "how did you know this wasn't Bodie?'

Candice shot Kitty an uppity glance over her shoulder. With a giggle she said, "Because a sign at the outskirts of town says 'Welcome to Aurora.'"

Kitty stopped walking and looked hard at Candice. She growled, "I thought you couldn't read."

Candice lightly replied, "Yeah, some of us hog farmers can do that, too."

"I hate you," Kitty screamed, drawing attention to herself.

Candice laughed and walked proper all the way to the stables.

Chapter 36

"I'm hungry and I'm sick of this town," Kitty spat as she hurried her pace to the stables. "I need James."

"I'm heeding the sheriff's warnings," Candice told her firmly. "We're gettin' our buckboard and we're goin' back to the mercantile to get supplies."

Kitty's frown fell and her eyes filled as she asked, "Is that the same place where you got that dress and hat?"

Catching the look on Kitty's face, Candice said, "Yes, but I bought their last dress."

Kitty's face reddened with anger. A moment later she lifted an eyebrow and calmly said, "We'll see."

"Hello, sir...I mean, ma'am. I took care of the horses for you as I told you I would." The young man, who had helped Kitty the night before, politely held his hand out. "I made sure they got fed good."

"Thank you," Kitty said in a flirty voice. The boy's head lowered, as did his hand.

Candice caught the disappointment in his eyes and asked, "Did she say she was gonna pay you?"

"Yes, ma'am." His voice jumped with excitement.

"How much did she say she was gonna pay you?"

The boy looked at Candice's fancy clothes and said, "Ma'am, this is between her and me, not you."

"She's my sister," Candice whispered. "If she owes you money, then I owe you money."

"Ma'am," the boy stood tall and said, "I ain't ever seen a whole dollar before."

Candice, expecting to pay a nickel, stopped in her boots and swallowed hard. Throwing Kitty a deep frown she said, "I'll be right back." She walked into the shadows of the stables and delicately pushed her breasts apart to grab the only coin she had ever owned.

She walked back over to the boy and said, "Don't spend this. Hide it."

The boy's face lit and a smile wide enough to dive into filled his face. "Yes, ma'am!" He hurried the horses to the wagon.

"Do we owe the stable hand any money?" Candice asked as she looked around for someone older.

"No, ma'am. My pa is supposed to be here. He's home takin' care of my ma. She's havin' a baby. I'll give you some oats to fatten them animals up." Arms straining, the young man lifted a fifty-pound bag of oats and eased it into the back of the buckboard.

"Are you sure they don't have any more of them fancy dresses?" Kitty asked with a raised eyebrow.

Candice just said, "Get up," to the horses, then glared at Kitty. "You really said you would pay that boy a dollar?"

"I hope that mercantile has somethin' to eat," Kitty sighed. "I'm starved."

The women threw each other a hard stare and then a grin.

"It's the prettiest dress I've ever seen," Kitty admitted. "How much did it cost?"

Candice's slow reply set Kitty's mind wandering. "I bet you paid handsomely for it."

"No," Candice lied. "They were tryin' to get rid of it and sold it to me cheap."

Kitty, far more knowledgeable about fine clothes, grinned and said, "I bet you paid four dollars for that dress." She studied Candice's fancy hat, and with a mile-wide smile said, "And about a dollar for that beautiful hat."

Candice's jaw dropped. "How did you know?"

Kitty rolled her eyes. "That hat's from Paris, and that dress is probably from France, too."

Candice's face went pale as she studied her own clothes. Before she could get a word out of her mouth Kitty added, "You got it for a fair price, and it becomes you."

Candice stopped the horses in front of the mercantile. Kitty glanced toward the large front window. "The sign says 'closed'. Are you sure you got it here?"

Candice, being careful not to dirty her new dress, gingerly exited the wagon.

"The sign says 'closed'," Kitty repeated in a testy voice.

Candice lightly knocked at the door.

Kitty stomped her right foot. "It still says 'closed.'"

Candice bit her upper lip and tapped harder on the door.

The door inched open. "Remember me?" Candice said with a smile. "I just bought this lovely dress from you."

An older woman, using a cane, inched the door open a bit farther. "I'm sorry," she whispered, short of breath. "My family is at church."

Candice helped the woman close the door. Kitty sighed as a frown settled on her forehead. "I reckon I won't get breakfast today, neither," she grumbled.

Candice offered her a short smile. Both women got back in the buckboard.

"Why is that man standin' in the middle of the street wavin'?" Kitty asked as Candice got the horses moving.

"I don't know." Candice slowed the buckboard again.

"I ain't goin' back to that jail," Kitty insisted. "Go around him."

"Why, it's Tim," Candice announced. "I think he wants me to stop."

"Who's Tim?" Kitty asked with caution.

A grin slid over Candice's face as she said, "He's the man that took you to the sheriff last night."

"Give me them that whip!" Kitty shouted. "I'll teach him."

"Stop it!" Candice barked. "His wife's dead." She rolled her eyes, and with an uppity tone said, "And he gave me your bottle of champagne last night."

Kitty reached for the long, leather horsewhip. Candice's layered dress blocked Tim's view. Candice stopped the horses.

"Mornin' again, ma'am. I forgot to tell you...." His words ceased as he stared at Kitty. His back straightened as confusion rang in his voice. "Isn't that the polecat I took to the sheriff last night?"

"What did you just call me?" Kitty spit back, her eyes tightening.

"Yes," Candice simply replied. "Why were you flaggin' us down?"

Tim's face reddened and filled with a puzzled expression.

Candice, in a louder voice asked, "Tim, why did you stop our buckboard?"

"Oh." He shook his head. "Oh yeah." He glanced down at the ground and scratched his head. "I was supposed to bring you breakfast. It was included in your room pay."

Kitty's back straightened. She brushed off her skirt and her voice lightened as she said, "Can you bring it to us now?"

"I reckon," Tim hesitantly replied. "But it's a mite cold."

Kitty's eyes widened. "Can I help you get it?" she offered.

Tim's eyes tightened. "You stay away from me, you polecat!"

Candice threw a dagger look at Kitty and calmly said, "I'll get the food. You mind the horses."

"That sure is the purtiest dress I ever seen," Tim said as he offered Candice his hand to help her out of the buckboard.

"It would look prettier on me," Kitty spat.

"What the heck are you doin' with her?" Tim asked as he escorted Candice up the wood steps to the hotel lobby. "I left the food in the kitchen. I'll go fetch it," he said without waiting for an answer.

Candice studied the lobby. "If you could add a bit more food to that breakfast I would gladly pay for it."

"If it's for that polecat, no." A second later Tim's tone lightened as he said, "Doggone it, where are my manners?" He appeared with a bulging sack of food. Candice had only expected a slice of bread and jam.

"I need to pay you for that," she said, staring at the sack.

Tim's eyes darted around the lobby. He shook his head. "Ma'am, you just have a safe trip. That'll be payment enough."

He hurried Candice out of the lobby and back to the buckboard. He helped her up, then handed her the sack.

"Are you sure?" she questioned. He raised his head for a second, winked at her, and blushed. "Yes, ma'am. I would say that is the most handsome dress I've ever seen."

An angry, high-pitched voice from inside the hotel sent Tim running. "You should get now," he whispered as he hurried back inside.

"Whatever's in that sack sure smells good." Kitty grabbed the sack. It was warm. She lifted it up and took a deep whiff. "Mmmm. I ain't had hot bread and ham forever." She tore the sack open.

Candice urged the horses forward as she shared a final glance over her shoulder with Tim.

"He even gave us butter." Kitty's voice jumped. "I think we should stay there, again sometime."

Kitty's high shrills of pleasure added to Candice's grin as their horses led them away from the comforts of town.

"Here, have some." Kitty handed Candice a thick ham steak, warm and dripping grease.

"Get that away from my new dress!" Candice squealed.

"You want bread around it?" Kitty asked with concern.

"I want bread, jam, butter, and anythin' else around that pig Tim gave us."

"What are you talkin' about?" Kitty slowed her chewing. "This is meat. It's from a cow."

Candice's eyes danced as she held back laughter. "Give me that pig," she demanded as she grabbed for the thick sandwich.

"It's meat and it's from a cow," Kitty hissed. "You need some schoolin'. When we get to Bodie, I'm goin' to help you get schooled."

"Ham is meat from a pig," Candice insisted in between mouthfuls.

Then what comes from a cow?" Kitty spat.

"Milk, butter, and steaks." No longer able to control her laughter, Candice roared, "Kitty, for havin' a fifth-grade education, you sure are stupid."

Candice's laughter ceased. Her eyes widened as she threw Kitty a hard stare. "You can't have breast milk, unless you've had a baby. I know. I've been around a lot more pregnant women then you."

"Leave me alone!" Kitty screamed. "All I want to do is marry James!" A second later she asked, "Do you want some more jam?"

"Sure," Candice simply replied. "Any more of that sweet butter left?"

Chapter 37

"We need to keep followin' the south ridge." Candice yawned as night fell.

"I don't think we should do that," Kitty slowly replied. "I don't remember," she said. "I think there's Indians there."

"But that's what the sheriff told me to do," Candice said, her mind made up.

"No, I'm sure James warned me about the south ridge."

"No," Candice lifted her head. "He was talkin' about goin' south around that lake."

"I don't remember," Kitty admitted, yawning. "Can't we stop here for the night?"

Candice stopped the horses.

"Unless you borrowed somethin' else that I'm goin' to get hung for!" Kitty shouted.

"You ain't ever borrowin' this dress," Candice growled. "It's mine! I'll get the horses."

"I'll make a fire and get the bedrolls," Kitty replied.

Without another spat, the women settled down by a fire. "Can I borrow that dress when I get married?" Kitty whispered above the crackling fire.

"Will you return it?" Candice asked. They shared a glance as grins settled on both their faces.

"I ain't ever had a sister before," Kitty remarked.

"I never knew havin' one would be such a worry," Candice offered with a yawn.

"Oh my darlin', oh my darlin', oh my darling Clementine. Get up, mule!" A crusty old voice hollered. "I am lost and gone forever, goodnight Clementine."

The mule came to a halt. A stout, unshaven miner swayed, then fell off the mule to the ground. Kitty and Candice readied their guns. The man didn't stir.

"We won't hesitate to shoot!" Kitty warned the prone miner.

The miner's round body rolled as he laughed and sang.

"We'll shoot you dead and take your mule," Candice growled.

Surprised by Candice's words, Kitty whispered, "Candice, you can't sound that mean when you're wearin' that purty of a dress."

The miner belched, then slowly stood up. His body swayed as he lifted his arms. His shirt was layered in sweat and grime and clearly hadn't been washed in a long time. "What did you do that fer, Bessie?" he mumbled, admonishing the mule.

The women were down wind and caught a whiff of him. They both grimaced. Kitty hollered, "Put them stinky arms down!"

Surprised, the old-timer said, "So what should I do now?"

Kitty threw Candice a quick glance. Both women stared at the stranger, guns aimed.

"Drop your gun!" Kitty demanded, rising to her feet.

The miner's legs trembled. "But this here gun ain't got any bullets in it," he whined.

"Drop your gun!" Kitty demanded again, cocking the trigger on her shiny six-shooter.

The miner groaned and shook his head. "I already told you, it can't do nothin' but add weight to my achin' hip." He caught a glimpse of Kitty's beauty and the fire in her eyes. "You can hold it, but you can't keep it. I traded my good mule for this gun, and you'll have to shoot me dead to keep it." He unhooked his belt and untied the leather string that fastened it to his leg. "Why would you want to kill me, anyways?" he groaned. "I ain't got nothin' but an empty gun and an ornery mule."

Kitty walked over to the miner and cautiously picked up his gun holster. She checked the gun's chambers. All were empty. She threw the gun at Candice and took a step backward. "So, tell us why you're here," she demanded.

The miner scratched his grubby beard. "I reckon I don't know." He gave his head a quick shake. "I reckon my mule saw your fire and invited herself in." A deep frown settled over his weathered face. "I should have eaten that mule a long time ago," he snarled.

The old-timer scratched his head again. Standing tall, he addressed his mule. "Bessie, I'm goin' to eat you for sure if you don't come to me." Looking straight at Kitty, he said, "If you're gonna kill me, I'd be obliged if you did it soon. I would have shot me myself if I had any bullets. My feet killed me a long time ago."

A puzzled expression settled on Kitty's face. Cautiously, she asked, "Where are you headed?"

"To California." He drew a deep breath. "I know more about minin' than any of them young whippersnappers out there. Bessie and I can smell a strike from a mile away." He hiccupped, belched, and fell backwards, landing hard on his drawers."

Kitty and Candice shared a glance and a cautious giggle.

"Where the heck is that mule? He stood back up, swayed, and hollered into the darkness, "Bessie, where are you? I promise you, I'll buy you oats."He stumbled again. Cussing and spitting, he growled, "I'll eat you for sure if you don't come to me. Where the heck are you?"

"What do you think?" Kitty whispered, holding back her smile.

"I think he stinks bad and we have his gun," Candice yawned. "I'm gettin' some sleep."

Kitty lowered her gun and curled next to Candice, her gun still ready.

The miner dropped close to the fire. Kitty sat up and cocked her pistol. "I don't know you, and I don't care who you are." Her face turned black with anger, "But you need to get on that thing you call a horse and get!"

"Can't find her," he bellowed. "I should have shot her…" he shook his head strongly… "when I had bullets."

Kitty studied him hard. The stranger's body shook with shivers.

"I ain't good at talkin'," he said as his teeth clattered. "But I give you my word I won't touch you if you let me get warm by this fire."

Kitty watched him edge closer to the fire. "Don't you have a blanket?" she asked.

Shivering, the miner quickly replied, "No, ma'am. Them got stolen from me and Bessie a long time back."

Kitty studied his chattering teeth. The miner was shivering so bad she began to feel sorry for him. "You can share ours," she offered.

The miner kept an eye on Kitty's faltering gun. Kitty stood up, surprising the miner, and with the gun still in hand she said, "It isn't 'good night Clementine.' It's 'dreadful sorry my Clementine.'"

The miner's eyes narrowed. He hugged the fire some more.

Chapter 38

"This dress hurt me while I slept." Candice yawned.

"How?" Kitty yawned too. "It's soft and beautiful."

Candice studied the lay of the land. "Is that smelly man gone?"

Kitty sat up. After looking around, she said, "I think so."

"Well, is he or ain't he?" Candice snapped.

Kitty slowly pushed to her feet, shielding her eyes from the piercing morning light. "I don't see him. I think he's gone."

Candice stretched. "I ain't ever wearin' this dress to bed again."

Kitty offered Candice a short smile. "I didn't kill him, if that's what you're thinking." Her grin widened. "I just woke up and he was gone."

Candice yawned again and said, "He sure left in a hurry, it looks like." She bent down to check on the gold dust she had hidden in her boots. It was gone.

"What?" her voice jumped. "Give it back to me or I'll shoot you dead right now!"

Startled, Kitty turned, and with a raised eyebrow barked, "Are you talkin' to me?"

"Gimme back my gold!" Candice demanded, raising her gun.

"I ain't got..." Kitty's voice fell, and then she shouted, "It's *our* gold, not *your* gold!"

"Why the heck are you yellin' at me?"

Candice aimed the gun.

"Are you crazy!" Kitty screamed. "Are you still on the opiate powder?"

Candice drew a deep breath. Slowly, with the gun still trained on Kitty, she bent and checked her boots again.

"You stole it!" she screamed, stiffening her back. "That gold was for Sam and me."

"I didn't take it," Kitty cried, her gun raised and aimed, too. "And I still ain't sure about Sam." Her eyes tightened.

"Why did we trust him?" Candice screamed.

"Who?' Kitty shouted, confused.

"The miner!" Candice groaned. He took my gold!" Candice's head fell. "He took our dreams."

"No, he didn't," Kitty spat, her face reddening in anger. "I'll catch him and kill him twice and I'll get our gold back." She unhitched one of the horses from the buckboard.

"It's too late!"Candice cried. "He's on a mule. We can't catch him."

Kitty, her face still darkened with anger, asked, "Why not?"

"Cuz mules can climb places our horses can't. And…" Candice bawled…"oh why did we trust a man!"

Kitty caught a glimpse of the disappointment in Candice's eyes. "I reckon it's my fault." She stopped unhitching the horse and admitted, "He was old and drunk and cold. I didn't think he could cause us harm."

Candice wept and shook her head.

"He couldn't have gotten far," Kitty offered, leading the horse away from the buckboard. "Can this buckboard work with one horse?"

Candice nodded.

"Stay here. If I ain't back by tomorrow's sunset," she lifted her head and solidly eyed Candice, "you find Sam and go your own way."

"But," Candice wiped her tears away, "You told me you hate horses. We don't even have a saddle. How are you goin' ride that horse?"

"It don't matter," Kitty spat. "I'll learn or die tryin'." She stared long and hard at the horse, and without another thought, grabbed at its mane and pulled herself up onto its back.

Candice wiped back tears and stared.

Kitty leaned forward, and in a frightened voice said, "Go." The horse didn't move.

Surprised at Kitty's tiny voice, Candice offered, "Kitty, it's a horse, not a man. You need to make your voice louder."

Kitty sat up a little straighter on the horse's back and a second later, stretched out face first along its neck. She hollered, "Get up." The horse turned its neck and looked up at Kitty. It shook its back. Kitty's body exploded in movement. She grabbed the horse's mane. Her face went pale.

Candice roared, "I think we have a better chance of catching him together in this buckboard."

Kitty, still glued to the back of the horse, lightly said, "If you teach me how to ride these things when we get to Bodie, I'll teach you how to read."

Candice drew a deep breath. "How did you know I can't read?"

Kitty gave her a short smile and said, "The sign that you said you read headin' into the town of Aurora, doesn't say welcome to Aurora."

"What does it say?" Candice asked, her tears slowing. "It said…" Kitty cautiously lifted her neck while still planted on the horses back. "I ain't goin' to tell you."

Candice hollered, "Get up!" at the horse. Both horses leaped forward. Candice held tight on the reins of the horse still hooked up to the buckboard. The other horse shot forward.

Kitty cried, "Stop!"

Candice, her reddened eyes open wide, screamed, "I'm sorry! I didn't know he would listen to me with a person on his back."

"I hate you!" Kitty cried as the horse galloped away from Candice's sight.

Candice flew around the campsite picking up their belongings. She jumped into the buckboard and shouted, "Get up!" at the single horse attached to it. The horse didn't budge. It turned its head and stared at where the other horse should have been. "Get up!" Candice shouted again, slapping the reins. The horse refused to budge. "She lifted her pistol, and in and angry voice screamed, "Get up!" again. She raised her pistol and fired off a shot. The horse leaped forward.

"I'm commin' Kitty!" Candice cried. "Don't die on me. If you don't die on me, I'll tell you where the other sock of gold is."

"Ma'am," a deep voice shouted, "Why are you runnin' a single horse that fast?"

Surprised at the voice, Candice threw a quick glance to a soldier on a chestnut horse matching her pace.

"My sister's in trouble!" she shouted. "And I intend to help her."

"Slow your horse," the soldier hollered over his shoulder, "I'll get her." His horse flew past the buckboard and disappeared into a cloud of dust.

Candice caught a glimpse of his blue uniform as he flew past. "Whoa!" Her strong arms pulled tight on the reins. The buckboard slowed.

The soldier caught up to Kitty's running horse. "Hold on," he warned. He kicked his horse and abruptly turned sharply, directly in front of Kitty's horse.

His horse resisted and bucked. Kitty's horse threw its neck up and was forced to abruptly stop. Kitty flew unnaturally forward over her horse's neck. The young man lost his seat and shot into the air. Both of them slapped the dirt, hard, a few feet apart.

"Who are you?" Kitty asked with a cough, lifting her head.

"Are you all right, ma'am?" The young man sat up and shook his dizzied head. "Are you all right ma'am?" he asked a second time.

"I…" Kitty's head drooped and she closed her eyes.

Candice slowed the buckboard. When she saw Kitty's stilled body, she cried, "I killed her!"

The young soldier, still woozy, simply said, "I reckon."

Candice leaped out of the buckboard and ran to Kitty's side. Throwing the solider a frown, she said, "I'm sorry Kitty. I didn't know the horse would do that."

Kitty opened her eyes, her head still spinning. Simply, she said, "You promise me I can borrow that purty dress when I get married?"

Before Candice could answer Kitty's eyes closed and her body stilled.

"I'm sorry, ma'am. I did the best I could," the solider offered lightly. "If she's dead, I'll bury her for you."

Candice glanced up at the soldier and cried, "If she's dead, you can bury us both. She's my best friend. If she's dead then I'm dead!"

The solder scratched his thick dark hair hard and said, "I don't understand. You told me it was your sister, and now you're tellin' me you want me to bury you with her?" He shook his head. "I ain't ever been in this sort of a situation before. I reckon I should get the captain to figure this out." He jumped on his horse and flew from sight, leaving a long dust trail.

Candice fell to her knees and delicately lifted Kitty's head and laid it on her lap.

"I'm sorry I killed you by a horse," she cried. "I'll bury your share of the gold with you." Her eyes welled with tears.

"What did you say?" Kitty asked quietly, her eyes still closed.

"You're alive!" Candice sniffled. "On my life I didn't think that horse would run. If you want this fancy dress, you can have it right now."

Kitty slowly lifted her head. In a tiny voice she whispered, "I don't want to know nothin' more, ever again, about horses." She drew a deep breath and sat up. "My head hurts somethin' awful." She dropped back to the ground.

Candice offered, "Can I get you anythin'?"

"A new head." Kitty begged. "I want to shoot this one off."

Candice grinned. "I can't do that. I'm savin' the bullets for that miner."

Eyes still closed, Kitty lightly nodded. Her head dropped. Her body stilled.

Candice's face turned pale. "Kitty, don't die on me," she demanded. "We've got to get to Bodie."

Fast-approaching horses caught Candice's ear. She glanced over her shoulder. Her trigger hand twitched.

"Company halt!" A rail of a man with a thin, graying beard held his right arm up high. He looked like a cold, unpleasant man.

The young soldier directly behind him stopped on his command. "These are them, sir," he said.

"Dismount!" the captain shouted. The private jumped off of his horse and straightened his back.

Candice, her eyes open wide, looked around for more men.

"My private said Indians tried to kill you. But I don't see any arrows. Were they Comanche?"

Candice threw the private a confused glance. He shrugged his shoulders.

Another horse flew into view and slid to stop only inches away from the captain. A thin-faced man jumped off his horse and threw the captain a salute, "Yes sir!" the man shouted. His back straightened. His voice lightened. "I'm a medic. Let me take a look at your sister."

"What's a medic?" Candice nervously asked, her gun hand still fidgeting.

A short grin flashed across his face."Ma'am, I fix ailin' people." He eyed Candice's nervous hand out of the corner of his eye. "Don't shoot me," he warned. "I'm here to help you."

Candice eased her scowl as they shared a quick glance.

"There are no tracks of unshod horses or anything else around here," the captain shouted, mounting his horse. "Fix her or bury her and get back to the men."

"Yes, sir," the medic replied with authority.

The captain turned his prancing horse, studied the afternoon sky, then kicked the animal forward. The private followed him.

Candice grimaced. "Is she dead?"

The medic held her wrist. "She's got a pulse." He quickly unbuttoned Kitty's blouse and dropped his head to her chest."

"I'll shoot you if you do anythin' not descent!" Candice growled.

"Her heart sounds good." He lifted his head. "Do you have any cold water?"

Candice stared at the man.

"Get me some water!" he demanded with a scowl settling on his forehead.

Candice, with one eye watching the medic, hurried to the buckboard and grabbed a canteen.

"Hurry," he insisted. "My captain's not a patient man."

Candice handed the canteen to the medic. With her trigger finger calmed, she asked, "What are you goin' to do?"

His short grin offered Candice hope. "I'm goin' to wake her up and check her eyes."

Candice took a step backward. Her eyes widened.

The medic gently dripped water onto Kitty's face. She didn't stir. His grin faded.

Candice took a step closer. "Are you sure she's not dead?"

The concern in her voice set the medic into motion. He poured water out of the canteen at a much faster pace.

Candice watched with fright. Kitty coughed. "You're alive!" she cried.

"Ma'am, please be quiet. I've got some things to check."

Candice took a step back as a frown, deep enough to fall into, settled on her face.

"You need to open your eyes and look at me," the medic demanded of Kitty.

"My head is spinnin'," Kitty grumbled. "My eyes are too heavy to open."

The medic's voice grew with alarm. He gently pried Kitty's eyes open.

"I know you can hear me. I need to know if you can see me," he insisted.

Kitty drew a deep breath and lifted her heavy eyelids. "I see you, and I can hear you, but I need you to shoot my head off. It hurts real bad."

"Ma'am," the medic said gently, "you have a concussion."

Kitty closed her eyes again.

Candice took a deep breath. "Will she live?"

"Yes, ma'am. She worried me a mite, but with rest she'll be fine."

"What do I do?" Candice asked, puzzled.

"Don't let her ride horses without a saddle," the medic teased, jumping onto his horse.

"Wait!" Candice shouted. The medic turned his horse. "Will you help me get her into the back of the buckboard?"

The medic slid off of his horse again, his head shaking. "That captain is drivin' me so hard, I forgot my manners." He scooped Kitty up and laid her dead weight gingerly into the back of the buckboard.

"Thank you,"

Candice's worried eyes caught the medic's attention. "She'll be good in a day or two," he offered climbing back on his horse. He stopped a second later and said, "If her head gets bumped hard again, she might not wake up."

Candice nodded, offering him a short smile. Daylight faded. Candice remembered what the medic had said and carefully chose the horses' path. Kitty cried and mumbled when the buckboard rocked or jumped. She pushed the horses at a crawl, day and night, only stopping to feed and water them.

Below the tree line Candice turned the horses southwest. Hard gray clay gave way to soft white sand, slowing the horses' pace. She followed a narrow wash that snaked around steep canyon walls and dropped into a flat valley dotted with clumps of creosote bushes.

Kitty moaned much louder, then cautiously sat up. "That hurt worse than any hangover I ever had," she whimpered. Her eyes were glassy.

Candice glanced back at Kitty and lightly said, "Welcome back. I missed you."

"That soldier doctor said your head would be mighty sore. He also said if you fall like that again you won't ever get back up."

"What happened?" Kitty softly asked. "All I remember is...." She blinked long and hard. "You said our gold got stolen and I got on that stupid horse and... somethin' about gold we still have, and...."

Candice shot a glance back at Kitty and offered her a short smile.

Kitty's eyes fell. Her shoulders drooped.

"Don't you worry," Candice offered. "By the time you remember it all we'll be in Bodie."

An arrow sailed down a steep canyon wall and landed on the wooden seat inches from Candice's left leg.

"What?" Candice blinked. Then her eyes shot upward. Arrows sailed downward like a hailstorm. "Hang on Kitty," she screamed. "Get up!" She grabbed the horsewhip and snapped it with furry. "Hang on!" she shouted, using the whip again.

Soft sand slowed the buckboard's progress. "I'll get them," Kitty groaned. Her gun exploded.

Candice glanced over her shoulder into the back of the buckboard. Kitty was reloading her gun with one hand and holding her spinning head with the other.

"We're almost out of this canyon, Kitty!" she hollered, "We can make it!"

An arrow fell and tore through Candice's flesh. Her body shook. Her vision began to blur.

"What the heck are you doin'?" Kitty cried. "Why are the horses slowin'?" She lifted her dizzied head and shot a glance at the buckboard seat. Her face went pale. Candice's bloodied body dropped to the seat.

"I'll kill you all!" Kitty screamed. She crawled over the seat and grabbed the reins.

"I hate horses!" Her face darkened with anger. "If you want to kill me, then catch me!"

She whipped the horses, tearing their flesh. The horses ran through the canyons, their backs lathered with sweat. Kitty whipped them harder.

Arrows whizzed by her. She ducked screaming, "I hate horses and I hate men!"

The canyon walls exploded with music. Arrows slowed and abruptly stopped. Kitty braced herself in the seat and pulled back on the reins. The lathered horses stopped in their tracks. "Get up" she hollered. The nervous horses jumped forward. "No, stop!" she barked.

The music echoed off the canyon walls again. Kitty glanced at Candice, then at the horses, and then at the steep canyon walls. She cautiously sat up, her hands still tight on the reins. The music echoed up and down the steep canyon walls.

It spooked the horses. They bolted forward.

"You stupid horses!" she cried. "That's music!" Her head slammed into the side of the buckboard seat as she latched hard onto the snaking reins.

Her head dropped. Her hands opened. The horses picked up speed.

Chapter 39

"Get that wagon!" a deep voice commanded.

"Yes, sir!" a shadow of a man replied, kicking his horse forward.

"Sergeant!" the voice demanded. "Check the arrows." The commanding officer slowed his horse.

A horse thundered past the captain. Its neck jumped as the rider turned it. "Sir! We've got them in a draw."

The captain's cold eyes hardened. "How many?"

"I reckon a dozen or two," he replied.

"Are there twelve or twenty-four? The captain's face reddened. "How many?"

"About twelve," the young rider shouted. His horse nervously pranced and circled. "Sir! What should we do?"

"Kill them all!" the captain growled. "I ain't takin' any prisoners."

"Yes, sir!" The soldier spun his horse around, then kicked it forward. It jumped and disappeared in a trail of dust.

The captain looked up. He stared long and hard at his surroundings. "I will kill all of you," he said, his face blackened with hate. "I'll kill you, and your kin."

"Sir," a voice shouted. "These aren't Comanche arrows."

"Captain!" the medic shouted. "I stopped the buckboard. It's the same women we helped a while back."

"Company halt!" the captain roared to a group of soldiers approaching on galloping horses. "Corporal, get your men out of this canyon and circle to the north," he ordered. "Sergeant, take the left flank around the east slope. Wait for us there. If it's a trap we'll lead them directly into you. That tall outcropping of rocks in the distance should hide you. Spread out."

"Yes, sir," two reckless and eager young men replied in unison with authority.

"What do I do with the women?" one of them shouted.

"Take them with you to the safety of the rocks." The Captain kicked his horse and shot a quick glance at a man whose horse was keeping pace with his. "Charge!" he ordered. The soldier riding alongside him whipped out a bugle and made it sing.

The men scattered. The captain led them out of the canyon and joined the soldiers who circled to the north. "Watch your flank!" he called out. "I said, spread out!"

The men's horses flew up a steep hillside made of shale. The soft rock shattered beneath the horses' hooves, slowing their run. The captain's vast experience in these matters was apparent. His horse never missed a step.

The bugler sounded off again. Horses leaped and slipped from rock to rock. A soldier not old enough to shave rolled backwards off his horse. His horse stopped. The soldier shook his head, grimaced, and jumped back into the saddle.

The soldiers crested the hill. "Company halt!" the captain ordered as they caught up with him. Indians, their bows and arrows lying by their sides, were seated in a tight circle.

"Sir!" an officer approached. "They put their weapons down and sat on the ground as we approached. I couldn't order the men to kill them in cold blood."

The captain's eyes flared. "I gave you orders. Now shoot them!"

Guns aimed and exploded. The smell of gunpowder and blood filled the air as the men grimaced in horror.

In a blistering voice, the captain shouted, "Sergeant! If you ever disobey my orders again, I'll have you court-martialed."

The sergeant straightened his back. "Yes, sir!"

The captain shouted, "Head down that northern pass." His horse circled on command. "If they were a scouting party, their tribe won't be far behind."

"Sir!" the sergeant hollered. "We need to bury them."

The captain stopped his horse in its tracks. It turned, prancing. "Let the crows eat 'em," he spat.

The men stared at their doings. "This ain't right," the youngest cavalry soldier said out loud.

Bodie or Bust

"I'll shoot the first one of you who doesn't follow my orders!" The sergeant flashed his gun as a scowl deepened on his face.

"Sir!" a solder cautiously said, "I agree with him. It ain't decent to not bury the dead."

The sergeant straightened up in the saddle, his gun hand nervous. He shouted, "Company up!"

The men shared looks of confusion but they willingly followed their commanding officer. They positioned themselves safely behind rocks and eased up on their triggers as the captain approached.

The captain, not waiting for his horse to stop, jumped off. He dusted his uniform off and calmly said, "We killed them. We didn't lose even one man."

The men crawled out from the shadows behind the rocks.

"How many were there?" an anxious soldier asked, out of line.

"It's not your business," the captain spat, his face reddening with anger. He studied the lay of the land. "If that was a scoutin' party the rest will be comin' down from that high valley."

"Yes, sir!" the young soldier said, standing at attention.

"What's your name, boy?" the captain growled.

"I'm--" He hesitated, swallowing hard. Proudly, he said, "My name is Jeremy, sir."

"Take care of my horse, Jeremy." The captain's step slowed as Jeremy slid from his horse and approached.

"You ain't ever travelin' with me no more!" The captain slugged Jeremy in the head with his gun, drawing blood. Jeremy dropped.

The captain hollered, "Men, I'm your commanding officer! I don't care if you like me or not. If them Indians were scouts, then we need to head southeast now!"

The men glanced at Jeremy who lay twitching in the dirt. Their backs straightened. "Yes, sir!" they shouted.

"Sir?" the medic called out. "I warned this one about hittin' her head, and I don't think she'll pull through. This other one has pretty thick skin, though. She's the lucky one."

"What does that mean?" the impatient captain barked.

"I reckon," the medic lowered his head but quickly lifted it again, "this one will live." He pointed at Candice.

The captain spat, "We have a hard road to travel, and these women ain't welcome."

"But sir!" the medic pleaded. "I can't fix them if we leave them."

The captain's scowl deepened. He threw the medic a hateful look. "You didn't save my wife. We'll follow the river south and meet up with company B at Tonopah. You have three days. Heal them or bury them."

The medic jumped to attention. "Sir, your wife needed a hospital. I did my best."

The captain saluted the medic, then turned his horse.

"Sir, yes, sir," The medic stood at attention and saluted his commanding officer.

The captain's horse leaped forward. The soldier with the bugle followed the captain, matching his pace. He lifted his bugle and blew out his commanding officer's orders.

As the men kicked their horses forward, the medic watched in disappointment as his companions galloped away.

He tended to the women. "Don't you move," he instructed Candice. "I pushed the arrow through your shoulder. It's got to be a mite sore."

Candice tried to sit up. The right side of her body refused to obey. She squirmed and tried to roll, but the right side of her body shook in pain.

"I warned you," the medic said in a much lighter tone. "You lost a lot of blood, but I got the bleedin' stopped, so I reckon you'll live. Ma'am, don't you fuss on them thoughts. My name is Eric and I'm here to doctor you."

Candice closed her eyes.

"It's your friend-- or sister," the medic said, mostly to himself, "I'm worried about. Her pupils ain't responsive."

He walked back over to Kitty and changed a cold compress on her forehead. "You're the purtiest girl I've ever seen. I would be a mite mad at myself if you died."

He forced her to drink from his canteen. "I know you don't want water, but If you don't drink it, you'll die."

Three days passed. Neither woman responded to the medic's treatment.

"I just can't leave you here," he said loudly to himself. "But my captain will be full of vinegar if I don't get back."

Shaking his head in disappointment, he collected his horse and saddled it. With a heavy heart he kicked his horse forward.

Darkness fell. Coyotes howled as they circled the still campsite. A full moon offered them a good look at the women's inert bodies.

A young pup crawled forward, his sharp teeth snapping. Another older coyote with a limp followed close behind. The coyote pup cautiously sniffed Kitty's hand, then licked it and ran. His back raised and he returned snarling.

An arrow flew with accuracy, killing the coyote. The other coyote ran as fast as his wounded body would carry him.

Indians, bows and arrows raised, cautiously approached the campsite. A young brave with fire in his eyes screamed as he lifted Kitty's blonde head up. He pulled his knife out from its sheath and shouted to the moon as he bloodied Kitty's scalp.

Before he could do a proper job of scalping her, an arrow with perfect aim stopped him. His hand shook and his knife dropped. His body stilled.

Braves jumped off of their horses and screamed at the coyotes. Candice and Kitty's seemingly lifeless bodies pleased them.

An Indian on a prancing mustang slowly circled the campsite. He looked at the full moon and joined his braves, hollering his victory to the coyotes.

Another brave grabbed his knife and hid a grin as he headed toward Kitty's blonde locks. The Indian on the prancing mustang got a glimpse of the brave's raised knife and screamed at the moon as he urged his horse forward, running the brave down, his face blackened with anger. The other braves threw looks like daggers at their chief, challenging him. His horse pranced and circled close to the women's stilled bodies. Raising a long spear, thick with feathers, he shook it at the moon. His horse pranced around the campsite as he joined his braves, howling at the moon.

Chapter 40

"Ow, my head hurts," Kitty whined as her eyes opened and she sat up. She startled a young Indian girl who was touching her golden hair. "I'm sorry," she said, after she caught a glimpse of the fright in the child's eyes. "You can touch it. I didn't mean to frighten you."

Not understanding a word Kitty said, the girl ran from the teepee.

The chief entered the teepee. His large shadow overwhelmed Kitty's thoughts. He stared at Kitty's golden hair. She jumped to her knees and grabbed for her gun. He threw her a mean glare as a frown settled on his weathered face. Kitty glanced down at her clothes. They weren't hers. Her eyes narrowed as she spit, "If I had my gun I would have killed you dead!" Her body swayed and her knees buckled. She fell to the dirt. The chief's frown deepened. He shook his head, then turned around and left the tent.

The young Indian girl reentered the tent and sat as far away from Kitty as the small space would allow. Her eyes followed Kitty's every movement.

Kitty offered the girl a short smile. "My name is Kitty," she told her.

The young girl stared at Kitty's blonde hair.

"You've never seen blonde hair before, have you?" Kitty leaned her head toward the girl. "You can touch it if you want."

The young girl cautiously extended her hand and touched Kitty's blonde hair. She giggled.

Another young Indian girl entered the tent and sat down. She whispered something to the first girl. They shared a glance and a giggle. Not sure of what to do or say, Kitty surprised herself when she said, "I make real good biscuits. Would you like me to show you how to make them?" She lifted her hands high above her head and stretched. Her movements startled the girls. They ran from the tent.

Kitty knew she was in an Indian camp. What she wanted to know was why. And how had she gotten here? She thought about Candice.

The chief reentered the tent, and Kitty saw worry on his face. She submissively lowered her eyes. When he spoke his voice was loud and his words sharp. Even though she didn't understand a word he said, she knew something bad was going to happen. So she jumped to her feet and punched him in the face. His eyes crossed and he shook his head. Her fist tightened, and without warning she jumped as fast as a rabbit to his left side and punched him again.

His calm composure confused her. He turned, and as she tried to connect another blow, his left hand caught her flying arm. Without a word he threw her across the tent.

Seeing her body curl, he turned to leave the tent. She sprang on him like a wild animal, latching her arms around his neck as she jumped on his back.

He flew forward out of the tent with Kitty glued onto his back. He spun, not sure how to get rid of her. She kicked him and bit at his ears. "You ain't gonna scalp me, and I would have killed you twice if I had my gun," she screamed.

Braves, alarmed by the unusual noise, hastened into the fray, their bows and arrows raised. But soon they began to roar in laughter. When one eager brave tried to help pull Kitty off of the chief's back, she kicked him in the shin. He howled in pain and hopped in a circle. The squaws watched from shadows and choked on their laughter, hiding their grins with their hands.

One brave drew his bow and arrow and took aim, but his hands had to dart up and down so fast he finally gave up. Shouting out in anger, he finally lowered his weapon.

"Kitty!" Candice shouted. "What are you doing?" Candice appeared from inside a tent and ran over to the chief. "Get off of him!" she screamed. "He ain't gonna hurt you."

Kitty accidentally kicked Candice in the face as the chief spinned. Candice flew backwards. The braves exploded in laughter, some dancing, others chanting.

"That hurt!" Candice growled as she leaped on top of Kitty's spinning back. Candice's heavy weight surprised the chief. His legs buckled and his body flattened to the ground like a pancake.

"Get off of me!" Kitty growled, not knowing it was Candice.

"Stop it!" Candice screamed. "What did you do that for?" She shook her head and stood back up. Kitty let go of the chief and rolled off of his back. She jumped up, fists raised. "I'll kill all of you!" she cried, swinging wildly.

Candice took a step back and screamed, "Kitty, it's me!"

The chief crawled away from the two arguing women. The braves whooped and danced.

Kitty froze,."Candice?" Her arms dropped to her sides. "You're alive? But I thought these Indians killed you."

"I thought you were dead, too," Candice replied as a smile shot onto her face.

Meanwhile, the riled braves chanted and danced in a wide circle around Kitty and Candice.

"They think you're good luck," Candice said, raising an eyebrow. Sarcastically she said, "Boy, are they wrong."

"Why would I be good luck?" Kitty giggled as she watched the men dance.

"I think it's because of your blonde hair," Candice simply replied. "But I'm not sure." Then Candice said, concerned, "After embarrassing their Chief like that, I wouldn't be surprised if he eats us for dinner."

"Do you know how to get us out of here?" Kitty whispered as the braves' screeching voices grew louder. "I have a bad feelin' about all this."

"Fall down," Candice whispered. "Do it now."

Kitty faked a fall and stilled, peeking at the braves with one eye half closed. Candice faked a fall right next to her. She winked at Kitty, and in a whisper said, "Don't move or open your eyes. When they carry us back to the teepees wait a short while. I'll get our horses and meet you at your tent."

"Are you sure this will work?" Kitty asked in a tiny voice.

"I don't know," Candice said. "But I have a bad feelin', too."

The braves whooped and hollered as they jumped and danced. A small brave, not much taller than Kitty, shouted something to the braves. They ignored him and danced faster.

The smaller brave stopped dancing and walked over to the two women curled up in the dirt. He scratched his head and kicked Kitty's back. She bit her lip and didn't move. He shouted louder to the men. Again, they ignored him. A scowl crept onto his face. He walked over to a squaw and shouted at her. Lowering her eyes, she hurried to the women. She shouted to other squaws and three women came running. Three dragged Candice in one direction and one dragged Kitty in another.

The young Indians inside both Candice's and Kitty's tents listened to a squaw call them to supper. They both stood up and left the tents.

Kitty stole a glance around the tent, only lifting one eyelid. Candice did the same. Candice knew her way around the camp. Her shoulder still smarted a mite, but she had helped prepare meals with the women for days. She knew how short a window of time she had to escape. She crawled underneath the back of her tent and stayed in the shadows, heading toward the horse corral. Voices were in full vigor, which was good.

Their buckboard was nowhere in sight. Candice swallowed hard. She crept inside the corral, and using two ropes from a large pile strewn in front of the corral's closed gate, she threw them around the necks of the first two horses she could catch.

Slowly, she opened the gate, praying it wouldn't squeak. It didn't. Flanking the horses, one on each side of her, she lowered her head and used them for cover, walking them as fast as they would let her toward Kitty's tent. "Kitty," she whispered. "Don't go out the front of your tent. Slide out the back.

"What took you so long?" Kitty asked, her nerves jangling. "I don't feel right about them men."

Candice nodded and handed Kitty a rope.

Kitty stared at it and cried in the tiniest voice she had, "You know I don't do horses. Where's the buckboard?"

"I can't find it," Candice cried in a stifled whisper. "If we don't get now, we'll be dead by mornin'. I'd rather die by a horse than an Indian."

Kitty nodded her head at first in agreement. But then she stared at the horse, shaking her head in disagreement. Candice, however, would have none of it. She gave Kitty a leg up onto the back of the horse.

"I don't like this," Kitty complained in a whisper.

"Walk 'em light," Candice whispered back, heaving her heavy body up onto the back of her horse.

"Where did you learn to do that?" Kitty whispered.

Candice didn't answer. Instead, she leaned her body forward and laid her chest on the horse's neck. As she squeezed its girth lightly, it moved forward at a slow pace.

Not sure of what Candice was doing, Kitty followed Candice's movements as best she could. "This ain't so bad," she whispered to Candice. "I reckon I shouldn't be so afraid of these horse critters."

Candice glanced over her shoulder. Kitty was leaning dangerously to one side, close to falling off of the horse's back. "Kitty," she whispered, "Keep centered."

"What does that mean?" Kitty asked, her back stiffening. Too late, her body slipped to the ground and her horse took off running.

"Ow!" she screamed. "That hurt."

Candice swallowed hard as her face darkened with fright. "The dancing has stopped," she cried. "Kitty, I think we're gonna be their fun tonight."

Kitty glanced down at her clothes, and without a worry said, "These clothes make me itch. What the heck are you talkin' about now?" An arrow sailed past Kitty and slammed into the dirt. "Throw me your gun!" she screamed as she ducked for cover.

"I don't have one!" Candice screamed back. "Jump on!"

Shaking her head, Kitty grabbed at Candice's lowered hand, and Candice helped her onto the back of the prancing horse.

"Hold on!" Candice warned, kicking the horse forward.

"I got a bad feelin' about this!" Kitty screamed, grabbing onto Candice's thick waist.

"Keep your weight even with mine!" Candice shouted, ducking another arrow. Her horse leaped forward and ran like the wind. Arrows flew and missed their mark.

"He won't last much longer," Candice cried. "This horse is tired. We ain't gonna make it."

Chapter 41

"Kick this horse harder," Kitty cried. "They're gainin'!"

"I'll head him to that outcropping of rocks," Candice shouted, turning the horse abruptly left. The move sent Kitty flying off of the horse's back.

Candice cried, "No!" as arrows flew and dropped like rain around her. She screamed, "No!" again as she ducked and headed for the safety of the rocks.

"Charge!" A strong, authoritative voice hollered out. A soldier flanking his commanding officer raised a bugle and blared the captain's command to the company of men close behind.

Soldiers appeared over a bluff and raced toward Candice as fast as she raced away from the Indians.

The bugle blared again. The soldiers charged downhill and raised their guns.

Candice slowed the horse, and a second later turned it back toward Kitty.

"Ma'am!" a soldier shouted, "Get back into those rocks!"

Another solider hollered, "You ain't safe. Turn around!"

But Candice's grin just widened. As she raced past all the men, they threw each other looks of confusion because she didn't have a saddle or bridle on her horse, and the animal's back was foaming sweat, showing its exhaustion.

"Kill them Indians!" she screamed. "I need to save my friend." She slowed the mustang and brought it to a sliding halt.

The soldiers charged past her.

"I'm sorry," Candice cried. "I thought it would be better to die by way of a horse instead of an Indian."

Kitty stirred and groaned. "I hate horses," she moaned.

"You're not dead!" Candice cried.

"I wish I was," Kitty snapped. "That hurt somethin' fierce."

The bugle blared again. An angry sound rose from the men as guns fired.

"You're alive!" A man veered away from the troops and stopped his horse in front of Kitty. An arrow flew dangerously close to his left cheek. He ducked. "I don't know how you two made it through what you did, but if we stay here much longer, they're gonna have to bury all three of us."

He ran his hand lightly across the sweat on Candice's horse. "This animal won't get you to safety. We're gonna have to battle it out from the safety of them rocks over there."

Kitty sat up straight. "Give me a gun!" she demanded. "I'm killin' every last one of 'em."

Another arrow whizzed by the soldier's horse and fell inches from Kitty's feet. "You can kill me!" she screamed. "But you ain't gonna scalp me!"

The medic scooped Kitty up and threw her over his horse just before he swung into the saddle.

Candice followed his lead and leaped onto the mustang, her arms straining as she pulled her heavy body up.

Arrows rained down on them. "Give me a gun!" Kitty cried. "I can kill them all twice!"

The medic sheltered himself and Kitty as best he could as he ducked and positioned himself close to his horse's body. He shouted at his horse and kicked it into an unsafe gallop.

Kitty reached over his leg and grabbed the gun out of his holster. The wild movements of the horse jolted her as she tried to take aim. The gun exploded. The medic's horse bucked and threw its head. "I'll kill you twice next time!" Kitty shouted as she watched the brave fly off his horse to the ground. She aimed and fired again.

"What the--?" The medic heard the gun and Kitty, but was confused about what was happening. He focused on the safety of the rocks and hills in front of him and pushed his horse faster.

Candice's horse slowed. The medic's horse raced past it.

"Keep your head down!" Kitty shouted. "There's a brave right behind you." The gun exploded. Another brave dropped to the ground. Without a rider, the Indian's horse raced past the medic's horse.

"Slow this animal!" Kitty demanded, her voice panicky. "I can't kill these Indians if I can't see 'em. Candice, duck to the left!" she screeched as she let off another shot, missing the brave. He lifted a spear and hurled it at Candice.

"Duck!" Kitty screamed as she aimed and fired again. The spear hit dead center on her horse's hindquarters. The mustang kicked its back legs outwards as it slowed.

"I got you, too!" Kitty proudly shouted as the Indian brave slid off his running horse. Kitty glanced back toward Candice. "What are you doin'? Don't slow down! Kick him harder!"

Candice's horse abruptly stopped and dropped. Candice jumped off and screamed, "Kitty, throw me the gun!" She watched Kitty and the medic reach the safety of the hills.

"Are you crazy?" Kitty cried as she watched Candice fade from her view. "You're the one who knows how to ride. Kick him harder!" Sensing something was wrong, Kitty snaked her neck around as best as she could and shouted, "Turn back, my friend's in trouble!"

The medic ignored Kitty's pleas and ran his horse up a slight embankment toward a tumble of shaded boulders. Without warning he slid Kitty off of his horse's neck, surprising her. Her arms flew wide, steadying her fall. With his gun still in her hand she fired, accidently pulling the trigger.

The medic's face wilted along with his body as he fell off the horse.

"I'm sorry!" Kitty cried. "I didn't shoot you on purpose."

She stared at the prancing horse and the saddle. "If you kill me," she spat at the animal, "I'll kill you back." She tucked the gun in her squaw's clothes, and with a deep frown settling across her face, she set her foot into the stirrup.

"That was a lot easier," she said nervously as she swung her right leg over the horse's back and slid her foot into the stirrup on the right side of the horse. These are like buckboard reins," she proudly said to herself as she grabbed the thin strips of leather fastened to both sides of the horse's neck. She whipped at the reins as she had learned to do on the buckboard. She said with confidence, "Get up."

The horse threw its neck around and up. "What are you lookin' at?" Kitty spat, "I said, "Get up."

The horse neighed, shook its head, and freed itself from Kitty's grip. Within moments he was nibbling on thin grass tucked between the rocks.

Kitty's face reddened with anger. She screamed, "Get up!" The horse lifted an ear, but kept munching away. Kitty stood up in the stirrups and dropped back down in the saddle. She froze, expecting the horse to fly forward. It didn't.

"What the heck is wrong with you?" she screamed, slapping its neck with her left hand. The horse merely shook dust off of its neck.

"I hate horses and I hate men!" Kitty screeched. Her bloodcurdling cry sent the horse into motion. It bolted forward. Kitty bent down, grabbing at the horse's mane, her chest painfully hitting the saddle horn. She glanced down and latched onto it, stabilizing her movements. "I can do this!" she cried as her face went pale. "Good horse!" she shouted while her knuckles turned white and shook.

"Candice waved her arms. Kitty turned the horse left. A grin settled on her face as she cried out, "I'm doin' it! I'm riding a horse!" Her face was still pale, and her left hand was still fixed onto the saddle horn.

Still hiding in the shadows behind a small rock and worried about Kitty's fast pace, Candice, shouted, "Slow down!"

"I got a gun!" Kitty shouted back, her smile widening.

Candice shook her head. "Why are you on the medic's horse?" she cried.

Kitty, still proud of her new-found riding abilities, simply said, "I shot him."

Candice studied the mayhem surrounding her, then tucked deeper behind the rock. She waved her arm at Kitty.

Kitty flew past Candice.

"What the heck are you doin'?" Candice screamed.

With a proud voice Kitty shouted, "Look, Candice. I know how to ride a horse."

"Turn the horse!" Candice cried, ducking back behind the rocks.
"How do I stop it?" Kitty screamed, her voice suddenly shaking.
"Pull back on the reins!"

Kitty cried, "I hate horses!" as she jerked hard on the reins. The horse abruptly turned, throwing Kitty hard to the right, but her left hand held tight onto the saddle. "I didn't mean to kill him, but I think I did!" she shouted.

"Kill who?" Candice shouted back, waving her arms with panic as Kitty's horse didn't slow.

"How do I stop him?" Kitty hollered in a panic.

"Pull back on the reins!" Candice instructed again.

Kitty yanked on the reins, her thin arms trembling. The horse slid to a fast stop. She flew forward, careening over the horse's neck while Candice watched in horror.

An arrow dropped, creasing Candice's skirt. She hurried to her feet and grabbed the horse's reins. "Kitty," she cried, "We need to get, now!"

A military bugle blared again as Kitty pushed to her knees. "I hate horses and I hate Indians!" she said furiously.

"I ain't dyin' here!" Candice screamed as arrows whizzed around her.

"Well, I ain't gettin' back on that horse!" Kitty snapped.

Candice threw her leg into the saddle, circled the horse, and with a worried look in her eyes, offered a thick arm to Kitty,. "Get on!" she demanded. "We need to get to that ledge of thick rocks, now!"

"You promise I won't fall off?" Kitty asked, shaking her head with doubt.

A frown settled on Candice's face. "Shut up and give me your arm!"

Kitty latched onto Candice's arm and pulled herself up onto the horse's rump, right behind Candice. "Hold on!" Candice warned, kicking the horse into a run.

A soldier's horse flew past them on their left. Another horse drew up beside them, flanking their right side. "Turn, you horse!" the soldier demanded in a strong voice.

"No!" Kitty screamed at Candice. "We need to get back to the medic. Go straight."

The soldier who had run past them came charging back. He slowed his horse and demanded, "Where did you get this horse?"

"From the medic," Kitty shouted. "Follow us."

The men exchanged a confused glance, but with the women sandwiched between them Kitty guided them to the medic.

"There, over there!" Kitty yelled, her hands still tight around Candice's thick waist.

Candice turned the horse right and slowed it.

One of the men hollered, "You go get the captain. "I'll stay here with them."

"Yes, sir." The soldier on the left disappeared at a fast pace.

Candice leaned forward.

"What are you doin'?" Kitty nervously asked.

"Gettin' us up these rocks," Candice barked. "If you fall off it's your own stupid fault."

Kitty straightened her back and let go of Candice's waist. "You're doin' this on purpose, ain't you!" she groused.

"If you don't lean forward, you'll roll of this horse again!" Candice warned.

"I hate you and I hate horses!" Kitty snapped as her body swayed backwards. Her arms flew forward, latching back on to Candice. "I will never get on a horse again!" she spat, tucking hard into Candice.

Candice shook her head. "I don't see him. Are you sure you got this far up hill?"

"I think so, "Kitty said, cautiously looking up. A second later she said, "No, I think it's that big rock over there."

The soldier kept a safe distance behind their horse, his gun hand ready. Fewer arrows fell as their horses climbed.

"I'm sure it's that rock," Kitty insisted, pointing to a rock in the distance. Candice turned their horse again.

"What are we doin' up this high?" Kitty asked, leaning deeper into Candice's back.

"What?" Candice barked. "What did you say?"

"Maybe I'm wrong," Kitty said in a light tone. "I was sure I left him behind one of these big rocks."

"Hold on!" Candice ordered, "I'm turnin' this animal around."

Kitty shouted, "It was that big rock!"

The strength of her voice surprised Candice. Candice halted the horse's steep descent and threw Kitty a dagger glare over her shoulder. "I ain't goin' any farther. If you don't know where he is...." She shook her head. "Then I'm gettin' off of this horse and I'm goin' to let *you* figure out how to get it to go back down this mountain."

The soldier still covering their rear shook his head, listening to their spat. After studying the hillside he shouted, "He's over here!"

Candice threw Kitty a frown, then turned the horse and followed the soldier.

"How does he know where he is?" Kitty asked, sitting farther back but still holding on to Candice.

"I don't know," Candice spat, shaking her head. "This is down hill. We'll *both* fall off this horse if you lean back much farther.

"I don't like riding downhill," Kitty cried. Their horse slowed its pace, his back rocking dangerously.

"What do I do?" Kitty wailed. "Do I lean *with* him or *against* him?"

"Follow his legs," Candice barked back.

"I ain't goin' to look down at his legs!" Kitty cried. "How the heck did we get up this high?"

"There he is!" the soldier hollered, stopping his horse to study the battlefield below.

"I'm not sure if we've won the battle," he said as he glanced at the women. "But I think we have them on the run."

"Where is the medic?" Kitty shouted. "I don't see him."

The soldier turned his horse around to address her squarely. "Ma'am," a scowl filled his forehead, "he's back down there, right where you left him."

"I knew we didn't get this high," Kitty replied in an uppity voice.

Candice and the soldier just shook their heads as they led their horses down the steep embankment.

"I don't know how horses do this," Kitty said. "They've got much better feet than us, I suppose."

"Shut up!" Candice ordered. "You're annoying."

The soldier threw a quick glance at Candice and smiled. Candice caught it and her frown lifted into a smile.

The private hurried his pace, widening his distance from the women. "What the heck took you so long?" the medic called out as he approached.

"Sir," the private said. "We thought you were back at the camp. How did you get out here?"

The medic, with his back pressed safely against a thick rock ledge said, "I was headed back. But I caught a glimpse of those women and they looked familiar to me. So I turned back and followed them for a closer look."

A look of confusion fell on the private's face but he respectfully said, "Yes, sir." He studied the surrounding rocks and then settled his gaze back on the medic. "I don't see the arrow, sir. Did you break it off?"

The medic's face darkened with anger. "I've been shot with my own gun by a damn woman! She shot me!" he snarled.

The soldier straightened. "Sir...." A puzzled expression crept over his face as he studied Candice and Kitty's slow descent off the mountain. "Sir, which one?"

"The blonde one," the medic mumbled.

"Should I shoot her?" The private's eyes flared wide as he readied his gun hand.

"No!" The medic's lips tightened. He shook his head and admitted, "It was an accident. I can't believe both of them women are alive. I left them for dead."

"There he is!" Kitty shouted, shifting her weight and nearly toppling Candice.

"Stop moving," Candice warned. "This trail is really steep."

"What did I do wrong?" Kitty grumbled, her eyes widening as their horse stopped and tucked in its back legs.

Candice grimaced and her voice shook. "I ain't too sure about this," she cried.

"I don't like that tone in your voice," Kitty whined. "Can't you find an easier way down?"

Tired of Kitty's patter, Candice grinned. "Well, you led me up here." She kept the horse at a stop. "I'm gonna get off of this horse and let you lead it back down."

"I didn't do it on purpose!" Kitty screamed. "No! I ain't steering any horse ever again." She grabbed Candice's waist with both arms. "You're drivin' this animal, not me. I was just lookin' for the rock I left the medic under."

Candice kicked the horse and got it moving again. "So why isn't the medic on his horse, and what the heck is he doin' under a rock?" Candice asked.

Kitty hesitated, and in a tiny voice said, "Because I shot him."

"What?" Candice frowned. "You shot the medic? What fer?"

"I didn't do it on purpose!" Kitty snapped. "It was an accident."

Candice's frown deepened. "Is he dead?"

"I don't think so. I told you I didn't do it on purpose!"

"If he's dead, nobody will believe a girl over a soldier's word!" Candice snapped. "We're gettin' out of here." She tried to stop the horse from its sharp descent and turn it back uphill. It refused and fought her. Rocks crashed down the hillside.

Both men looked up. "What the heck are they doin' to your horse?" the private asked, mainly to himself.

Chapter 42

"I'm not dyin' by a horse!" Kitty screamed.

"And I'm not gettin' hung!" Candice spat back at Kitty. The horse's back legs buckled and its rump slapped the hard ground. As it desperately tried to get back up on all four legs, both women flew off of its back.

Without the women's weight on its back, the horse regained its footing, bucked, and ran fast, downhill.

As both men watched, their deep-set frowns disappeared from their weathered faces. They grinned. "I thought the one with red hair knew what she was doin'," the private quipped as he shook his head.

Both women rolled downward, like barrels. "I hate you!" Candice cried.

"I hate horses!" Kitty screamed.

"They've got more lives than a cat." The medic chuckled.

Candice landed first in a pile of dust and gravel. Kitty's tumbling body slowed and came to a halt a few feet away from Candice. Both women just layed there, still as corpses.

"Are they dead?" the private asked the medic.

"I hope so," the medic snapped. "I've had enough of these two."

Kitty sprang to her knees and reached for her gun, surprising both men. "Don't you move," she shouted. "I know how to use this." Her body was swaying. Both men chuckled and eased up on their itchy trigger fingers.

Kitty barked, "Do you think my gun is funny?" Her gun hand shook and dropped. She fell, head first, to the dirt.

"I guess that one's alive," the private quipped. The medic nodded. Both men glanced at Candice. Her body remained still.

"I'm kind of glad the blonde one is still alive," the private admitted with a slow grin. "I reckon she's too purty to be dead."

The medic nodded, then looked around the rocks. "Where are the rest of the men?" he asked in a serious voice.

"I sent Daniel back for reinforcements, sir." The private's back straightened. "Sir, can you ride?"

A bugle blared, catching both of the men off guard. "Yes, I can ride. She only winged me," the medic answered.

"What do we do with them?" the private asked as he glanced down at the women.

"Let Daniel figure it out," the medic replied with a frown. He moaned and limped over to his horse. He patted its thick neck and checked the leather cinch holding the saddle on its back. "Mount up, soldier," he commanded as he swung into the saddle.

"Yes, sir!" The private swung into his saddle and turned his horse. The medic kicked his horse into a run, and the private followed at a close pace.

A cloud of dust blanketed a hillside to the south. "It looks like we've got them on the run, sir." the private shouted.

The medic, stopping his horse, bellowed, "I can't do it."

The private slowed his horse and studied the countryside. "Sir, they're headed south, so why are we stopping?"

The medic shook his head as he bit his lip. "I took an oath and I've got to go back and help them women."

"But," the private scratched his forehead, "what about Daniel?"

The medic turned his horse and headed back toward the steep hillside.

"Yes, sir," the private said with a note of confusion in his voice. He turned and followed the medic back toward the hillside.

The early afternoon sun was burning the women's delicate skin. "Help me get them to the shade of those rocks," the medic commanded, his limp deepening.

"Sir?" The private saw the pain on the medic's face. "Sir, I can get the women. That shade over there might offer some comfort to you."

The medic nodded and hobbled over to a long, shaded rock shelf where his bloodied right leg promptly collapsed. He moaned and dropped to the hard dirt.

The private scooped up Candice first. His back shook and his knees trembled under her weight. "This one is really heavy," he groaned.

The medic chuckled, "Don't drop her, private; she might break your toes."

The private's face reddened and his breath labored with each step. A horse flew over the ledge the medic sat under, startling both men. The private dropped Candice. She landed on his boots. He howled in pain. The medic shook his head and roared in laughter.

The soldier on the horse stopped and watched in dismay. "Sir," he questioned, "what's so funny?"

"Daniel," the private shouted. "Get off your horse and help me."

Daniel jumped off of his horse and threw his commanding officer a salute. Hurrying to the private's side, he said, "Why is that woman on top of your boots?"

The medic roared. "She was helpin' him shine 'em."

"Oh." A puzzled expression filled Daniel's face. "How do I lift her, sir?"

"I don't care how you do it; just get her over here and out of the sun."

"Yes, sir!"

Daniel pulled Candice's feet off of the private's boots. Both young men respectfully lifted her body and carried it over to the medic.

Kitty moaned, grabbing the medic's attention. "Hurry up, get the other one," he said.

The men hurried. They bent down to pick Kitty up by her shoulders and feet. She sat up and flashed her gun.

The startled men stepped back. Both instinctively drew their guns. She fired.

"Put your weapons down!" the medic ordered. Confused, both men lowered their guns. Daniel's shoulder was bleeding.

"Sir," he shouted. "She shot me!"

The medic's eyes flared. "Why can't you just die!" he barked at Kitty.

The young soldiers stared at Kitty's beauty.

When she caught a glimpse of the hunger in their eyes, she said softly in a teasing voice, "I'm sorry. I thought you were Indians." She pretended to faint and fell dramatically to the ground.

Both young men ran over to her. "Ma'am," Daniel said. "You must be delirious. I'm not mad at you anymore. Wake up, now."

The other soldier said, "You're bleeding. I'll help her."

"Stop fighting over her!" the medic snapped. "And get over here, you fools."

Kitty slipped her gun back into her skirt pocket as the men gingerly lifted her.

"Get my kit from my horse and my canteen," The medic demanded.

The young soldiers hurried to do his bidding.

Kitty opened her eyes, and with feminine charm said, "My name is Kitty."

A frown settled on the medic's face. "I don't care what your name is, and I've already doctored you once." His voice tightened. "And I hope I won't ever have to doctor you again."

The young soldiers returned and knelt down close to Kitty. "Back up!" the medic snarled. "How the heck can I doctor her with you two sittin' on top of her?" They inched backwards, away from Kitty.

Kitty threw them a wink. They threw her a short smile back.

Candice stirred and moaned. "My arm hurts."

The medic rolled up Candice's sleeve and slowly moved her arm. "That hurts!" she cried, her eyes still closed.

"It's broken." He sighed. "I'm gonna have to put it in a splint. Daniel, let me look at that shoulder next."

"It's only a flesh wound," Daniel insisted. "It don't hurt real bad."

The medic drew a deep breath and went to work. By sunset he had set Candice's arm, removed the bullet from Daniel's shoulder, and bandaged Kitty's bloodied hands.

"Sir," the private asked, "why haven't they come back for us?"

Exhausted, the wounded medic answered in a whisper of a voice, "The bullet in my leg is too deep. I can't get to it. Get me the provisions from both horses and ride like the wind to catch up to the rest of the unit."

"Yes, sir!" the private replied, then flew into action. The medic's heavy eyes drooped.

Chapter 43

A bugle blared, awakening the troops with the lively strains of reveille.

"Captain, they're in that ledge at the bottom of that mountain," a young soldier reported as men dressed in military uniforms with morning dew still on the ground. They thundered onto their horses, the early rays of sunlight piercing their eyes.

"Company halt!" The captain slowed his horse. It pranced in place. "It could be a trap," he stated, squinting into the distance.

"Sir, I don't see any more arrows flying," the young soldier replied respectfully.

The captain distanced himself from his men, and the young soldiers closely watched him. Abruptly he jumped off of his horse and fell to his knees. After a few minutes he jumped back on his horse and kicked it into a run. "Charge!" he roared, sending the troops into frenzy. The men kicked their horses into a dead run, their sabers and guns raised.

"What *is* that noise?" Kitty yawned. "Eew, my hands have blood on them," she commented, wiping her hands on her skirt. Thundering hooves caused her to look up.

"It's Indians!" Kitty cried, grabbing for her gun.

"No!" Daniel and the medic shouted at the same time, just as the captain's horse flew over their ledge.

Kitty aimed and fired. Daniel flew at Kitty, dropping her to the ground. He struggled to follow the movements of his commanding officer's horse. Daniel saw his captain fall from his horse and onto his knees.

"I thought it was an Indian!" Kitty sputtered, her gun still lifted and ready.

"Don't shoot!" both Daniel and the medic hollered, ducking for cover.

The cavalry swarmed their campsite, the men wide-eyed and their trigger fingers itchy.

"I didn't mean it!" Kitty shouted. "I thought he was an Indian." She dropped her gun.

As the medic leaped up, pain shot through his leg, forcing him back down. He cursed under his breath.

"Hold your fire! We're not Indians," Daniel shouted, dropping his gun.

The soldiers' horses pranced and circled. The men stared at their commanding officer, who was spread out, face down on the ground.

Kitty's face reddened with anger and she kicked the hard ground. She cried, "I didn't do it on purpose!" The morning sunlight danced upon her blonde locks. When the young soldiers' eyes fell onto her green eyes and delicate features, they, lowered their weapons.

Daniel flew to his captain's side. The medic dragged his leg, and with pain slicing across his forehead, he hurried his pace behind Daniel.

"Sir!" He swallowed hard. "Sir, I was headed back to camp when I saw these women needin' my doctorin'."

"Who shot me?" The captain coughed, and a deep scowl settled on his face.

"She did," everyone within listening distance, replied, pointing at Kitty.

"What?" The captain shook his head and dusted off his pristine uniform. "I ain't ever been shot by a girl before." He shrugged his shoulders and studied his body, looking for blood.

"She missed." He chuckled glad to be standing.

"Sir," Daniel said with worry in his voice. "Your horse never got back up."

The captain's jaw dropped. He hurried to his horse's side. "Hurricane, get up," he demanded. The horse's neck lifted, and the animal desperately tried to get to its feet. Exhausting itself, its neck fell back to the ground.

The captain studied the blood flowing down the horse's rump, then threw Kitty a hateful glare. His men stepped back.

"I didn't mean to shoot you or your horse!" Kitty cried. "I thought you were Indians."

The captain drew his weapon from its holster, aimed and fired. Hurricane's neck fell; its eyes closed. With his gun still raised and his trigger finger ready, he huffed, "I don't care who you are, and I don't care that you're a woman." His voice shook with anger in a tone none of the soldiers had ever heard before."If you hurt one hair on any of my men or their animals, I will personally hunt you down and kill you in your sleep!"

"I didn't do it on purpose!" Kitty sputtered. The young men watched her, enjoying her feminine movements. Lustful thoughts filled their young minds.

The captain's face darkened with hatred. He walked over to a young soldier who was ignoring him, still caught up in Kitty's beauty. The captain pulled the soldier off his horse. "If any of you listen to her," he snarled, "I'll slice your heads off!" He threw Kitty another hateful glare, whipped his saber from its sheath, and raised it in a threatening manner.

The bugler still atop his mount joined the captain's side. "Sir!" He saluted. "The Indians are forming on the north slope. We can't outrun them there."

The captain jumped into the now vacant saddle of the young man's horse the soldier he had just unseated. He yelled out a blur of commands. Soldiers flew in different directions. The bugler's horn blared.

"I'm tired of all their noise!" Kitty complained, "and I'm hungry." She glanced around, and spying her gun, picked it up.

Daniel shook his head as she approached. "I don't know why I got stuck with you," he said, "but I'm supposed to take you through Snake Canyon and let loose."

"Don't you men ever eat?" Kitty whined.

Daniel glanced at the medic, who was still sitting and nursing his leg, then at the dead horse, then back at Kitty. He said in a cautious voice, "If you put that gun down, I'll find you some rations."

Kitty stared at the dead horse. Bored, she said, "I hate horses, but I didn't mean to kill one."

Daniel's eyes filled with worry. Soldiers appeared in the distance. raising a thick cloud of dust behind them. His focus changed, as did the medic's. Both men eased their weapons from their holsters.

Kitty caught the worry on Daniel's face. "I'll kill every last Indian I can!" she growled, raising her gun.

"No!" both men shouted, falling to the ground.

Candice stirred and yawned. Stretching, she abruptly stopped. "Ow!" she howled as tears pooled in her eyes. "Who did this to me!"

Both men darted glances between the two women. "Sir," Daniel's eyes fell to the ground. "I ain't ever gonna look at another girl again. These two hurt my brain."

The medic sighed. "Not all women are like this sort," he told Daniel sagely.

As Kitty caught his words, she stomped over to the medic, swaying her shapely hips. "And what sort am I?" she asked evenly.

The medic slowed and he bit his lip, watching Kitty's feminine movements. "If you shoot me again," he said, "I'll shoot you right back. Now, ready that gun and get yourself behind some cover."

Daniel and the medic scrambled for cover as the thundering noise of horses' hooves approached. "Company halt!"

The choking dust behind the company rose like a black cloud, blanketing them.

"It's Indians!" Kitty cried as layers of dirt blocked her sight.

"Don't shoot!" both the medic and Daniel shouted.

"Kitty!" Candice cried. "What happened to my arm?"

"I don't know," Kitty said, her voice filled with alarm. She blinked hard to force the settling dust out of her view. "I hate it out here!" she cried. "It's dirty." A second later she screamed, "And I'm still hungry!"

The approaching soldiers readied their weapons when they heard Kitty's shrieking voice. They jumped to safety and hollered, "Sir, are you still alive!"

The medic shouted, "Put your weapons down. We're still safe."

The men cautiously pulled the women's buckboard forward, and Kitty lowered her gun. "Where's Lucky?" she cried.

The soldiers in the buckboard threw their commanding officer a puzzled glance.

Candice shook her head, and with the assistance of the medic, stood to her feet. "You did this to me, didn't you?" she screamed. "You broke my arm!"

"Oh, be quiet," Kitty barked back. "Candice, look. We have our buckboard back."

"Sir?" Daniel nervously asked, "What do I do now?"

The medic saw the confusion in the young soldier's eyes and jumped to his feet. His bad leg buckled, and Candice offered assistance. They caught each other's fall and threw each other a glance. The medic straightened up, but lowered his eyes as pain ripped through his body.

"I reckon I owe you," Candice gushed, glancing at her set and bandaged broken arm. The medic's scowl disappeared. "You told me she was your sister. You told me she was your friend." He shook his head and offered Candice a look of concern she had never seen before in a man's eyes. Her heart leaped.

"She's my *best* friend," Candice gushed.

"I reckon you don't remember my name," he offered. "These men call me the medic, but my real name is Eric. I offered it to you the last time I was doctorin' you, but I suppose you were too addled at the time to remember."

The soldiers still in the buckboard were watching Candice and Eric. They all shared a grin. "Sir?" one of the men asked the medic. "Can I go with you down Snake Canyon?"

The medic stood at attention but pain slowed his response.

Daniel shouted, "Sir, I need to get back to the captain's needs." A grin eased the shadows in his worried eyes.

The soldier driving the buckboard leaped out of the seat and dusted his uniform off.

Daniel said, "Which horse is yours?"

The young soldier grinned. "The one with four white stockin's."

Daniel jumped onto the grinning soldier's horse and disappeared.

The medic shook his head. "Private, what is your name?"

The soldier ignored his commanding officer as he stared at Kitty.

Kitty eased the grip on her gun.

"Are we safe here?" Candice asked as her eyes darted toward the rocks.

"Don't know," the medic replied, his voice tightening as he helped Candice into the back of the buckboard.

"I think we should stay and eat," Kitty whined. "I'm starved!"

The soldiers seated in the buckboard nodded in agreement. After studying the hillside, the medic offered a short nod. "We all could use some food, but make it quick."

"I'm starved," Kitty whined again. "What do you have to eat?" She stood up and dusted off her skirt, then threw a short smile and a wink at the soldiers.

They blushed and piled out of the buckboard. "Why, ma'am, I've got fresh ham, and if the medic gives me enough time, I can make beans and biscuits."

The medic shook his head. "There are Indians watching us. Look at those smoke signals. If you two fools are dying to fall in love right now, I'll put you out of your misery right now!" He took aim at them with his sidearm.

Both men dropped to the dirt, spilling the food in their hands, studying their commanding officer's movements.

As she watched the meat drop to the ground, Kitty screeched, "What is wrong with you?"

The medic's frown deepened. "Let's just make this fast. We're not safe here."

Both men rose from the dirt. Throwing each other a confused glance, one offered in a submissive voice, "Sir, the weather is light and the day is young. Shouldn't we get outa here while the getting's good?"

The frown on Eric's brow eased. He threw Candice a glance. "No, men," he replied with authority. "This woman is wounded, and that loud mouth over there needs to eat. I have a feeling if we don't eat now she'll complain until she kills us with that darn chatter of hers. I'd rather die by the hands of the Indians than by her darn chatter."

The soldiers nodded. "Yes, sir!"

Kitty walked over to Candice and sat close. "I swear I didn't do that to you."

Candice lifted one tired eyelid. "I know, Kitty." She turned to look at Eric.

Kitty caught Candice staring. Miffed, she complained, "What is wrong with all of you? How come no one is hungry but me?"

A cluster of small rocks rolled down the hillside. Both soldiers drew their guns as they jumped up from the fire they'd been starting. Kitty flattened to the dirt, her head narrowly missing the fire. Candice and Eric shared a concerned glance. Everyone quit talking.

"Ma'am," one of the young soldiers whispered to Kitty, "we've got you covered. Get away from the fire before you get burned."

Clearly, those tumbling rocks had been a false alarm, so Kitty rolled to her back, sat up, and smiled at the soldier who'd been cooking the meat. In a girly voice she drawled, "Well, I do declare, you're the most handsome man I ever met. I'm real hungry. It sure smells good."

The soldier blushed, then swallowed hard. "Ma'am, I'm gonna cook you the best meal you ever et."

Eric, the medic, barked, "What's takin' so long! Hurry up with that grub! Them smoke signals is gettin' closer."

"Yes, sir!" The soldier hastened his pace.

Kitty rolled her eyes. "He sure is grumpy. What did you say your name was?"

"Kitty," Candice shouted. "Be quiet! Didn't you hear what Eric just said?"

"Why is everybody so grumpy?" Kitty snapped. "All I want to do is eat."

A single arrow sailed down the hillside and landed inches from Kitty's feet. She jumped to her knees, then flew for cover.

Bodie or Bust

The two soldiers cooking the food leaped to the safety of the rocks.

"Mount up!" Eric ordered. The men hurried, grabbing everything their arms could carry.

"Wait!" Kitty balked. "What about the meat?"

"We've got you covered," one of the soldiers shouted. "Run, now!" He aimed his pistol in the general direction of where the arrow had come from.

"No!" Kitty screamed. "I'm not leavin' this meat for the Indians. I'm hungry."

The nervous men darted glances toward the smoke signals and back down at Kitty. Kitty calmly pulled the arrow out of the dirt and brushed it off. She stabbed the meat with it, then calmly said, "This meat sure smells good." She raised the skewered ham up high, showing it off. A scowl settled on her face as she screamed toward the Indians, "You can have my scalp, but you ain't gettin' my breakfast."

Everyone shook their heads. Candice shouted, "Kitty, I'm not dyin' over a piece of meat. Get in this buckboard, now!"

Eric hobbled to the buckboard, and with great effort pulled himself up into the driver's seat. Candice, sitting in the back of the buckboard, slid to safety behind the seat, her gun raised.

One of the soldiers untied a horse alongside the buckboard and jumped on. The other soldier jumped onto Eric's horse and kicked it into a run, circling the campsite.

Eric whipped the horses and spat, "I ain't comin' by you twice, girl, so jump on!"

Kitty slowed her step and looked up. "What's all the ruckus about?" she questioned. "I don't see a thing."

Drums echoed down the snaking canyon walls, driving birds to flight. "What do we do, sir?" one of the soldiers asked impatiently, fear showing in his eyes.

"Flank us on both sides!" Eric ordered. "Stay as close to the buckboard as possible."

"Yes, sir!" both men snapped with fear in their voices.

Slow down!" Kitty shouted. "All that dust will get my breakfast dirty."

Eric slid the buckboard to a stop and offered Kitty his right hand. "I saved the meat from the Indians," she snapped. "Don't you try to take it away from me."

Eric's face darkened with anger. "I ain't ever left a girl before, but you sure are tempting my patience."

Candice, tired of Kitty's nonsense screamed, "Kitty, shut up and get in the buckboard!"

Kitty, with a close eye on the meat, grabbed onto Eric's hand and pulled herself up into the swaying buckboard. Before she was seated Eric whipped the horses into a fast run. Her thin frame flew backwards over the seat and landed directly on top of Candice.

Candice howled in pain. *"What is wrong with you!"* she cried as tears pooled in her eyes.

"He did that, not me!" Kitty protested. In an uppity tone she huffed, "I don't see any Indians or arrows. I think these soldier men are joshin' us about us bein' in danger."

"If you weren't my friend I'd kill you!" Candice cried, tears flowing down her face.

"If you weren't my friend I wouldn't share this sweet piece of ham with you," Kitty shot back.

The drums abruptly stopped.

Eric's face darkened with anger. "I hope the trail of dust we're leavin' will hinder their aim," he shouted. The soldiers keeping pace on both sides of the buckboard nodded, their trigger hands itchy.

Chapter 44

"Hold on!" Eric hollered as the buckboard jumped in a shallow riverbed.

"What are we in such a hurry for?" Kitty cried as she tried to take a bite of the hot meat.

"Indians," Candice told her as she wiped tears from her cheeks.

"What Indians?" Kitty asked, irritably. "I'm hungry and I can't eat this ham when we're movin' this fast!"

"He's a soldier!" Candice replied in a puny voice. "He knows all about this stuff much better than us."

"He's just a man." Kitty rolled her eyes. "I think all they want is our favors."

"You are the dumbest person I've ever met!" Candice cried, still wiping tears away to clear her vision.

Kitty abruptly sat up in the rocking wagon. "Dumb! I'm the one that can read and write," she huffed. "I'm much smarter than you or any man!"

"I hate you!" Candice cried, protecting her broken arm as best as she could in the jostling buckboard.

"Sit down, ma'am!" the soldier closest to Kitty demanded. "We're under attack!"

"But I don't see any Indians!" Kitty pouted. "And I don't see any arrows! You just want our favors, don't you?"

Dust dimmed the soldier's view for a second. He shouted, "Ma'am, hide in the shadows!"

"I hate dust!" Kitty screamed, her body swaying dangerously.

"Shut up and sit down!" Candice demanded. With her good arm she grabbed at Kitty's swaying skirt.

Gunfire exploded. "With all of this dust, I can't see nothin' to shoot'!" Kitty cried.

Candice peeked up at Kitty. "Kitty," she said with worry, "I don't know if we'll get through this, so I just want to tell you...." A smile eased the worry on her face. "I love you."

"What the heck does that mean?" Kitty cried, waving her trigger hand at unfamiliar noises.

The buckboard slowed and came to a gradual stop.

"I knew it was you men all along!" Kitty shouted. "I ain't givin' any of you men my favors until I eat!"

Dust settled. The soldiers' horses that had been flanking them came in view, their saddles empty.

Kitty lifted to her knees and glanced over the seat. Eric's body lay still and bloodied. Carefully, she tucked behind the wooden seat again. "Candice," she cried, "I think they were real Indians."

Candice gave Kitty a comforting smile. "We almost made it to Bodie, didn't we?"

Kitty nodded. "I wanted to have the grandest saloon."

"And I would have liked to come visit it." Candice offered Kitty a short smile, the fright on her face fading.

Both women hid as best they could in the shadows of the buckboard, their guns ready.

Chapter 45

A bugle sounded, awakening the hillside. Both women arose with caution. "Are we or ain't we dying here?" Kitty asked.

"How far did you say Bodie was?" Candice asked back.

"I miss James." Kitty said.

"And I miss Sam," Candice whispered, her gun still aimed.

"I already told you," Kitty warned. "He's no good!"

An arrow pierced and shattered wood way too close to their hidden bodies.

"I ain't gonna die in the shadows!" Kitty screamed. She jumped up and fired her gun.

Candice rose up and fired twice.

"I hate men," Kitty cried. "And I hate Indians!" She reloaded her gun as fast as her shaking hands would allow.

Candice covered Kitty's back and reloaded her gun as Kitty's gun exploded.

"Shoot him!" they cried to each other as Indians jumped from their horses and lunged at the women.

A bugle blared again, this time closer.

"I don't think we're gonna make it!" Candice cried. "I'm almost out of bullets."

"Me, too!" Kitty shouted as her gun exploded again. "Duck, Candice!" she screeched, squeezing off another shot.

A regiment of soldiers on horseback flew past the buckboard. Their horses raised a thick cloud of dust, limiting the women's view. Kitty fired her gun and hit a soldier. He dropped from his horse and fell to the dirt.

"Don't shoot!" Candice cried. "They're on our side!" Candice's face paled. "We're gonna get hung for sure." She stared at the soldier lying in the dirt.

"I thought they were Indians!" Kitty shouted as she dropped her gun.

"I hate you! Candice spat. "Now look at what you've done!"

Kitty's back straightened. "I didn't do it on purpose! I couldn't see them. I thought they were Indians."

"That was your excuse last time and the time before that," Candice yelled.

An officer rode in. He trotted his horse in a large circle around the buckboard and the stilled bodies. When he looked up at Candice and Kitty, his face tightened and his eyes flared wide and filled with anger. "I don't believe it. It's you two again!"

He slowed his horse. His voice rose dangerously. "I already warned you two women what I would do to you if you harmed any more of my men. This one doesn't have an arrow in him, so which one of you shot him?" He aimed his gun at Candice.

"Sir," a private cried out as he rode in. "We killed 'em all. You were right, sir. It was that renegade band of Apaches. Look, sir, two of them had guns." The private offered the guns to the captain.

The captain glanced at the six-shooters the soldier had in his hand, he glanced back toward the women.

"I told you," Kitty barked. "We didn't kill anythin' but Indians! And," she said in an uppity tone, "we only killed the ones who were tryin' to kill us." She threw Candice a wink and shrugged her shoulders.

Eric moaned, grabbing Candice's attention. She turned toward him.

The captain swung off of his horse and walked past two sprawled Indians to get a better look at his downed soldier. Kitty caught a subtle movement from one of the downed braves out of the corner of her eye.

As the captain dropped to one knee and studied the soldier's wound, one of the Indians jumped up and attacked him with a knife.

Kitty grabbed her gun and fired, startling everyone within listening distance. The bullet whizzed past the captain's left shoulder, creasing his uniform, then slammed into the Indian's chest. The brave's knife fell from his hands and he dropped to his knees. The captain aimed and fired twice. The Indian dropped face first to the dirt.

"Men!" he hollered. "Still your weapons! Go check each stinkin' Indian and make sure they're really dead!" He cautiously rolled the other sprawled Indian directly in front of him onto his back and callously shot him at point blank, in between the eyes, mumbling something under his breath.

"Them Indians are sneaky devils," Kitty quipped, her gun still raised.

"Put that gun down before you shoot yourself!" the captain barked.

"Is that all you have to say?" Kitty rolled her eyes and teased, "Why, I do declare Candice, I think I'll shoot this soldier just out of spite."

"You are by far," the captain shook his head, "the nosiest, most cantankerous woman I've ever tangled with! Now put down that darn gun, now!"

"I just saved your life," Kitty shouted, lowering her gun. "You sure ain't very grateful. Why, if someone just saved my life I would offer them a hot meal and the finest champagne money could buy."

"Private," the captain ordered. "Shut that woman up!"

"Yes, yes sir!" a wild-eyed, baby-faced man shouted. "Sir," his voice dropped, "how, sir?"

The captain spat, "I don't know, just do it!"

"What kind of champagne do you have?" Kitty asked the young soldier.

"Ma'am, we don't have any liquor. It's not allowed."

"Well, what do you have?" Kitty asked, dusting off her clothes.

"I can rustle you up some grub; will that slow your tongue?"

"Maybe," Kitty replied. "Wait a minute. What happened to my ham?" She frowned, studying the ground around the buckboard. A second later her voice calmed. "What kind of grub?"

She jumped out of the buckboard and followed the soldier, talking out loud mainly to herself about the types of food she liked. As her voice faded the frown on the captain's forehead melted.

"Let me take a look at that wound." The captain helped Eric out of the buckboard and sat him against the wooden wheel. "I know you're the medic, but I think the best thing for this shoulder is for me to push the arrow all the way through."

Eric grimaced and closed his eyes. "I think so, too, sir," he replied.

"This is gonna hurt," the captain warned. Still wearing his riding gloves, he broke off the tip of the arrow, and in one swift movement, pushed it deeper into Eric's flesh and out the front of his upper shoulder. Eric's body trembled, and blood pooled on the front of his uniform.

Candice went pale and looked away. "Is he gonna live?" she asked.

"He's gonna be a mite sore, and he's lost a lot of blood, but I reckon he'll live." The relief in the captain's voice was apparent. A second later his tone deepened. He stared at Candice, making her feel uncomfortable. He said, "You ain't like that polecat, Kitty. What are you doin' with her?"

Relieved at what she'd heard from him, she offered the captain a short smile and simply said, "She's my friend. Were goin' to Bodie and have the grandest saloon ever built."

"Bodie?" The captain's back straightened. "That's a lawless town. Only fools and gunslingers go there."

Candice in a light, polite tone, raised an eyebrow and glanced over to the Indian Kitty had just killed. "Well...I guess she's the gunslinger." Then she glanced down at her broken arm and said, "I reckon that makes me the fool."

The captain shook his head and finished bandaging Eric's shoulder as best he could.

Eric opened his eyes and managed a slight grin. "Captain, I left these two women for dead. If anyone can make it in Bodie, I'd bet an entire year's pay these two could." His grin faded and his eyes closed a second later.

"He ain't goin' anywhere today," the captain said out loud, mainly to himself. " I hate to lose a full day's light, but I reckon the troops could use a day of rest." He studied the surrounding hills and nodded to himself. "Water is close by, and there's enough grass to feed the horses. We'll stay here for the night."

"Candice!" Kitty shouted. "They have lots of food! I want to become a soldier."

The captain cringed. "You stay away from our food and my men!" he ordered tightly.

"You sure are bossy," Kitty barked back. "Why, I bet you ain't even married. No girl would marry a person as bossy as you. And look at your uniform. I thought soldiers were supposed to keep their uniforms clean."

The captain threw Candice a frown. "I'll keep her fed if you keep her quiet," he told her.

"I'll try," Candice said with honesty. "I've been tryin' to do just that all the way from Reno."

"Candice, look. They have bread and honey. I brought you a piece."

The captain walked away as Kitty approached. "I'm gonna join your troops, Captain," Kitty proudly said with her mouth full.

The captain lowered his head and headed over to his horse, throwing out commands like a barking dog. His men hurried, and in a short time their surroundings were dotted with tents, grazing horses, and campfire pits.

"Why are they settin' up camp so early?" Kitty asked as she sat on the back of the buckboard eating bread and honey.

"Eric and the other men need to rest for a day," Candice replied. "The lieutenant said his men needed a rest, too."

A twinkle grew in Kitty's eyes. "Some of these men are really handsome."

"No!" Candice insisted. "I promised the captain I would keep you away from his men."

Kitty raised an eyebrow, and with feminine charm said, "And how are you gonna do that?"

Candice growled," Kitty, let's take their hospitality and then get."

"But they have money," Kitty moaned. "And some are real handsome."

"Kitty," Candice warned, "I'll get us packed up right now if you don't promise me you won't visit these men tonight."

"But I miss men," Kitty whined. "And they're young and...."

"No!" Candice screamed again. "I'll get the horses, and we're leavin' now!"

Two soldiers appeared, both with wide eyes and wearing reckless smiles. One stiffened his back and said, "Ma'am, the captain wants me to escort you over to the base of that hill."

"No," Kitty replied. "I like it right here."

The soldier cleared his throat. "Ma'am, it's not a request. It's an order."

Kitty shook her head. "Why would I want to camp way over there? No."

"We ain't campin' here tonight," Candice said, biting her lip. "We need to get. The day is still young."

"Yes, ma'am," both of the men said, dropping their smiles. "Can we hitch the horses for you?" one offered, staring at Kitty.

"Please," Candice said. "With this busted arm, I'm just not able to do it today."

"I ain't goin' nowhere!" Kitty snapped.

Both men threw each other a puzzled look. One said, "Am I or ain't I hitching up the horses?"

Candice raised her voice. "Yes, you are. She has a mind of her own. Please don't listen to her."

"Are you sure we can't set you up a camp over yonder?" the soldier staring at Kitty asked. "We get hot stew and biscuits tonight."

"I'm stayin'," Kitty said with a decisive nod.

"No, you're not!" Candice shot back.

"Well," one soldier said. Both soldiers shook their heads. "I reckon we did what the captain asked, didn't we?" They turned to head back.

"I think so," the other soldier replied. "She sure is purty, though. I ain't ever seen a girl like her before." The men shared a grin and a nod.

"Why ain't those two women movin'?" the captain demanded as the men approached.

"Because they're leavin', sir." At least one of 'em is."

"When?" the captain asked.

The men exchanged a glance of uncertainty. "The redhead is goin' and the blonde one is stayin'."

The captain shook his head. "I knew I shouldn't have sent babies to do a man's job."

He checked to make sure his gun was loaded, then hurried over to the buckboard. Kitty was still eating, swinging her legs off the back edge of the buckboard. Candice was busy, checking and adjusting leather on the team.

"You told me you would control her!" he shouted at Candice in an angry voice as he approached.

"No, I didn't," she replied with a sigh. "I told you, I've been tryin' all the way from Reno."

"Here, let me help you with this," he offered. "You can't hitch a team with one arm."

"I'll manage," Candice said, shifting her weight, her breath labored.

"No, you go sit; I'll get the team harnessed," the captain insisted, though not exactly sure why he'd just offered to help.

Candice took a deep breath and wiped the sweat off her face. "Is it always this hot in California?"

"Don't know. I'm from Oregon."

"Where is that?" Candice asked as she sat down to rest in the shade of the buckboard.

"It's up north," he said. "We get a lot of rain up there."

"I don't like the rain in Reno." Candice stared at the captain. "It's bitter cold, that rain."

The captain nodded. "It's not like that in Oregon, unless the clouds set themselves up deep." He double-checked all the leather attached to the horses and said, "Them Sierra Mountains are wicked. I've only had to pass through them once, and I almost lost a toe from frostbite. My advice is that you get, and you get quick before fall sets in."

"I ain't goin'!" Kitty informed the two of them, her stomach full. She stretched and yawned. "I'm stayin' right here and takin' a long nap."

"I'll give you two weeks' provisions and blankets if you get her out of this camp now," the captain offered, dead serious.

"That would be appreciated, "Candice replied lowering her head respectfully. "Wait!" she shouted as the captain walked away. "Where is Eric stationed?"

The captain's face hardened as he turned. "He's from Fort--" his voice deepened. "I don't want you or her visitin'. Now, do you or don't you want them provisions?"

"Please," Candice said. "They'd be most welcome."

"I ain't goin'," Kitty snapped as the captain walked past her.

He shook his head so hard he dizzied himself. He ground his teeth and didn't miss a step as he walked past Kitty.

Chapter 46

"Kitty," Candice rose from her seat in the shade, "I can't lead these horses with this busted arm of mine." She watched Kitty playfully swing her legs. "I need you to."

"It's kind of hot here," Kitty said. "But I want to stay."

"That man is bringin' us back two weeks' food," Candice informed her. "Kitty, if we leave now, and if you can drive the horses, we could get to Bodie before the weather stops us."

Kitty stopped swinging her legs. "I suppose you're right," she said in a less insistent voice. "James said nature would kill us if we tried to get to Bodie any time except the spring." She jumped down from the wagon as the weary captain approached again. She said to him, "You're right, we've got to get. Thank you for the vittles."

The captain and two soldiers with itchy gun hands approached the buckboard. Kitty's movements captured their attention. Candice threw the captain a short smile. "Kitty, get up here and help me with these horses."

Kitty paused and her eyes widened as she eyed a young soldier so handsome he took her breath away.

Disgusted, Candice yelled, "Get up here now or I'll shoot you!"

"Drop the food and blankets in the back of the buckboard and get back to camp," the captain hollered.

"I do so want to stay," Kitty pouted.

"I won't talk to you ever again unless you get these horses movin'!" Candice demanded. Reluctantly, Kitty complied.

The men took a step back from the buckboard, all of them shaking their heads.

"What do we do?" the youngest soldier asked.

The captain, surprising himself, said, "We need to get back to our business."

"Yes, sir." They all hurried away from the buckboard.

"Hold the reins tighter!" Candice instructed Kitty. "Don't push them that fast."

The captain and the two soldiers watched and listened to the two women argue as the buckboard abruptly turned left and then right, disappearing in a cloud of dust.

"Sir," the youngest soldier said with respect. "I didn't know that women could hurt your brain this bad."

The captain stared into the young soldier's eyes. "What is your name, soldier?"

The young soldier stood at attention. "My name is...." He lowered his eyes, then lifted them. "Sir, Bartholomew, but I go by the name of Buck."

"Buck?" the captain threw him a hard stare. "Buck, you're goin' to escort them two crazy women to the outskirts of Bodie. Then you head northeast and catch up with us in Sodaville."

A deep frown settled on Buck's face. "Sir, I ain't good with women. Them two gave me a headache." His head shook as though a cluster of bees were buzzing around it.

The captain grinned. "Soldier, grab your belongin's and catch up with them two before they kill themselves."

Buck lifted his head, and in a respectful yet sad voice replied, "Yes, sir."

The other young soldier smiled and said, "Sir, there are two of them women. Can I go?"

The captain, catching the restless and eager look in the young soldier's eyes, said, "No. You can go help the cook."

"The cook?" He sighed. The captain glared. "Yes, sir," he said and swung back into the saddle.

"Kitty," Candice said with a drawn sigh. "Why do you tease men the way you do?"

"That's a stupid question," Kitty snapped.

"What's so stupid about it?" Candice asked, raising her voice.

"Because I can!" Kitty smugly replied.

"But you're beautiful. You don't have to," Candice offered in a soft tone.

"Men will be men," Kitty growled. "It's that simple."

"Don't shoot!" Buck shouted as he caught sight of the racing buckboard.

Both women looked over their shoulders, then threw each other a frown.

Candice grabbed her gun with her good arm. Kitty shook her head and said, "I knew it wouldn't be that easy. That captain figured out I shot his soldier."

"I don't think we can outrun him," Candice shouted. "And he ain't shootin', so maybe we should see what he wants."

"No," Kitty insisted. "I know men, and I ain't dyin' today." She pulled the whip out and slapped the horses' rumps. They picked up reckless speed.

"We're goin' too fast!" Candice hollered. "Slow down!"

"I told you," Kitty shouted, "I'm not dyin' today." She whipped the horses again.

The buckboard jumped, flipped on its side, and careened forward, only to come to an abrupt stop.

The soldier close behind, stared in horror. He kicked his horse into a faster run and shouted, "I'm comin'. Don't die on me. The captain will be awfully mad at me if I tell him you're already dead."

Candice coughed and spit dust out of her mouth. She had landed in soft dirt. She heard what the soldier had said. She grimaced and sat up, holding onto her throbbing arm that was hung up in a sling. "So you ain't here to kill us?"

The soldier jumped off of his horse, his face filled with confusion. He rushed to Candice's side. "Ma'am, why would I do that? Let me help you. Are you hurt?"

She drew a hard breath and slowed her racing heart as he helped her out of the dirt. "Ma'am, I'm so glad you ain't dead," he said.

Kitty moaned from underneath the buckboard.

"Ma'am, I'll get you next! Dang! I have a bad feelin' about this." He moaned as he helped Candice over to some rocks and eased her down in the shade.

"I hate horses," Kitty mumbled in a puny voice, lifting herself out of the dirt. She had landed dangerously close the horses' hind legs.

One of the horses pooped. It had landed inches from her head. "What's that awful smell?" she cried.

Buck looked around, his gun hand itchy. "Ma'am, I don't see or smell nothin'. Are you hurt badly?"

The other horse pooped. It splashed onto Kitty's left hand. "I hate horses," Kitty barked as she scrambled to her knees.

The soldier said, "Ma'am, I'm glad you're alive. Are you hurt?"

"What were you followin' us that hard for?" Kitty snapped, her trigger hand itchy.

"Well, I sure didn't want your company." The soldier frowned. "You give me a headache." He shook his head. "The captain gave me direct orders to make sure you get to Bodie. And right now, ma'am, that headache is comin' back."

Candice and Kitty shared a confused glance.

Kitty brushed off her clothes, and with feminine charm said, "So, do you know how to drive that buckboard?"

"Yes, ma'am," the young soldier replied. He stared at Kitty and his jaw dropped.

"What are you starin' at me like that for?" she asked as her knees buckled and she fell to the ground.

"You're bleedin' real bad!" he shouted as he rushed to Kitty's side. He swooped her up and hurried her over to the shade. "Don't die on me," he demanded worriedly. "I don't want to get shot by my captain."

Candice's face paled when she saw Kitty's condition. "Put her down here," she cried, pointing to a patch of shaded soft sand close by.

"I ain't a medic." Buck's eyes widened. "And I ain't knowin' what to do."

He shook his head and stared at the bleeding. He threw a worried glance at Candice. "I ain't good at this. Are you?"

"I'll try." Candice got up and hurried over to Kitty. She fell to her knees and grimaced at the red stains across Kitty's blouse. Kitty's body unnaturally shook.

A sweet smell filled Candice's nose. With a shaking hand she touched Kitty's stained blouse, then cautiously sniffed her red finger. Then she licked it.

The young soldier scratched his head and dropped his jaw, his face still plastered with worry.

"It's not blood," Candice announced, her worry evaporating. "It's jam."

Buck couldn't believe it. "I'll put her out of her misery," he offered, his face thick with worry.

"Kitty, wake up!" Candice shouted. "You scared the pants off of me!" Candice lightly slapped Kitty's face.

The young soldier shook his head and grabbed his gun. "Ma'am, it ain't goin' to do any good. She's lost too much blood. I'll get you to Bodie, but her time is up." His voice hardened as he bit his lower lip and complained into the air, "Captain, I promise you, if you keep me away from women, I'll never, ever not listen to you again."

Candice giggled. He threw her a look of scorn. "What's so funny?" he bellowed.

In one swift movement, Kitty sat up, surprising Buck. He jumped back and his face went pale as he fumbled for his gun.

"Don't shoot her!" Candice howled, "or you'll kill her all over again."

Nervous, Buck stepped backwards and hid in the shadow of the rock.

"I thought you were dead!" Candice cried, her smile widening.

"I hate horses!" Kitty groaned in a tiny voice, her head still spinning. "What is that fruity sweet smell?" she asked, wrinkling her nose.

"It's you," Candice said, holding in her laughter.

Kitty looked at her stained blouse and sniffed it. Her voice tightened and her face filled with disappointment. "This was a special gift from the cook after I gave him my favors!"

"You did what?" Candice said, appalled. "For a jar of jam?"

Kitty rolled her eyes at Candice. "He was handsome and he gave me fresh bread too. I was grateful."

The soldier, still hiding in the shadows, shook his head and lowered his gun. He cautiously stood up.

Both women stopped their squabbling and glanced at him.

When he caught them staring he nervously said, "I don't want nothin' to do with you two...." He scratched his head. "But the captain says I have to take you to Bodie."

Kitty and Candice shared a glance. Kitty studied Buck, and with a teasing voice said, "I ain't dead, and I do declare, you are very, very handsome." She threw Buck a wink and dusted off her skirt.

Buck grinned, but a second later he caught the scorn on Candice's face. "Yes, ma'am." His voice shook. "I mean, no, ma'am." He turned away from the women and shouted, "Captain, you did this on purpose, didn't you?" He composed himself, and in a worried tone said, "Ladies, I ain't good with women. I sure don't want to get shot by her." He threw Candice a glance, meaning Kitty. "And I don't want to get caught enjoyin' her favors." He glanced at Kitty, then lowered his eyes. "Not that I wouldn't love your favors... but the captain will shoot me if I do." He walked a little ways away from the women and loudly shouted to nobody in particular, "All I ever wanted to do was kill the rebels."

"What rebels?" Kitty said, still sashaying.

"Ma'am, we've been chasin' a pair of redskins for a time. They've ravaged everythin' in their path."

"Did you kill them?" Candice asked, lowering her voice.

"No, when we took our horses for a drink we found them dead, floatin' in the river."

Kitty flashed Candice a short smile.

"Now I don't know you, and I don't want any of your guff!" the confused soldier blustered.

"Do you know how to get us to Bodie?" Candice asked with caution.

"No, ma'am. I mean, yes, ma'am."

"What does that mean?" Kitty barked.

The young soldier scratched his head, gathering his thoughts. "The captain said to head southwest until we fell into a pocket. Then he said to head southeast. Then he said don't go up the incline, head back."

"So," Candice offered with a short smile, "you know about as much as we do?"

The soldier bowed his head and gave it a shake. "I didn't want to be here. I was happy where I was."

Both women grinned. "Buck, we could use a man's strong back," Candice sighed with relief.

"Does that mean you're gonna help me set this buckboard back up?" The frown on Buck's face lifted.

"What can we do to help?" both women asked at the same time.

Buck straightened up, clearly pleased. "I ain't sure this will work, but we can try." Carrying himself tall, he unhooked the team.

Kitty and Candice sat down in the shade. Buck shook his head time and time again, hooking and unhooking leather.

"Should we help him?" Kitty giggled.

"I don't think we could do any worse." Candice smiled, struggling to contain her laughter. "Buck," she said, hiding her smile, "all you have to do is hook one horse up, not both of them."

Buck shook his head again. "I ain't never worked with this much leather before."

"Buck," Kitty said. "When I get to Bodie, I get to own the grandest saloon ever built."

Confused, Buck turned to Candice. "Show me what you know about hitching horses," he said.

Candice unhooked the thick leather that snaked around the horses' backs, walked around the buckboard, and lashed it around metal grommets.

"You make the horse move at a slow pace, and Kitty and I will call to you when the buckboard is up."

The soldier nodded, ran to the buckboard, and pulled out the whip. He threw Candice a nervous stare when she hollered, "Now!"

Kitty shook her head and glanced down at her jam-soaked blouse. "I can't believe you ruined my clean blouse!" she complained.

"Shut up and help me!" Candice demanded. "I need your help."

Watching Candice, Kitty frowned. "I think you did this on purpose." She sat back down and mumbled under her breath as she busied herself cleaning her shirt.

"It's not working!" the soldier cried. "Maybe we should stop."

Candice walked over to Kitty and slapped her face. "What the heck is wrong with you?" she snapped. "We're almost to Bodie, and you're worried about your blouse?"

"What is wrong with *you*?" Kitty fired back. "I can't go to Bodie now."

"What?" Candice lightened her tone. "Why not?"

"Because I ain't got a clean blouse left," Kitty replied in an uppity tone.

"Well, you can borrow one of mine," Candice offered.

"But it would be too big," Kitty said with a worried look.

"Kitty," Candice said, raising her voice, "you are the dumbest person I've ever met. Get off of that tiny butt of yours and help us out!"

"I've been schooled!" Kitty shrieked. "I ain't dumb!"

Buck looked over his shoulder, shook his head, and murmured, "Captain, if I get back safely, I promise you I'll help the cook every night if you promise me I don't have to put up with womenfolk ever again."

The frown on Candice's forehead eased. "Kitty, we're close, real close, to Bodie. And I know we can make it."

Kitty glanced up. "Are you sure?"

Candice nodded and a smile filled her face. "I'm lookin' forward to seein' your grand saloon."

Kitty stopped cleaning her blouse and jumped up. Her eyes gleaming, she said, "What can I do to help?"

Buck kept an eye on both women, glad to be farther away from their squabble.

Kitty hurried to Candice's side and said, "Do I push it or steady it?"

"Both," Candice replied with a nod, readying her strong arms. Then she shouted, "We're ready. Buck. Try it again."

"Okay," Buck hollered back. The horse eased forward. The leather between the horse and the buckboard tightened. "Tell me when!" he shouted.

"Now!" Candice yelled. "Push hard," she shouted at Kitty. "It's movin'." The buckboard moaned and shook. Dirt and dust flew as it slowly righted itself.

"That's good!" Candice cried as the buckboard's wheels slammed to the ground.

"We did it!" Kitty shouted.

"Yes, we did," Candice offered Kitty with a short smile.

"I did it!" Buck shouted. Checking his own excitement, he cleared his throat. "I'm goin' to get you two to Bodie as fast I can." The worry on his face gone now, he politely asked, "I ain't much at cookin'. Do either of you know how to cook?"

With thick smiles still on both women's faces, Kitty asked, "Do you like biscuits?"

Candice walked around the buckboard and said, "We spilled the supplies, but if you help me fetch 'em, I reckon we can cook."

"Yes, ma'am." Buck said, dropping the horse's reins and hurrying to help Candice.

Kitty lifted her head. "Why are you leavin' that horse in leather?" she asked.

"Ma'am, yes ma'am." Buck turned around and ran back to the horse he had been using to right the buckboard. Out of breath he glanced back at the women and mumbled, "I sure hope Bodie is close."

Chapter 47

"Where are you goin?" Candice asked Buck in a testy voice. "You need to tell us if anythin' is broken on the buckboard."

Buck dropped the heavy harness attached to the horse, shook his head, and turned to hurry back to the women. "Yes, ma'am."

"Kitty," Candice said in a stern voice, "I'm still mad at you, and I'll shoot you if you tempt him again."

"This jam is sweet and a bit bitter at the same time," Kitty simply replied, smacking her lips. "I'm mad at you, too!" A second later her voice settled. More gently she said, "How far did you say Bodie was?"

Buck stopped short of the women, his eyes filled with worry. "If either of you women would help, I would be obliged."

Candice threw Kitty a hard stare. "If we're gettin' to Bodie...."

Kitty frowned and raised an eyebrow. "I know how to handle horses," she said. "I'll help Buck."

Kitty's feminine movements arrested the soldier's thoughts. "Ma'am," he said, "I reckon I don't need your help."

Candice caught the fright on Buck's face. With a wide smile she said, "What can I do?"

"Get your friend away from me, that's what. I'm studyin' this situation real hard, and I don't like it."

Candice offered him a short smile, then said with a long sigh, "I wish I could do that, but I've been trying to keep her under control all the way from Reno and I ain't had any luck so far."

Buck said, "All right, then. I reckon I can figure the horse out and the rest can wait." He hurried to Candice's side. "Ma'am, I reckon you need rest and some shade."

Candice nodded, and with heavy-lidded eyes said, "Thank you."

"Where are you goin'?" Kitty shouted from a distance.

Candice and Buck looked up.

"I think Bodie is right over this next hill," Kitty shouted with excitement. "I want a nice glass of champagne. We need to get goin', now!"

Buck shook his head and hollered, "No, Ma'am. I know what the captain said, and that ain't the area."

"What do you know?" Kitty spat. "You don't even know how to unhook a horse."

Buck moaned and threw Candice a worried glance. Candice tried to control her labored breath as Buck steadied her broken arm.

"Ma'am, you rest here." He helped Candice to a shaded patch of overgrown shrubs. Grateful, she nodded and fell to her knees.

"What are you waitin' for?" Kitty screamed. She ran back to the buckboard and hurried around it. "Is it workin' or not?" she demanded, her eyes lighting up.

"No!" Candice moaned.

"Yes," Buck replied.

"Which is it?" Kitty huffed, throwing Buck a wink and Candice a frown.

"Kitty!" Candice cried in a puny voice. "We ain't gettin' to Bodie today. I'm hurtin' real bad, and if I hear your voice again, today…I swear I'll shoot you!"

Buck took a step away from both women and shook his head.

Kitty screamed, "It's not fair. I found Bodie, and now I can't go there."

"Ma'am," Buck said frowning, "I already told you, that ain't Bodie."

Kitty's voice filled with anger. "I hate men!"

Buck turned to face Candice and shrugged his shoulders, clearly looking for her help.

"Kitty," Candice moaned. "Buck has food, lots of food."

Kitty stilled.

Candice winked at Buck, then settled into the comfort of the shade.

Wary, Buck didn't know what to expect next from Kitty.

Kitty threw Buck a wink and raised an eyebrow. "What kind of food did the captain give you? Let me see it."

"Ma'am," Buck quickly replied, "You can have everythin' the captain gave me if you just stop talkin' and leave me alone."

"What does that mean?" Kitty spat. She wiggled her hips and threw Buck a smile. "When was the last time you had a woman?"

Buck shook his head so hard he got dizzy. "Now, you stop that!" he said as polite as he could manage. "The captain would shoot me if I touched a hair on either of you."

Kitty stopped flirting. "What kind of food did you bring, Buck? Do you have any more of that pomegranate jam? What about honey? Do you have some of that?" Stopping only long enough to grab a breath, she said, "I hope you have some of that fresh bread."

Buck drew a deep breath and his eyes widened. "I don't know, I just brung it."

Kitty hurried over to the spilled supplies."Why, I do declare," her voice sang. "We have fresh meat and," her face lit up, "another jar of that sweet pomegranate jelly."

Buck kept his distance. "You said you can cook biscuits, so cook them." He distanced himself from Kitty and sat next to Candice, hunting for shade. "If you don't mind," he politely asked, "can I share the small patch of shade with you?"

Candice nodded and scooted a few inches left. "Don't let her tease you," she yawned. "Kitty's real good at that."

"Ma'am," Buck admitted, "I already know that." He asked a second later, "How do I train her?"

"I already told you," Candice sighed. "I've been tryin' to train her all the way from Reno."

"Can I offer you some water?" Buck asked, glad to be away from Kitty's incessant chatter.

"No," Candice replied with a sigh. "I would be appreciative if you'd make sure she doesn't burn down anything, especially the buckboard."

Buck jumped to attention. "Yes, ma'am." His voice fell and a worried expression filled his face. "Ma'am, I don't know nothin' about cookin'."

Candice smiled, then sighed. "Neither does Kitty."

Buck frowned as he stood up. Candice closed her eyes and her smile faded. He checked to make sure she was comfortable, then he headed toward Kitty.

"Well, it's about time I had some help!" Kitty shouted, watching his approach out of the corner of her eye.

"Let me get something clear here," Buck growled, his face tight. "I don't like you, and I ain't goin' after your favors. I just ain't good at this."

Before he could finish his thoughts, Kitty barked, "How am I gonna cook without wood? Go fetch me some wood."

"Yes, ma'am." Buck saluted Kitty, being used to following a command, then blushed.

"I'm sick of men," Kitty snapped. "Why don't they listen' to me anymore?" she frowned. "What is this?" She untied a gunnysack and peered inside. "Snake!" she screamed, jumping to her feet. Her hands fumbled for her gun. She got off a shot, then another one.

Buck flew to the ground and raised his gun. "Are you hurt?" he shouted.

"I killed it," Kitty said proudly. She caught Buck's flattened body and raised gun. "What the heck are you doin'?" she asked. "You ain't gonna kill a snake lyin' next to it."

"Where?" Buck jumped to his knees and wildly pointed his gun toward several places around the dirt.

"I already killed it," Kitty informed him, her tone testy.

Buck stood up, dusted off his uniform, and with caution walked over to Kitty.

"See?" she proudly said, pointing to the gunnysack.

"Put your gun away," Buck demanded, bending down to get a better look at what was inside the bag.

"You idiot!" he shouted. "The snake was already dead. That was part of our grub!"

"You can't talk to me like that!" Kitty snapped. "How do you know it was already dead?"

"You are the--" Buck caught the ire in his tone and bit his lip. "The cook told me he packed me somethin' special."

"What does that mean?" Kitty shouted, still mad at being called an idiot.

"It means...." He took a breath and lowered his head. A second later he raised it again and in an angry voice hollered, "Captain, I ain't ever doin' women duty again."

"What does that mean?" Kitty planted her hands on her waist, and with her nose in the air, walked in a short circle around the bag. "Are you sure it's dead?" she asked with caution.

"I already told you it was dead before you shot it again," Buck said.

"I don't believe you," Kitty snapped. "I killed it, and you're just jealous." She rolled her eyes at Buck. "It's a snake. Why would anyone put it in a bag?"

"I already told you that, too!" Buck's voice rose. "It's the somethin' special the cook packed for me."

"You mean," Kitty's eyes darted back and forth. For a minute she remained deep in thought. "I shouldn't have given him my favors!" Candice was right. Not for a jar of jam."

"What?" Buck said, his face turning shades of red. "You favored a man for a measly jar of jam?"

"It ain't your business!" Kitty snapped. "Where's that firewood?"

Buck stood back up and walked with slow steps to where he had dropped the firewood, thinking about what Kitty had just told him. "I'm droppin' you off and runnin'," he shouted over his shoulder at Kitty.

"I don't care!" Kitty shouted back. "Hurry up with the wood. I'm hungry!"

Kitty surprised herself at how fast she cooked the meal on an open flame. "You know, biscuits shouldn't be cooked like this," she warned, offering Buck a short smile.

"Yes, ma'am." He nodded. "Is there anythin' I can do to help?"

Kitty stretched her arms and looked around at her hard work. "I reckon not." A second later she said, "Yes, please help Candice to supper. I'll get the plates."

"You have plates?" Buck asked, a grin easing across his face.

Kitty glanced over her shoulder at Buck and said teasingly, "All ladies eat on plates."

Buck found his manners, and his tone of voice offered respect. "Yes, ma'am." He walked over to Candice and dropped to his knees. "I hope you slept hard and well. It's time to eat."

Candice opened her eyes, then closed them again. She curled as tight as her broken arm would let her.

"Ma'am," the private said, being careful not to upset her. "You need to get up and eat."

"What's takin' you so long?" Kitty shouted. "These biscuits are gettin' burned."

"She won't wake up," Buck shouted back.

"Slap her!" Kitty hollered back.

"What? No ma'am!" Buck jumped up. "I ain't ever hit a lady, and I ain't gonna start now!"

Kitty demanded, "Well, pick her up and bring her to the food, then."

"Yes, ma'am." The deep frown that had settled on his face earlier returned. He put one arm under Candice's neck and the other underneath her knees. Embarrassed at touching a woman so close, he blushed as he lifted Candice up.

Her weight slowed him, and he steadied his back with effort.

"I already told you!" Kitty shouted again. "These biscuits are burnin'. Hurry up."

"Ma'am, yes, ma'am." Buck steadied his knees and carried Candice to the fire, nearly dropping her several times along the way.

Candice opened her heavy eyelids midway. "I don't want to break anythin' else," she said as she held on tight and Buck tucked her closer into his straining arms.

"I'll wake her up," Kitty shouted in a testy voice. "She's been sleepin' a lot more than me anyways."

"No," Buck demanded. "You leave her be. She's hurt."

Kitty threw Buck a mean glare. "I've been hurt, too, and she's my friend. Drop her gently."

Annoyed, Buck shot back, "But a minute ago you told me you were gonna slap her."

"A minute ago I didn't know how bad she was hurtin'." Kitty rolled her eyes again. "I don't care if you eat, but I'm gonna feed my friend and then I'm gonna to eat right after her."

"Thank you, "Buck replied, huffing and puffing as he set Candice down by the fire. "I'm sure glad Bodie is near." I don't think I could take much more of this. What did you cook?" he asked, staring at the grub.

"Hot biscuits, roasted meat, and pomegranate jam," Kitty replied with a proud smile.

Buck nodded with respect and eagerly filled his plate. He bit into a rattlesnake tail. He politely turned his head and pulled it out of his mouth. When he saw the rattlers, he spit the remanding food out of his mouth completely.

"What are you doin' now?" Kitty asked, feeding Candice.

"Nothin', ma'am." Worried, Buck studied his plate, chewing carefully.

"Did you like the roasted snake?" Kitty asked with pride in her voice.

"Yes, ma'am," Buck lied.

"Sorry I burnt the biscuits," Kitty apologized. "I ain't used to open fires."

"And I ain't used to women," Buck replied, pushing the food around in is plate with his fork. "How much farther away do you think Bodie is?"

"I already told you," Kitty snapped. "Its right over that next crop of hills."

Buck smiled. "Thank you, ma'am, for supper." He put his full plate of food down.

Kitty narrowed her eyes. "Ain't you hungry?" she asked. "I thought you were hungry."

"No, ma'am," Buck replied in his kindest manner.

"So why did I go to all of this work!" Kitty shouted.

"I told you I would shoot you if you didn't shut up today," Candice mumbled. "What is this meat with all the bones? I've tried to bite into it and all I hit is bones."

"It's the rattlesnake that Buck brought," Kitty said with a smile. "I ain't ever cooked a snake before, but Buck said the cook said it was special…so I cooked it for us."

"Did you chop the head and tail off before you cooked it?" Candice asked, spitting the meat out of her mouth.

"No. Why would I do that?"

Candice grimaced and shook her head. "I hope we all don't die tonight by snake poisonin'."

Buck nodded and his face grew taut with worry.

"What is wrong with you two?" Kitty growled. "I've been cookin' over an open flame for three hours and you're spittin' all my hard work out. I'm gettin' the horses and headin' over that hill and goin' to Bodie right now."

Chapter 48

"No, ma'am, I can't let you." Buck said with authority.

"Who's gonna stop me?" Kitty asked, stiffening her back.

Buck glanced at Candice, hoping for support. Candice opened her eyes and shook her head.

"I already told you," Buck shouted louder. "I don't like you."

Kitty rolled her eyes. "I know that, and I'm goin' to Bodie right now."

Buck hurried over to Candice and whispered, "I told you I'm not good at women. What do I say now?"

"Nothin'. You go hobble the horses and she won't figure it out. She's educated."

"Yes, ma'am." A short grin replaced the worry on Buck's face. He hurried to hobble the horses as Kitty, in the back of the buckboard, surveyed all the provisions they had.

"I know you hurt," Kitty offered Candice. "And, I ain't mad at you." She took a long time collecting her thoughts. She shrugged her shoulders and said, "I just need men and champagne." The excitement in her eyes dimmed as she said, "I'm leavin' you all the food and blankets." But her eyes danced a second later. "I'm goin' to be in Bodie tonight!"

Candice bowed her head. Buck watched out for Kitty as he tied leather around all three horses' front legs. He hastened back to Candice the moment he finished.

"Do you reckon she'll figure out what a hobble is and leave us here?" he asked, worried.

"Nope," Candice replied with sly confidence, throwing Buck a tiny smile. "I ain't feelin' as good as I hoped I would after that long sleep. I apologize...." Her words failed her as she dropped to the dirt to rest again.

Bodie or Bust

Buck frowned, not sure he had done the right thing by hobbling the horses.

"How come this horse won't move?" Kitty screamed.

Buck and Candice shared a nod.

"I spent my entire night cookin', and you two tricked me, didn't you?"

Buck covered his mouth, choking on laughter. He shot a glance at Candice. "Are you sure?" he whispered."

"Buck," Candice said in one short breath, "she's city folk. She ain't goin' nowhere without our help."

Buck glanced in the distance at Kitty and back at Candice. "If she kills our horses we ain't goin to get much farther."

"What is this?" Kitty cried, eyeing the hobbles and dropping to her knees. "I hate you Candice!" she screamed.

Candice assured the worried Buck. Lifting one eye, she said, "I know her better than you. Relax."

Relieved, Buck asked, "Ma'am, but what do I do now?"

"Get some sleep," Candice replied. "She'll get over it by mornin'."

Confused, Buck sat at attention, his nerves jangling.

Candice curled up in the shade and dozed off.

"I'm goin' to Bodie if I have to kill you!" Kitty screamed. Her tiny hands pulled at the leather that hobbled the horses' front legs. "How do I get this contraption off?" she cried.

"Will she shoot me?" Buck whispered nervously.

Candice opened her eyes, drew a breath, and sighed. "I don't know. She gets mighty stubborn now and then."

Buck lifted his head to the sky. "Captain, you are a hateful man," he growled.

"You know horses!" Kitty shouted toward Buck. "Did you do this to the horses?"

Buck glanced at Candice and stood tall. "I'm tired of your patter!" he said. "Your friend can't travel any farther today, and so that means we ain't gonna go any farther today."

Kitty stood up and stiffened her back. "And, are you goin' to stop me?"

Buck's face reddened with anger. He jumped up and ran at Kitty, intending to topple her.

She laughed and said, "You'll never catch me. I'm a girl."

He hit her with full force. They both fell hard to the dirt, Kitty on the bottom.

"That hurt!" Kitty mumbled, looking up at the worry in Buck's eyes. "That never happened before," she complained, shaking her head to clear it.

"I'm sorry, ma'am. I ain't ever done that before." Buck helped Kitty to her knees and apologized. "You need to sleep. We can find Bodie after your friend heals."

Kitty, still dizzy, said, "What did you say your name was?"

"I already told you!" Buck shouted, "I don't like you and you ain't takin' them horses. Now go get some sleep."

Chapter 49

"What was that noise?" Kitty yawned.

"What noise?" Buck pushed to his feet and grabbed his gun.

Kitty yawned again and sat up. "I don't hear it now," she said.

Buck lowered his gun and his nervous eyes settled on Candice. "Ma'am, did you sleep good?"

"Why didn't you ask *me* that?" Kitty mumbled, frowning.

Buck looked over his shoulder at her. "I already told you, I don't like you."

Kitty raised an eyebrow and stood up. "Buck, can you fetch me a canteen? I'm awfully thirsty."

"Yes, ma'am, I suppose I could do that."

Candice stretched out her good arm above her head. "How long have I been asleep?" she asked, watching Kitty and Buck walk away. "Buck!" she screamed after them. "Don't!"

Buck turned. "Don't do what?"

Candice hurried to rise. She drew a deep breath and shook her head. She screamed, "Kitty, I'm gonna kill you!"

Kitty laughed as Buck untied the leather hobbles keeping the horses from moving with any speed. "I'm still not mad at you!" she shouted. "I just need a man and champagne."

Buck called to Candice. "Ma'am!" he shouted, "I already told you, I ain't good at this."

Candice's head drooped, but she grinned and said, "Buck let her go. She ain't gonna get far on a horse anyways."

Buck untied the hobble on the horse directly in front of him. "Yes, ma'am," he replied.

"I'll meet you in Bodie, "Kitty shouted, cautiously pulling herself onto the back of a horse. "You better not hurt me," she demanded of the horse.

Buck and Candice shared a glance and grin.

Kitty raised an eyebrow and said, "I hope James is there. I miss him something bad."

Buck stood up and distanced himself from Kitty, shaking his head as he watched Kitty balance herself on the back of the horse.

Candice said, "Buck, Kitty's not good with horses, so stop worryin' so hard about her."

"I ain't worryin' about her horse skills," Buck bellowed. "I'm more worried about her loud voice when I have to pick her back up off the ground after she falls off."

Candice chuckled. "Buck, you're a smart man. Why did you volunteer to escort us to Bodie?"

"I already told you, I didn't volunteer. The captain ordered me to." He looked up at the stars, "Well I'll be danged."

"What does that mean?" Candice asked as she glanced up, too.

"She's right. Well I'll be danged," Buck said again.

Candice's face filled with a puzzled expression. "Who's right?" She hesitated, then asked, "Right about what?"

"She's right about Bodie. We've been headin' up hill for three days. Bodie can't be much farther."

"But earlier you said Kitty was wrong. How come she's right now?"

"I guess I forgot some of what the captain told me. I was payin' more attention to what direction we were headin' in, and I reckon I should have paid more attention to our surroundings." Buck sighed. "Ma'am, I'm kinda new at this. And I ain't for sure I'm right, but I remember the captain sayin' don't drive the team hard the last three days because the elevation was steeper than it looked." He grinned. "And that's what we've been doin' for the last three days."

Candice took a deep breath. "Kitty!" she shouted, suddenly filled with excitement. "Buck thinks you might be right. Bodie might be just past that next bluff."

"I told you." Kitty rolled her eyes and dared herself to sit upright on the horse's back instead of hugging its neck. "I knew I heard something earlier." The horse was walking in a slow circle and paid no mind to Kitty as she kept kicking its ribs and in a whisper kept repeating, "Get up slow now."

"Don't get me wrong, but I'm lookin' real forward to gettin away from you, too," Buck shouted. "Would you mind if I get you there tonight?"

"As long as I can sit in the buckboard," Kitty compromised. "I hate horses, and this one is real stupid."

"I sure would love a hot bath and soft bed," Candice sighed.

Buck's grin widened. He helped Kitty down from the horse, and with the help of a full moon, hooked the team of horses up to the buckboard. He dashed around camp as though his legs were on fire, picking up everything and throwing it all in the back of the buckboard.

"If I didn't know better, Kitty laughed, "I would think you wanted to get to Bodie more than we do." Candice nodded and threw Kitty a wide smile.

"No, ma'am," he said, his breath labored. "I just want some peace and quiet."He helped both women into the buckboard, and before Kitty was seated he jumped up in the driver's seat and urged the horses up the slope.

"I think you're right," Candice giggled. "He is in more of a hurry than us."

At the crest of the next hill, Buck slowed the horses. A sea of lanterns lit the surrounding hillside a short distance away. When he stopped the team, everyone's eyes widened in astonishment. "Are all of them lights lanterns?" he asked.

"Look at all of them lights," Candice said. "Why, they must be a mile wide and just as deep." She smiled at Kitty. "We did it, Kitty! We made it to Bodie."

"It sounds real loud from way back here," Buck exclaimed. "How can anybody get rest down there?"

"I don't intend to sleep for a month," Kitty teased, a ring of feminine charm in her tone.

"Thanks for gettin' us here." Candice offered Buck a short smile.

Buck's back straightened and he scratched his head. "I reckon this is Bodie, and I reckon I got you here safely, so I reckon I can leave now." The worry on his face disappeared as he listened to himself. He glanced at Kitty. "Do you reckon you can get from here to there without tippin' the buckboard?"

Kitty rolled her eyes. "I hate horses, but I know how to drive this thing."

Buck glanced at Candice. "I can't say it's been nice knowin' you. I've had a headache from the minute you showed up in camp. The captain said I wasn't to go into town, just get you here safely. Well, I reckon I've done that."

He handed Kitty the reins and jumped out of the buckboard. "Goodbye," he shouted as he untied his horse from the back of the buckboard and eased into the saddle. He turned his horse around and kicked it into a full run.

"I want the best champagne money can buy!" Kitty shouted to the heavens.

"We ain't spendin' our gold on expensive champagne," Candice cried. "We're goin' to share a hotel room, take a bath, and get some sleep."

"I didn't say I was gonna pay for the champagne." Kitty raised her eyebrow, and with pure feminine charm said, "I already told you, I don't pay for food or champagne."

"Hush up and get this thing movin'," Candice barked. "My arm is achin' somethin' fierce."

"I need a man and champagne," Kitty snapped back.

"You ain't whoring in this town. Remember you're the one that told me that."

"I changed my mind," Kitty shouted, moonlight causing the twinkle in her eye.

"I ain't givin' you gold dust tonight, and you're not gettin' out of my sight."

The women's patter was drowned in music and laughter as they slowed the buckboard and walked the horses up the main street of Bodie.